A FREQUENT PEAL OF BELLS

TED TAYLER

vinci
BOOKS

Vinci Books

vinci-books.com

Published by Vinci Books Ltd in 2026

1

Copyright © Ted Tayler 2018

The author has asserted their moral right to be identified as the author of this work in accordance with the Copyright, Designs and Patents Act 1988. This work is a work of fiction. Names, characters, places and incidents are the product of the author's imagination or are used fictitiously. Any resemblance to actual persons, living or dead, places and incidents is entirely coincidental.

All rights reserved. No part of this publication may be copied, reproduced, distributed, stored in any retrieval system, or transmitted in any form or by any means, including photocopying, recording, or other electronic or mechanical methods, nor used as a source for any form of machine learning including AI datasets, without the prior written permission of the publisher.

The publisher and the author have made every effort to obtain permissions for any third party material used in this book and to comply with copyright law. Any queries in this respect should be brought to the attention of the publisher and any omissions will be corrected in future editions.

A CIP catalogue record for this book is available from the British Library.

Paperback ISBN: 9781036700591

The EU GPSR authorised representative is Logos Europe, 9 rue Nicolas Poussion, 17000 La Rochelle, France

contact@logoseurope.eu

By Ted Tayler

The Phoenix

The Olympus Project
Gold, Silver and Bombs
Nothing Is Ever Forever
In the Lap of the Gods
The Price of Treachery
A New Dawn
Something Wicked Draws Near
Evil Always Finds A Way
Revenge Comes in Many Colours
Three Weeks in September
A Frequent Peal of Bells
Larcombe Manor

The Freeman Files

Fatal Decision
Last Orders
Pressure Point
Deadly Formula
Final Deal
Barking Mad
Creature Discomforts

Silent Terror

Night Train

All Things Bright

Buried Secrets

A Genuine Mistake

Strange Beginnings

Dead Reckoning

A Normal November

Into the Sunlight

Tame the Storm

One True Friend

Whispered Truths

A Morning Murder

Quick to Anger

Red Herring Season

Gathering Clouds

Still Standing

Chapter One

Monday, 29th September 2014

Henry Case left the Olympus car with the transport section, collected his bag from the boot, and walked to his quarters in the stable block. He was tired but happy. The weekend in Surrey with the Reverend Sarah Gough had flown past.

Henry couldn't believe twelve weeks had passed since his first visit. That crazy weekend in mid-July, when Sarah invited him to the annual flower show and fete, was a high summer spot for her parishioners.

Sarah had booked him into the Hurtwood Hotel on that occasion, three miles away in Walking Bottom, Peaslake. Modesty was the order of the day. Her neighbours mustn't catch a whiff of scandal in the air, she had told him.

Last Friday evening, Henry had arrived at the vicarage and parked in front of the main house. He checked his jacket pocket as he stood on the doorstep with his dozen red roses. Yes, the surprise was still there where he had put it before leaving Larcombe Manor.

"Hello, darling," cried Sarah as she threw open the door, "come inside."

Henry followed her indoors. Sarah took his bunch of flowers and went to the kitchen. She found a vase in one of the lower cupboards, arranged them to her satisfaction, and then topped up the glass container with water.

"There," she said, "now for a proper welcome."

Sarah took Henry by the hand and led him to the bottom of the stairs.

Henry stopped.

"Before we go any further, there's something I need to do," he said.

Sarah gave him a quizzical look.

"Not more revelations, surely?"

Henry smiled. His mother had always told him the truth will out, and it did two weeks ago. Sarah now knew most of his duties at Larcombe for the Olympus Project. She had come to terms with them. His concerns over whether they could ever have a lasting relationship were over. He was ready to move forward to a bright future.

"Nothing sinister, I promise," said Henry, taking the small box from his pocket.

"Will you marry me, Sarah?" He opened the box, revealing the elegant diamond solitaire he bought in Bath. Sarah's only response had been to extend her left hand so that Henry could slide the ring onto her finger.

"It's perfect, Henry," she said, "yes, I'll marry you."

"Excellent," said Henry, "now let's carry on what we had started."

The vase of red roses remained on the work surface in the kitchen for several hours as the happy couple made love upstairs. There was no question of Henry needing to drive

A Frequent Peal of Bells

to Walking Bottom tonight. The car could stay in the driveway.

"Oh, Henry," sighed Sarah, "that exercise has made me hungry. So let's walk up to the Royal Oak for a bite to eat and a few drinks. I'll keep flicking my hair out of my eyes until someone notices the ring. That should start the tongue's wagging."

"The sooner the locals see us together, the better," said Henry. "I expect they've wondered why I haven't been back."

They dressed and returned downstairs.

"Did you bring a bag?" asked Sarah.

"It's still in the car," Henry replied. "I waited until you accepted my proposal before moving my gear indoors. Regardless of your answer, I wasn't driving to a damn hotel."

"That would never happen, darling," said Sarah.

The couple had strolled up the street to the pub, had a meal and shared a bottle of wine. When the Royal Oak landlord called time, Sarah and Henry were threading their way through a crowded bar. Several customers spotted the new adornment their vicar had acquired. Drinking-up time ended before the well-wishers let them leave.

Henry and Sarah had returned to the vicarage arm in arm. There were no furtive glances or snatched goodnight kisses behind the greenery this time. Instead, Henry stopped to collect his bag from the car. Sarah let them into the house, and although the downstairs lights went on to appease the neighbours, the newly engaged couple had headed upstairs.

On Saturday and Sunday, Sarah had parish duties to fulfil. She disappeared on her bicycle to spend an hour or two fulfilling her commitments, and when she returned, the couple discussed their plans.

"Where shall we marry?" asked Sarah.

"I thought you wanted the service here," said Henry.

"If we were to live here as husband and wife, and I continued to work in the parishes this ministry covers, then yes, it makes sense. However, I'm not sure that's practical."

"What do you propose then?" asked Henry.

"I wasn't born here in the village, so I have no strong ties to the place. My parents lived in Hungerford, and that was where they raised me. My father died when I was in my early twenties. Since my mother's funeral three years ago, I've not returned to the place. There are happy memories there, but nothing that makes me yearn to marry in the church where I was christened and confirmed."

"Where do you wish to marry?" Henry asked.

"If Annabelle agrees, I would love it to be at Larcombe Manor. Neither of us has a large family to invite, and your friends and colleagues live there. I can ask a friend to officiate. She shares duties with me in the four parishes we cover."

"What are your plans following the wedding?" asked Henry.

"I'll call the Bishop first thing on Monday and ask him to look for a move further west. If he asks, how soon will the wedding be?"

"There's no cause for concern, is there?" asked Henry. "We haven't taken precautions this weekend."

Sarah dug him in the ribs with an elbow.

"My first job when I get back is to explore the possibilities of moving into the main house," said Henry, rubbing his side. "Rusty moved from the stable block with his good lady, and they aren't married yet. My quarters are no place for a married couple to live. Your new position may come with a vicarage, but it's not practical for me to live off-site while I work for Olympus."

"Right," said Sarah, "that's settled. We set a date as soon as I secure a new parish near Bath. If Annabelle agrees, we'll get married in that delightful church on the estate and live in one of the apartments. I know from my visits how comfortable they are. We can make a home there. If we're blessed with a child in time, it will be an idyllic setting to raise a baby. Hope thrives on it."

They visited the Royal Oak for refreshments between the wedding plans and Sarah's parish duties. Henry felt the effects of the superb food on his waistline. It had been a memorable weekend. Now, it was Monday lunchtime. Henry had missed the morning meeting and had a long list of jobs that needed his attention. As he reached the door to his quarters, all he planned to do was drop the bag and sleep.

Hugh Fraser heard Henry's door close. He checked his watch; someone had a good weekend, he thought. Hugh was leaving the estate to drive to Manchester later. Tomorrow at three fifteen, he was attending the funeral of Monty Jacks, the disabled ex-serviceman murdered at New Street station, Birmingham. Monty was the first casualty suffered by the Irregulars.

The logistics officer worked with Phoenix in the orangery over the weekend. Phoenix was keen to keep the pressure on organised crime gangs across the country. It didn't matter where you looked; even the most unlikely towns added to the statistics.

Hugh Fraser knew only too well those areas in Glasgow

where crime was rife. It was nothing new in Drumchapel and Govan. They had been in the Top 10 for decades. Even in Scotland, he had raised an eyebrow when violence or burglary became a hot topic in the smaller towns in the countryside. Phoenix and Rusty kept turning over stones in affluent areas of the South or the Midlands, and the worst low-life criminal crawled out.

Despite the authorities' claims of an improving picture, crime was no longer under control. On the contrary, it spread further than ever before and faster than a forest fire. Olympus did what it could, given its resources, but the battle would be lost unless they reversed cuts to services.

The ringing phone interrupted his thoughts. Ambrosia was calling him.

"I wanted to catch you before you left," she said. "I've just learned from Zeus that the funeral for the other agent murdered in Winson Green is on Friday."

"Finn's family came from Rugeley, in Staffordshire," said Hugh, "I had better attend."

"We'll go there together," said Ambrosia. "I told Zeus I thought a senior Olympian should be present and offered my services. When will you arrive in Leeds?"

"I'm leaving Larcombe within the hour. Olympus has booked me into a budget hotel tonight. The funeral in South Manchester tomorrow is mid-afternoon. I should be with you by seven in the evening."

"I can't wait for you to taste my food," said Ambrosia, "it will be a pleasure to cook for someone. Living alone makes it easier to eat out or get a takeaway."

Hugh thought of the lonely nights after his wife had moved out. He had the local pizza parlour, chippy, and Chinese restaurant on speed-dial on his phone. Things had moved fast with Ambrosia. She was ambitious and knew what she wanted. Who was he to complain?

"I'm sure I'll enjoy everything," he said.

Hugh heard Ambrosia's trademark giggle.

"Don't worry, I'll make sure of that," she replied.

"I must drive back to Larcombe on Wednesday morning," he said. "Unless I can persuade Phoenix, I'm owed two days' leave."

"Stay with me," begged Ambrosia, "we need to discuss future roles for the Irregulars. I'll clear it with Zeus if there's a problem. We'll make our way to Rugeley on Friday. You can head home after the service, and I'll return here. Can I convince you to spend time with me?"

"Do you have an extensive range of dishes to tempt me with?" asked Hugh.

Ambrosia laughed out loud.

"My skills in the kitchen only stretch to enough dishes to feed you tomorrow evening. After that, we'll phone for a takeaway. I only want to get out of bed for food, don't you?"

"That sounds good," he replied, "I look forward to seeing you tomorrow evening."

"Drive safe," said Ambrosia, "and sleep well tonight."

Hugh listened to her laughter before she ended the call. Then he packed a bag for four nights away from Larcombe. When he moved south from Scotland, he had known that this was a tough assignment, but someone had to do it. Hugh puffed out his cheeks, hoisted his bag on his shoulder, and left the stable block. It was time to drive to Manchester.

Athena was wondering why Henry Case hadn't been present in the meeting room this morning. She knew he planned to spend the weekend with her friend, Sarah, but had assumed he would return late on Sunday evening. It was unlike Henry to miss a meeting without warning.

Her husband was taking the others through the mission plans agreed upon for the coming week. Phoenix had disappeared for half a day on Saturday and Sunday to work on them with Hugh Fraser in the orangery. It was for a good cause, but it would be nice to spend quality time together. A week ago, Phoenix had started delegating tasks to less senior agents. Stress affects everyone in time, no matter how tough they appear.

"Will these missions cause the Grid any long-term damage, Phoenix," asked Minos. Athena forgot Henry for now and switched her attention to the matter at hand.

"I think we've used this comparison before, Minos," replied Phoenix, "it's like that Whack-A-Mole game for kids. Heads pop up all over the place, and we try to hit them. Every head we take out of the game hurts the Grid for a while; there's no doubt. How long it lasts depends on how soon they select another soldier to fill the gap."

"My concern is that we take risks every time we send agents into the field. First, they get killed, as we have on several missions in the past six months. Second, during those actions, our enemies uncover their identities. That poses a danger to everyone here at Larcombe."

"We take every precaution against both eventualities," said Athena. "Our losses are painful, but weighed against the benefits we have secured, they represent a low percentage of our assets."

"It's not our job to inflict lasting damage on the Grid," said Rusty, more animated than Athena had seen him of late.

"Exactly," agreed Phoenix, "our missions often target the vilest criminals. People we must eliminate before they can carry out any further crimes. On occasion, we encounter the soldiers, the low-level villains who operate in regions plastered across every media outlet for a few weeks. Then, we hope the nudge we give the police galvanises them into positive action. So far, that element of our strategy has yielded the smallest fruit."

"The authorities have been slow to respond in every arena," said Alastor. "One can understand the logic behind not spending money you don't have. But this extended period of austerity is punishing the wrong people. Whoever said crime doesn't pay was a fool. The Grid has increased the profits from organised crime in the last month by a percentage that is manna from heaven for any of the world's leading companies."

"I have been distracted of late, with good reason," said Athena, "and I haven't kept up to date with your reports, Alastor. I apologise. Can you bring us up to speed? It might help everyone here."

"Please don't apologise, Athena. No matter what we face at Olympus, the family must always come first. I introduced the Grid into this conversation because something concerns me with the latest figures from the Glencairn Bank. Things moved on since the Spring when we sought the identity of the elusive 'H'. The ice-house named him Ardal James Hannon, an entrepreneur who five years ago lived in Cricklewood. Everything in his background suggested he was the perfect fit for the mastermind behind the Grid's increasingly cohesive network."

"Matching locations of a string of deaths to the letter 'H' was down to Orion's work," said Rusty. "We then discovered Hannon had changed his name, didn't we?"

"By the end of April, we knew Hannon had gone to ground five years ago. When he opened the Glencairn

Bank, he had taken his mother's maiden name, Hanigan. He ditched his first name. In his new persona, Hugo Hanigan controlled the bank and out-performed the opposition on every level. Hanigan covered his tracks well. Any photographs of him from his youth were useless. There were no current photographs of him online. In the summer, we stationed an agent on Gresham Street to capture images of frequent visitors. His vigil has been intermittent for security reasons. The images he has sent through to Giles left us with eight possibilities. We deferred progress on nailing the identities of those men whenever another crisis has arisen."

"We've had people work on those images, Athena," said Artemis, "but most are likely to be seasoned criminals. They are skilled in avoiding being caught on camera. A quick dash from a car to the bank gives us little to work with."

"However, we named five of the frequent visitors," said Giles Burke, "and none of them was Hanigan or Hannon. We have three sets of photographs of men who often visit the Glencairn, but we can't trace them anywhere. They are of a similar age, white, and well-dressed. As Alastor pointed out, getting a face for Hanigan has been a lower priority in the past ten weeks. He may be among those three, or our agent could have missed him altogether. Who knows how often he visits the bank? He could work from home these days."

"Keep searching for those identities, Giles," said Athena. "Can we work back from the images of the three unidentified men to discover where they live? I know that's like finding a needle in a haystack, but it could help confirm who they are."

"If I may, Athena," said Alastor, "that's unnecessary. I've often seen those photos since the first ones arrived in early June. When I studied the latest batch from Gresham

Street, I spotted something. That's what raised my suspicions about last month's performance. One of the three men hasn't visited since before the Bank Holiday weekend. After being a frequent visitor for four months, four weeks is a long time."

"You believe the sudden improvement is due to a change of management at the bank?" asked Phoenix, "could that mean someone has replaced Hanigan? Or has he appointed a new person and given his total concentration to Grid business?"

"I checked the discarded photos in the latest batch," said Alastor, "the ice-house is focussing on the three that are still unidentified. A much younger man was snapped by our agent two weeks ago. He visited the Glencairn at the same time as one of its regulars. The image was sharp and in focus — no attempt to hide his face. I checked for him online, and in hours, I found him on social media. His name is Tyrone O'Riordan."

The room fell silent. The implication was evident to everyone sitting around the table.

"Tommy O'Riordan's son?" asked Rusty. "What is he doing at the Glencairn?"

"Tyrone and his sister Rosie lived in Marbella," said Artemis. "Tommy had a place out there. That was where the police arrested him for the murder of Michael Devlin."

"The two kids came home for the funeral," said Rusty. "Have they moved back in with their mother?"

"Not in the family home in Kilburn because they've sold that," said Alastor, "the Marbella apartment has gone too. With Tommy dead, I imagine money was tight, and Tommy's widow made cutbacks. She doesn't appear to have worked ever since she and Tommy married. I doubt she wants to start now."

"They will have done better than scrape by on his ill-gotten gains," said Phoenix. "I doubt she's living in poverty. I hope they don't blame me for getting rid of the family breadwinner?"

"We both had a hand in that," said Rusty with a grin.

"Giles, we need to learn more about young Tyrone," said Athena. "What's his history? Where does he live?"

"Will do, Athena," replied Giles, "should we add Colleen and Rosie to the list?"

"It can't do any harm," said Athena.

"I think what you have uncovered is gold dust, Alastor," said Phoenix, "well done. If we add other things into the mix, we could answer questions that have concerned me for a while. For example, who took over as leader of the Kilburn gang after we disposed of Tommy?"

"Tommy's deputy at the time of his murder trial was his brother-in-law, Sean Walsh," said Artemis, "he would have been Hanigan's first-choice. We must assume Walsh was the go-between for the gang while Tommy was in Belmarsh. With Tommy dead, Hanigan had to have let Walsh continue in the role unless he under-performed. Giles and I will check the current status."

"It may already be too late," said Phoenix. "We received intelligence that a member of the old guard, Michael Quinn, was murdered last month. It wasn't obvious whether it was an internal struggle for power in the borough, or the gang from Kilburn, next door, spreading its wings."

"So, the question I need to answer is, who succeeded Sean Walsh in Kilburn?" said Giles, "and are they looking to expand?"

"You two have got plenty to be getting on with," said Athena, "I suggest you get below to the ice-house and make a start. If you bump into Henry Case on your way, could you ask him to call into my office this afternoon?"

Artemis nodded, and she and Giles left the room. Athena looked at the others.

"I think we've found a chink in the Grid's armour, don't you?"

"Whatever role Tyrone O'Riordan plays, he's a different breed to Hanigan," said Minos. "His digital footprint is easy to track. It might be because he was thrust into a new role and hasn't learned to be more guarded in his actions."

"Or he's an arrogant sod, who thinks he's untouchable," muttered Phoenix.

"Either way, we can investigate his link to the Glencairn, discover what happened to Hugo Hanigan, and see whether the Kilburn gang's ambition has any limits."

Athena couldn't think of anything to add to Minos's comment, so she called the meeting to a close.

When they were back in the apartment, Athena was restless. Maria Elena had prepared them their lunch. She was helping Hope grapple with hers. Phoenix soon polished off his second sandwich and stopped to take a sip from his cup of coffee.

"A penny for them, darling?" he asked.

"I wanted to catch up with Henry to hear about his weekend. It's not vital, given what we learned from Alastor this morning, but all the same…."

"That's the first time since I've been here that he surprised me," said Phoenix, "he and Minos are such dry sticks. They churn out report after report. Their attention to detail is amazing."

"Yet, your in-tray is always full," chided Athena, "I have to pester you to take time to catch up with your reading."

"This was different," said Phoenix, "Alastor showed

initiative. Something bothered him in the numbers he saw from the Glencairn. Because those two delve into the minutiae daily, it registered with him. Normal people would have missed it. Or they would have dismissed it as a seasonal blip or an adjustment from earlier in the financial year."

"I've always told you not to underestimate them," said Athena.

"Fair point. As for what Alastor spotted in that photograph, I'm itching to hear what Giles and Artemis uncover regarding the O'Riordan family."

"I hope they can work fast; you'll be away after Wednesday."

Maria Elena had disappeared to the nursery with their daughter; Athena was still only picking at her salad. Phoenix rested his eyes and went through the actions planned for later in the week. It never hurt to check those plans.

When he opened his eyes, Athena was in the kitchen.

Phoenix walked to the door and watched as his wife stacked the dishwasher. Athena's heart wasn't in it; he could tell.

"Why don't you see if Henry is waiting for you?"

Athena looked at her watch.

"Where did that hour go?" she cried, flew along the corridor, and took the stairs to the administration area. Minos and Alastor were hard at work on their next batch of reports. Henry Case stood outside her door like a naughty schoolboy.

"Henry, you're alive and well. What a relief."

"Apologies for the late arrival, Athena," said Henry. "Sarah and I didn't want the weekend to finish."

"I'm only teasing you, Henry. Sarah called me yesterday on her way to church for evensong. She told me she left you snoring on the sofa in front of the television. I take it the food at the Royal Oak is as good as ever? Congratulations on your engagement. I didn't share your good news with the others this morning. You can do that yourself."

"Did Sarah mention the wedding?" asked Henry.

"No, she was too excited about the ring you gave her. I imagine you've started to make plans, though?"

"I won't put off matters," said Henry, "Sarah's calling the Bishop to ask for a transfer closer to Bath. Sarah doesn't want me to feel obliged to leave Larcombe and move nearer to her. If you agree, we want to marry in the tiny church. One of her colleagues has agreed to do the honours."

"That sounds lovely," said Athena.

"What are the chances of us living here afterwards? Not in the stable block, but in this building, the same as Rusty and Artemis."

"I'd be disappointed if you went somewhere else, Henry," said Athena. "This old Georgian manor house has eleven bedrooms and seven bathrooms. Daddy will move out in a few weeks, based on what he told me at lunchtime. Even if he stayed with us permanently, we could still find a spot for you both."

"Oh, jolly good," said Henry.

"I imagine the wedding date will depend on how soon the Church finds a new living for the soon-to-be Reverend Sarah Case?"

"Sarah has her heart set on Easter Saturday," said Henry.

"Well then, her matron of honour and the flower girl accept," said Athena. "That was another thing she mentioned during her frantic phone call last evening."

"I shall ask Giles to be my best man," said Henry, "he asked me if I would do the job when he gets married. Of course, I said I'd give it some thought, not realising I would be engaged only weeks later."

Henry trotted back to the stable block to call Sarah with the good news. He hoped she would receive positive news soon on her next parish. October was upon them. April seemed a long way off. If the last year had taught him anything, it was that things could change before you know it.

Chapter Two

Tuesday, 30th September 2014

"This makes a change, Mum. You are visiting me."

Tyrone O'Riordan welcomed his mother into his penthouse apartment with a peck on her cheek.

Colleen didn't hold with this foreign malarkey. She had been more used to getting a slap from Tommy. A kiss meant he wanted something else. She couldn't see anything wrong with shaking hands if it was business. People were too friendly by half these days. They didn't know how to keep their distance.

"I suppose you mean when you're here?" Colleen replied.

She sensed Tyrone's annoyance at finding she had paid a visit to the apartment while he was in East Anglia. The wall safe contained plenty of information the apartment's previous owner had gathered on his enemies and those who might have thought were his friends.

Hugo Hanigan's body was now somewhere on Hackney

Marshes among tonnes of the capital's waste. It was only natural the head of the network of organised crime gangs in the UK wanted access to that information. It could prove invaluable. Tyrone would have to get over it.

Tyrone shrugged. He knew better than to argue with his mother.

"Can I get you a drink?" he asked.

"It's not even eleven o'clock. OK, I'll have a gin and tonic with a twist of lime," Colleen replied, "easy on the gin. We've got matters to discuss."

"What did you want to discuss?" Tyrone asked.

"I don't want you to take me through your ideas on uncovering this so-called secret organisation you and Frank Rooney have dreamed up, that's for sure. Where you got that notion from beats me. I'm more interested in the Grid's major robberies in the lead-up to Christmas."

"When we pull those off, it will bring a whole new rival to Black Friday, believe me," said Tyrone.

"We'll see," said Colleen. "Who's running the show, and how much do we stand to make?"

"The team will be three Albanians who came to the UK six years ago. They claimed to be Kosovans fleeing the troubles but were seasoned criminals. They've majored in importing cocaine in the past, but there's big competition in that market, so they added to their skill set."

"Where do you go to do that? Night school, I suppose, or the Open University? Can you trust them?" asked Colleen.

"They understand the punishment if they try to cheat us," replied Tyrone. "As for the amounts involved, we have high hopes of collecting over one hundred million."

Colleen took a large sip of her drink and swallowed. A hundred million pounds? That would make the headlines. It could be just the push the Grid needed to prove its vice-like grip on the nation.

It would further emphasise the lunacy of cutting police numbers. If the Albanians got full credit for planning and executing the robberies, it would fuel the argument against open borders. The public would be outraged. The brazen disregard for law and order could topple governments. Serve them right.

"Did you want to go into the details?" Tyrone asked.

"Sorry," said Colleen, "no, not today; I'm having my hair done in an hour. Do you have a file on your computer you can send me?"

"I won't risk sending anything important in an email attachment," said Tyrone. "I'll drop a memory stick over to your place in a day or two. Don't worry. I'll show you how to use it."

"You're a good boy, Tyrone. We're going places, aren't we?"

"Onwards and upwards, Mum."

At Larcombe Manor, the ice-house team had worked their magic. Giles passed files around the table for the others to read.

"Tyrone O'Riordan, thirty-one-year-old son of Tommy and Colleen. His father insisted he stay in education until he had enough qualifications to make an honest living. Tommy had been keen for his children to stay on the straight and narrow. He's a qualified accountant and has an MBA. He lived in his father's place in Marbella rent-free. For the past decade, Tyrone has lived a high life. Fast cars, women, and late-night cocktail parties four or five nights a week. He has dabbled in drugs, but it's never become an issue. He picked up a handful of parking and speeding fines, but the Spanish police never linked him with anything more sinister. Members of crime families who knew, or worked for his father, have retired to Marbella over the years. Tommy O'Riordan kept his kids away from those people on holiday, but Tyrone chose to spend time in their company. He never got involved in criminal activity, but he likely gained the knowledge."

"So, his financial expertise marks him as the new head of the Glencairn Bank," said Athena.

"That's a fair assumption," said Giles, "as for Rosie O'Riordan, she's twenty-nine. Tommy used to call her his princess. She was a Daddy's girl. Rosie moved to Marbella, lived there on the cheap and got herself a sports car as soon as she passed her driving test at eighteen. At college in London, she had completed a hair and beauty course. Rosie partied with the same crowd as Tyrone and spent every euro she earned in Marbella's salons having a good time. She moved from salon to salon but was never out of work. Plenty of men have been prepared to spend their money on her because little Rosie is a beauty, as you can tell from her photos. There's no sign she's involved with anything criminal."

"Apart from the length of that skirt," said Minos.

"You're showing your age," said Rusty.

"If you've got tanned legs, you want to show them off," said Artemis.

"We red-headed Scotsmen keep our delicate skin covered," said Rusty. "The only tan I've worn was from my father on my backside."

"We can discount Rosie O'Riordan," said Athena, eager to make progress. "What do we have on Colleen O'Riordan, Giles?"

"Colleen will be fifty in a few weeks. She married Tommy at eighteen. Tyrone arrived ten months later. The gap between Tyrone and Rosie was eighteen months. Most accounts of her life with Tommy are anecdotal. He was a villain and treated her the same as most villains have treated their women over the decades. She stayed home, looked after the kids, kept the house tidy, cooked his meals, and kept her mouth shut. She's as hard as nails but has never had even a fine for dropping litter. Since Tommy got jailed for Devlin's murder, she has been active. As we discussed yesterday, this was a natural reaction to the drying up of the money supply."

"Did she begin that process before Tommy escaped from Belmarsh?" asked Phoenix.

"Yes," replied Giles, "the Marbella apartment was already on the market, and the cars the kids leased returned. The sale of the house in Kilburn brought in a million pounds, give or take. Oh, and she sent a Mercedes and an SUV to auction at the end of May."

"I told you Colleen O'Riordan wasn't skint," muttered Phoenix, "but if she needed cash to pay for Tommy's escape bid, it makes sense. He didn't enjoy his freedom for long. There would still be enough left for her to survive, especially as she forced her kids to stand on their own two feet."

"Rosie continues to live in Marbella?" asked Minos.

"Afraid so, Minos," said Rusty, "you're not likely to bump into her on one of your nights on the town."

The former High Court judge gave a thin smile.

"I wonder where the mother and son live?" he said.

"Colleen lives in an apartment on a property overlooking the City and the financial district. I expect she can see the Glencairn Bank. Tyrone doesn't live with her. Colleen ensured the kids couldn't run home by buying a one-bedroomed place. We haven't found the exact spot where Tyrone is living, but the way he approached the bank on foot suggests he's close."

"Hang on," said Alastor, "that makes no sense. He may be a financial genius, but there was no evidence of saving money in the past decade. Properties in that part of London are fetching exorbitant prices. You can't find evidence linking him to the purchase of a flat. Is he renting a place paid for by the Glencairn?"

"We never traced Hanigan after he left Cricklewood," said Artemis, "but he must have owned property near the City. If we found details of high-priced apartments sold around the time of the sale of that house in the suburbs, we might find where Tyrone now lives."

"You're not suggesting they're living together?" asked Athena.

"No, Hanigan hasn't been seen for weeks. I'm suggesting he's dead."

"Killed by Tyrone? That's a leap from speeding fines," said Phoenix.

"Who can say what he learned from those Marbella villains?" asked Giles. "Despite Tommy wanting his kids to stay away from a life of crime, perhaps it's a case of like father, like son."

"How does Colleen fit into this?" asked Athena.

"Her brother, Sean Walsh died in the Dominican Republic," said Giles. "His funeral was in Kilburn in the middle of last month. The local police report reported it as a professional hit."

"What was he doing in South America? Was he on holiday?" asked Alastor.

"An extended holiday?" asked Giles. "Or it could be related to his brother's escape. If he was behind it, supported by Colleen's cash, they might have told him to make himself scarce until the heat died."

"Who wanted Walsh dead?" asked Henry Case.

"Hanigan," said Phoenix, "the O'Riordan family didn't order a hit. If Walsh had gotten jittery, his family would have persuaded him to disappear for a while. But Hanigan wanted to ensure the prison escape and its aftermath didn't link to the Grid. Because we stopped Tommy from reaching Harwich, the blame for his death may have been aimed at Hanigan. Tyrone or one of the Kilburn gang killed Hanigan in retaliation for Tommy's and his brother-in-law's killings."

"So, who's head of the Kilburn gang, and who succeeded Hanigan at the head of the Grid?" asked Rusty.

"There aren't too many candidates for the first," said Artemis. She counted names off on her fingers: -

"Colleen, Tyrone, and whoever acted as second-in-command to Sean Walsh. It's hard to imagine them considering anyone from outside the families from the start."

Phoenix looked at his wife. It wasn't unheard of for a woman to control an unruly mob. Athena did it every day.

"Tyrone's the money man for the Grid, and we can discount him for the local leadership. We don't have a name for Walsh's deputy, which tells me he was a nonentity. No, Colleen O'Riordan is my bet for taking control of the borough. Giles said she was hard as nails. She would have learned the business from Tommy in thirty years."

"Are we overlooking someone senior from the other gangs in the network that may have replaced Hanigan?" asked Minos.

"If Colleen ordered the hit on Hanigan, she's unlikely to let a bloke from another gang waltz in and take the top spot," said Phoenix. "She would get the deed done and then bring the others into line with a show of force."

"Michael Terence Quinn, of course," said Artemis, "the jigsaw pieces fit together nicely."

"I doubt Quinn was alone," said Rusty, "if we dig, we'll uncover more bodies. Colleen O'Riordan has convinced the Grid to accept her as a leader by showing what happens if they disagree. Tyrone's work at the Glencairn is another way of showing the Grid members that they're better off with the O'Riordan family at the helm."

"What's next for the Grid?" asked Henry Case.

"We don't have the firepower to annihilate them, which is what they deserve," said Phoenix. "We'll continue hitting them as often as possible and avoid exposure. As for the Glencairn, if there's a way to reduce that improving trend in performance, we should explore it."

"Understood," said Henry, "but what do you think *they* will do next?"

"They've got fingers in so many pies, I don't know what they might do," said Phoenix. "I'd try something spectacular — the crime of the century. Hanigan was an arrogant swine and dreamed of controlling everything criminal from Land's End to John O'Groats. You know what they say about power corrupting. Colleen O'Riordan could plan something to bring the country to its knees."

Long after his mother left for the hairdressers, Tyrone was hard at work. He ignored Colleen's suggestion that a hidden hand in many recent Grid setbacks was far from genuine. Instead, everything he heard of the Malik story convinced him he was on the right track.

Tyrone studied a map of the UK on his computer.

Hugo Hanigan had kept a file that highlighted every gang headquarters. Few corners of the country remained where a number didn't appear; each number linked to that gang's leader, its strength, and whether it represented a general duties outfit or a group of specialists.

Tyrone made a few adjustments. Some gangs were parochial; their reach extended to the boundaries of a borough and no further. The next-door neighbours wouldn't appreciate them meddling in their affairs. Other gangs controlled large areas that crossed county barriers, even if much of it was countryside.

Two hours later, Tyrone could pinpoint the Grid's blind spots. Hugo had done him the favour of noting the few pockets of resistance. Those gangs that refused to join the network. Tyrone grasped the nettle. They must be put out of business if they don't join us.

Tyrone needed every inch of the UK covered. Any specialist outfit was exempt, but hundreds of street criminals would suffice. He could switch them from committing the petty crime to hunting for clues about this organisation. That meant minimal losses compared to the gains of removing the threat.

They would watch for the transport linked to the attacks. Tyrone was willing to pay a significant bonus for photographs of either of the two men most often seen during these attacks. If this organisation wanted to remain secret, they had to stay home. Wherever that home might be, their days of interfering in Grid business must end.

Tyrone took one last look at the amended map. Time for action. He called the heads of the gangs that surrounded these rogue enclaves. One by one, they received the same message: -

"Remove the top tier. Tell the others to fall in line or suffer the same fate."

He sent eight messages. They referenced eight areas that, when added, gave the Grid total control. They acquired extra foot soldiers to add to the band of watchers. Tyrone was content with his morning's work. Now, he must visit the Glencairn Bank. Tyrone expected more good news on the financial front to greet him when he arrived. Within an hour, he could stroll up Gresham Street to a French restaurant he loved. All work and no play never did anyone any good.

Tyrone returned to his penthouse at four in the afternoon. He phoned Frank Rooney.

"You might hear of activity in a few trouble-spots over the next day or two, Frank," he said, "don't worry; it won't affect you."

"Pleased to hear it," said Frank. He breathed a sigh of relief. His run-in with Colleen O'Riordan must have slipped her son's mind. He got on better with the son and hoped they could build a stable relationship. It seemed possible.

"I'm keen to build on the successes I expect before the week's out, Frank," Tyrone continued. "I'm implementing a country-wide search for these busybodies that keep hampering our activities. What I need from our gang leaders is eyes and ears on the street. Photographs too, if it's possible. Pick people you can afford to lose for a period, but make sure you can rely on them. I'll send the details to everyone this evening."

"Always glad to help," said Frank.

"I called you directly because we need to firm up our plan for this Trojan Horse."

"What's that when it's at home?" asked Frank.

He wasn't the sharpest knife in the box.

"It's from Greek myth, Frank. The story doesn't matter. You need to know that it represents a person we get inside this organisation. He will help us undermine and destroy it from the inside."

"Ah, the expendable scrote I thought of when you asked last week. Got it, we get our man picked up for questioning, and if this gang take him back to their headquarters, we've got them."

"Only if they take him back, Frank. Then, we need him to be useful enough for them to keep him alive. Otherwise, they'll interrogate him for information on us, and we'll become the target. What guarantee do we have they won't kill him? We need a strategy that works to our advantage, whichever way they play it."

"Tricky," said Frank, totally lost.

Tyrone expected nothing useful to come from the other end of the line.

"Leave the thinking to me, Frank. Make sure you have the right guy available when I call him."

"Got it, boss," said Frank.

Tyrone worked on getting their man on the inside and sending them details of the secret base's location. Whether that man came out alive afterwards wasn't relevant.

Wednesday, 1st October 2014

Phoenix and Rusty were on the road early, their destination North London. Day One of their missions against gangs of youths in the city had begun.

"We may miss an update on the O'Riordan's this morning," said Rusty as he eased into the flow of traffic on the M4.

"We can't help that," said Phoenix, searching through the glove-box for his CDs.

"Those changes at the top of the Grid came as a shock, didn't they?" asked Rusty.

"I remember Athena telling me it was vital to know your enemy. We had distractions this last month, but it's unacceptable to fall one or two steps behind, whether behind the Grid, the terrorists, or any opposition we face. The whole point of the ice-house is to keep us right on the money with intelligence."

"I'll have a word with Artemis," said Rusty, "tell her to pull her finger out."

"I don't blame Artemis or Giles. The system was state-of-the-art when Erebus had it installed. Things have moved so fast in that world. Your kit can be out-of-date within two years. We may need to consider forking out for an upgrade. Perhaps that's the best way to approach the matter with Artemis?"

"Try to blind her with the promise of something shiny and new? Rather than tell her, she's coming up short with the piece of kit she uses now? If that's your plan, I'll leave you to tell her."

Phoenix pretended he hadn't heard. He wondered what state the safe house was n they were staying at tonight. They were used to the place in Chiswick. It was easy to access from the M4, and generally, it was one of the better safe houses. But, on the other hand, the properties Olympus used in the north of the city were unfamiliar to him.

"We turn off at the Hogarth roundabout," said Rusty. "We should be in St John's Wood a half-hour later."

"What class of an area is it?" asked Phoenix.

"I'm not sure you'll be interested, but the safe house is a two-minute walk from Lord's cricket ground. The boundaries of St. John's Wood are the Regent's Canal to the south, Maida Vale to the west, Boundary Road to the north and Primrose Hill Park to the east. Little Venice and London Zoo are on our doorstep. It's a posh neighbourhood. If you own a property in NW8, you live in the fifth most expensive postcode in London. The rents for residents are the highest average in London."

"That's good to know," said Phoenix, "we should enjoy it while we can, though. If we need that computer upgrade, I suggest selling this place. We'll stick out around here."

"We're staying there for a reason. It's a hot-spot for this spate of attacks by kids on scooters."

"How did these things become such a menace?" asked Phoenix, "I can remember kids at school on mopeds and scooters. A few progressed to proper motorbikes, but they booked in for driving lessons as soon as the weather turned cold."

"Minos and Alastor analysed reports from last year of the sharp increase in offences committed in the capital. Minos reckoned the first six months of this year had seen a further steep rise in reported incidents. Our task is to nip this problem in the bud."

"Yeah, I read their analysis," said Phoenix, "well, I skimmed through it."

Rusty smiled. They had passed Reading. Another hour and they would arrive at the safe house. It wasn't difficult to understand the attraction for the feral teenagers of today. Easy enough to steal a scooter, and the second-hand market in the new iPhone was strong.

They stole a bike, covered their heads with helmets or balaclavas and rode away. The driver cruised the leafy streets around the affluent boroughs, and the pillion passenger grabbed handbags and phones. Easy pickings. The national pastime in the UK has become walking with a phone in your hand, not concentrating on your surroundings. Even when crossing the road.

When the lads moved into an urban environment, they added delivery drivers to their shopping lists. Vans and motorcycles stopped every few hundred yards in the city for at least sixteen hours a day. Mobiles were still a target, but the van drivers carried cash, too, so the older boys stopped and mugged them.

It was small-scale at present, but as Minos stressed, the police should do more to stop its spread. The public was as much to blame. They needed to be more aware of their surroundings. Rusty wondered why the scooter manufacturers and the phone companies didn't toughen up their security.

Rusty remembered the last sentence in the report. Calling on his years of experience in the High Court, Minos had warned that crime could shift up a gear. What starts as a rash of petty crimes escalates to a stage where serious offences are more common. Minos highlighted an occasional acid attack among the more severe incidents.

While Phoenix rested beside him, not offering to start a conversation or make him suffer a musical interlude, the traffic continued to build. They crawled through the streets from Chiswick to their destination, arriving at the safe house at eleven fifteen.

"This looks terrific," said Phoenix, "it's a shame it's only for one night."

The two friends moved their gear inside. The five-bedroomed detached house was several steps up the ladder from Chiswick; they found little or no food, as usual. So their first visit had to be to a supermarket. Parking looked like a nightmare in the district, so they elected to walk.

As they left the store with their provisions, Phoenix nudged his mate.

"Over there," he said, "where those scooters and bikes are in the staff section park."

Rusty spotted two lads, fourteen or fifteen years old. They were furtive in their movements, looking to see if anyone nearby was watching them. Then one lad darted to a scooter in the rack. He grabbed the handlebars and twisted them hard, breaking the steering lock. Rusty watched as the pair then wheeled the scooter away.

"They didn't bother to check for a tracker," he said. "I guess they'll whip out the ignition barrel, cross the wires, and be mobile in five minutes."

"Let's get these bags back to the house," said Phoenix. "Have a bite to eat, and then look for these little villains."

In the distance, they could hear the buzzing sound of a scooter revving its engine. Those kids were in business.

"What can they expect to earn from these ride-by robberies?" asked Phoenix.

"Two hundred and fifty quid for five minutes of work," replied Rusty.

Phoenix shook his head in disbelief. Minos had convinced Athena this caper was worthy of their time. He wasn't sure when it first surfaced. Olympus wouldn't take any of these kids out of the game permanently, and Henry didn't want them in the ice-house crying for their mothers. A short, sharp shock was what Athena had ordered.

If these muggings equated to three grand an hour, then it was well worth him giving these scumbags the shock of their young lives. All they had to do now was catch a few in the act.

The two agents left the safe house before five in the afternoon. They carried the gear they planned to use inside their zipped jackets.

Phoenix was the bait. He strolled along the pavement with an iPhone in his right hand. In his ears, earplugs suggested he listened to his beloved Judas Priest. He was in constant contact with Rusty, who followed him, at a distance, in the van.

Two scooters buzzed past the van like angry hornets. The leading bike slowed as he passed Phoenix. The second mounted the pavement and crawled up behind him.

"He's five yards behind you, Phoenix. Three, two, one….go," said Rusty.

As the pillion passenger made his move, Phoenix removed his left hand from his jacket. He batted away the grabbing hand with his right arm and used the stun gun on the rider. The young lad tried to accelerate away from danger, but three seconds was plenty to cause loss of muscle control and loss of balance and disorientation. The bike was on its side, and both boys lay on the floor.

Rusty had already pulled in front of them. He stopped the van, opened the doors and bundled the bike and the two lads into the back. Phoenix jumped inside with them; he covered his face and threw hoods over their heads, securing their hands behind their backs. Rusty drove back to the safe house. Less than ninety seconds had passed since the initial grab for the phone and the van leaving the scene.

At the safe house, Phoenix and Rusty dragged the boys indoors. Rusty took off the driver's helmet. He looked seventeen, maybe eighteen and had almost recovered. The stun gun Phoenix had used delivered a lower voltage than a standard Taser, and the buzz lasted only two seconds.

Henry Case reckoned the likely recovery period at ten minutes maximum.

When he removed his pillion passenger's helmet, Phoenix was shocked to find the boy looked about twelve.

"Time for you to listen, boys," said Phoenix, "you won't get a second chance."

"You ain't the police," said the older boy, "they don't care."

"Why do you do it?" asked Rusty.

"It's easy money. How else am I going to earn that much? We stick to our patch because we know the streets. If we go up West, we can hit rich tourists with better quality phones."

"Do you realise the harm you cause your victims?" asked Phoenix.

The older boy laughed.

"Are you for real? People can get a better phone tomorrow on their insurance. That's why the police don't bother with it. There are no victims here. They ain't going to chase us."

"What do you mean?" asked Rusty

"They can't follow if we aren't wearing a helmet. Health and safety stuff, so if we pick up a tail, my brother takes his off, and we're home free."

Phoenix took photos of both boys and the helmets they wore.

"What's that for?" asked the younger boy, whose swagger at the outset had disappeared. His bottom lip quivered.

"I told you when we arrived, this was your last chance. You're right. We're not the police, but we know how to find you, and you'll never identify us. One more slip and I promise you the punishment will be severe. Worse than what the courts could give you. Think yourselves lucky this time. We're taking you back when it gets dark."

Rusty drove the van back to Chalk Farm and the road where the youths had tried to snatch the phone at seven-thirty. Phoenix left them standing on the pavement.

"What about the scooter?" shouted the older youth, "how are we supposed to get home?"

"We'll drop it off somewhere safe, ring the police and say we found an abandoned scooter. The police will return it to its rightful owner, don't worry."

Later, Rusty pulled away from a supermarket car park, where they dumped the bike and headed back to spend the night in the safe house.

"Phoenix," he said, "can we take off the stupid Pinky and Perky masks now? It's getting hot under here."

Chapter Three

Thursday, 2nd October 2014

There was no warning a series of sudden deaths would dominate today's news headlines. Athena sat alone in the apartment at Larcombe Manor. Her husband was at the safe house in St John's Wood; he completed half of his mission yesterday. He and Rusty were returning later today. After delivering more shocks to the moped gangs that threatened the city.

Should she cancel it? These killings were a clear sign the Grid had toughened its stance against its opposition. News reports came in from around the country. Athena prepared for the morning meeting as usual. Her senior agents would help decide the best course of action. Minos and Alastor were wise and experienced. Henry Case, Giles Burke and Artemis were younger but equally adept at guiding her on the right path.

She called Maria Elena and asked her to look after

Hope earlier than usual. She wanted to watch the news updates on the large screen in the meeting room.

As the eight o'clock news summary began, Athena sat with a mug of coffee, listening to the latest from local reporters in each area. On the outskirts of Newcastle, three men had been shot dead in a bar last night. The men were known criminals involved in drug dealing, extortion, and loan sharking. A Detective Chief Inspector from Northumbria Police stood outside the pub and told the reporter it bore the hallmarks of a feud between rival gangs over disrespect. When pressed by the reporter, the DCI claimed gun crime was not out of control in the city. The public at large wasn't in any danger. Athena didn't think the reporter looked convinced. Anyone can get caught in the crossfire when someone enters a crowded bar, and both sides start shooting.

Before she had time to reflect on that attack, the next reporter appeared. The interior of the building looked to be Canning Place. It must be an Assistant Chief Constable from Merseyside. There must have been more trouble here to warrant the higher-ranked officer.

"How can you reassure the public the streets of the city are safe? There were five shootings between eight and one last night. Two men died as they answered their front door. One was riddled with bullets in his car when he stopped at traffic lights. A fourth man died in a drive-by shooting outside a pub. He stood with several others in the smoking bay. Three bystanders got hit but didn't sustain serious injury. The final man sat in a private booth in a strip club, enjoying a lap dance. The door burst open, and two masked men entered. One grabbed the girl and threw her to the floor, as the other opened fire with a machine pistol."

Athena closed her eyes as she listened to the ACC's response.

"A long-running investigation has monitored disputes between organised crime gangs on Merseyside. We have increased foot patrols. These shootings were on specific targets. I don't accept that the threat to the wider community has increased."

Athena wondered if these senior officers ever ran out of platitudes. The men that died were hardened criminals and senior people in organised crime gangs. The method used by the Grid was pre-meditated. Luck had governed that more deaths did not occur.

Liverpool and Newcastle now had several streets in gangland areas on lockdown. Armed patrols stood ready to strike if the violence escalated. Athena knew it was over. The focus would soon switch to another city, another region. The Grid had eliminated its opposition in the full glare of the media spotlight. They didn't fear the police, and they didn't consider the public. They wanted every gang leader to join their network.

It was now nine o'clock, and the meeting room was filling. Athena continued to watch.

"Have you heard from Phoenix?" asked Minos.

"We talked last night; everything went as planned."

Cardiff, Bristol, and Nottingham followed as the morning bulletins continued. The BBC studios at MediaCityUK saw a procession of experts who attempted to explain, calm, and excuse what had happened in front of the country's eyes.

The death toll stood at eighteen so far.

"What can we do?" asked Henry Case.

"We wait," said Athena, "this will be over soon. We can't strike until the media focus has moved to the next outrage, natural disaster, or sporting fiasco. Our time will come."

"How will the authorities react?" asked Alastor.

"The bulletins have ended so that they will wheel the experts into the studio after the weather report. Listen to what they say and make up your mind."

An interviewer asked in the TV studio about the availability of guns across the country. Experts explained that weapons came into the UK from Eastern Europe. Free borders meant just that. You lost the right to object to what entered. Opposition politicians pointed to years of severe budget cuts that hampered operations aimed at managing inter-gang disputes.

Athena and the others had agreed to set aside the planned agenda and watched and listened.

As the Grid cleared the three remaining areas of resistance, interviewers asked why these criminals thought it acceptable to attack people in daylight. In Tottenham, a husband and wife had left Tesco with a loaded trolley at one o'clock in the afternoon. The couple had reached their car, opened the boot and unloaded shopping bags.

A car pulled up behind them with its registration plates covered. A gunman forced the husband to his knees and shot him in the back of the head in front of his wife. The supermarket's CCTV caught every second of the action. They didn't air the actual execution —scenes of the police clearing the car park aired instead. They covered the body on the ground with a sheet. A reporter at the scene said the trolley attendant had told him he could still hear the wife's screams of terror.

"We'll be here for ages," said Athena, "we need to send out for lunch. Alastor, can you make the arrangements, please?"

"I'm not sure I'm ready for food," said Artemis. She wasn't alone.

Alastor left the room. Stewards carried the refreshments into the room twenty minutes later; there was no rush towards the table where they had left it.

"Do you believe we've heard the last of it now?" asked Giles.

"Hard to tell," said Athena, "unless you can tell me the exact number of gangs still operating outside the Grid?"

"Less than ten," said Artemis, "we mapped the locations of organised crime centres while I worked with the force. We knew the scale of their operations, the numbers directly involved, and the additional low-level criminals that had loose links with the main gang structure. But, monitoring it was one thing, having the capability to impact it altogether another matter."

"Gangs in the major cities are amorphous," Giles added. "They can split without bloodshed due to many reasons. The different factions then merge with a neighbouring outfit that's a better fit, whether it's because of its culture or its ambition."

The senior agents waited to see whether this marked a lull in proceedings or whether the carnage had ended.

"I'll call Phoenix," said Athena. "He and Rusty are due on the streets later this afternoon. They should be resting now. No doubt, they're watching this unfold. I want to add their thoughts to what we've discussed. They return home later tonight. We need to prepare for another long day drawing up our battle plans."

Athena made the call.

"Tell me your view, Phoenix," she asked, without her usual friendly preamble. "You're on speakerphone in the meeting room."

"Our list of opponents has reduced," he replied, "we understand the top-level command of the Grid far better now. Total control will mean a unification not only of personnel. Every member of the network will do as instructed in the future. They saw the alternative in graphic detail. That message was for the total Grid membership as much as the authorities and the British public. In a way, it makes our job easier. We are less likely to face the loose cannons that existed when it was a free-for-all. Life's about balance. This unification also means the Grid has improved its chances of identifying and countering our activities."

"I agree," said Athena, "so I advise caution. We must increase our level of security and delay any action against the Grid until we can ensure our anonymity."

"Are you suggesting we return to Larcombe at once?" asked Phoenix.

"The youths we are targeting aren't associated directly with the Grid's network," said Rusty, "they're street-level punks who could gravitate to more serious crimes in time. If we pull out now, there's a risk this moped gang menace will spread. I know we can make a difference through what we're doing. The risk of Olympus being seen as involved is low, and Phoenix and I can take extra precautions in light of what's been happening elsewhere. The spotlight is firmly on those killings. A few punishments in North West London will struggle to get two lines in a footnote in the media."

"We must be positive," said Athena, "go ahead with the mission, take care, and come home safe."

"If the authorities stamped out this threat from the outset, they wouldn't have the list of problems they face today," said Henry. "I agree with Rusty. The risk is low. The potential benefits are high."

After the conversation with the two men in St John's

A Frequent Peal of Bells

Wood ended, the team turned their attention back to the TV screen.

In the middle of the afternoon, Big Phil Sykes, a notorious criminal who never took a backward step in his life, stood on the cliff tops near Dawlish in Devon. He controlled large tracts of the South West with operations in four counties. The man facing him carried a sawn-off double-barrelled shotgun. Eye-witnesses a hundred yards away reported seeing the man continue to advance towards Sykes.

There were no shots fired. Sykes stepped back at last and lost his footing.

A seventh gang had lost its figurehead. The death toll rose to twenty.

As news of this latest killing was received, a Chief Constable sat in the hot seat. He called for communities blighted by gun crime to support the police. The interviewer interrupted his well-crafted prepared statement and switched the focus of her questions.

"How many more deaths are we going to witness today, Chief Constable?" she asked. "When are the police going to restore law and order in the country?"

"I can assure the public that my colleagues and I are doing our utmost to keep the public safe...."

"You realise many people are drawing comparisons between today's atrocities and those that plagued Chicago in the 1920s?"

A promising career in public relations crashed and burned as the unfortunate representative of what had once been a force with teeth struggled to find the correct answer:

"These inter-gang feuds have been with us in the UK since the 1920s. They're nothing new. It is just a readjustment of our organised crime power base. The public is not in danger."

The silence in the studio echoed the silence in the meeting room at Larcombe.

"Wait for it," said Minos, "he's left the door wide open. Here come the coach and horses."

The female interviewer couldn't believe her luck — an opportunity to be part of something meaningful on live TV.

"The police have failed to tackle organised crime for one hundred years. It's now established a power base that covers the entire country. Their activities threaten the economic fabric of this country. They reach into the deepest and most remote corners of our everyday life. Organised crime costs the economy between fifty and sixty billion pounds every year. How can you possibly maintain the public are not in danger? These killings may or may not be confined to criminals, but surely the British public deserves action against organised crime, not acceptance?"

"We have succeeded in combating organised crime on many occasions, young lady…."

"Oh, quit now," said Henry, "you're deep enough in it. Stop digging, you fool."

"Our viewers would be excused for thinking you've lost the battle given today's events. Let's join Sam for a summary of the news."

The focus switched to another newscaster on the other side of the studio. Sadly, for the Chief Constable, his microphone still broadcasts his comments. As the nation awaited the next catastrophe to hit the headlines, the senior police officer provided his own.

"You stitched me up there, didn't you? The sisterhood will be over the moon."

At Larcombe Manor, despite the seriousness of the situation, that remark brought a smile to several faces around the table.

"The BBC may have stumbled onto a winner," said Minos. "This could bring daytime TV viewers back in their millions."

"They're moving another expert in to take his place," said Giles.

"What a shame. I enjoyed watching that policeman squirm," said Artemis.

"I've seen this new chap before," said Henry. "That's Rod Nugent, a former Senior Investigating Officer with the National Crime Agency. He disagreed with how the force was going. Three years ago, he quit his job and now works in the private security sector.

Everyone's attention had switched to the big screen.

"Mr Nugent, you listened to our last guest give his views on today's events. How do you see the situation?"

"It's ludicrous to say the public shouldn't be concerned. A third of crime groups use violence or intimidation against non-gang members. Violence is many groups' stock-in-trade. They will likely carry through with threats against the public. They use violence to control their organisations daily. This level of violence ensures obedience, and as we've witnessed today, it eliminates competition."

"As shocking as today's events have been," said the interviewer, "most of the public won't experience it, so how deep does the problem go? How does organised crime affect the average person on the street?"

"We've seen examples in the media of high-impact crimes such as benefit fraud, business fraud, drug trafficking, intellectual property theft, and revenue fraud. Organised crime gangs are also responsible for stealing arts and antiques, illegal immigration, paedophilia, and vehicle theft, which impact a lower percentage of the public. Finally, you've got armed robbery, counterfeiting, kidnapping and extortion, pornography and prostitution. They have many options. Some specialise in a small number; others operate a pick-and-mix strategy. You were spot on with your comment earlier; it threatens our way of life. It's all-pervasive. Even if you don't come face-to-face with it, it will taint some part of your daily life's activities."

The mood warmed as another guest joined the discussion from a London studio. There was a pause, and the female interviewer said they had to interrupt the programme for a news flash.

The lull had ended dramatically. An eighth region of the country had suffered a gangland execution. A reporter stood outside a detached house in a smart residential borough of Southampton.

The garden swarmed with members of the emergency services. Parts of the building still smouldered. Their actions had limited the damage, but it was evident a serious incident had occurred.

"What can you tell us about what happened, Nick?" asked the newsreader at MediaCityUK.

"This is the home of Idris Johns, a sixty-one-year-old man known to have links to organised crime. He lived with his wife Megan, fifty-nine, their three sons, and two dogs. At around five o'clock, it's believed a group of armed men stormed the house. Megan Johns was in the kitchen. A gunman kicked in the back door and shot her dead. Idris Johns was asleep upstairs. The attack dogs always lay at the foot of his bed. The three sons sat in the lounge watching TV. After the first shots, the sons appear to have rushed towards the kitchen. Idris died on the stairs, and long bursts from submachine guns felled two of his boys as they exited the lounge door. People in the next street could hear the noise of gunfire. The third son dived through a front window onto the lawn and hid in the trees and bushes you can see on the right-hand side of the property. Reuben Johns, twenty-eight, tried to return to the house after the men had left, but the fires made it impossible. Reuben reported the murders to the police. The fire service chief told me his crew, wearing breathing apparatus, gained entry through the front door. They found three male bodies in the hallway. The dogs still lay on the stairs next to their owner. They died from smoke inhalation. The two sons who died were Lewis, thirty-three, and Dylan, thirty-one. All three sons were involved in criminal enterprises along with their father."

"That's where it ends," said Athena. "The Grid saved the most shocking attack to the last. Almost an entire gangland family wiped out."

"Those poor animals, too," said Artemis.

"Do we have a final death toll?" asked Alastor.

"Twenty-four," said Athena. "If that doesn't end resistance from groups who continued to go it alone, I don't know what will."

"What do you want us to do next?" asked Giles.

"Henry, I want you to review our security protocols. Not only here at Larcombe but across the board. Every safehouse must be invisible. Every agent needs to be reminded of their duty to keep Olympus safe. Our skills allow us to stay off the radar of the authorities. We must extend that to include anyone who might be associated with the Grid."

"Understood, Athena," said Henry.

"Giles and Artemis, return to the ice-house. Gather every scrap of intelligence on these killings today. Use whatever CCTV and communications data you can access to discover who carried out these attacks, Trace the killers to their origin if you can. We will act when the time is right. Switch personnel from other duties. I'll leave you to assess priorities for the short term. Phoenix and Rusty need someone on their shoulder this evening. The targets they seek have been active in the region for weeks. These aren't new to the game. Liaise with Phoenix and guide him towards the specific riders we want. There's little to gain from a random stop. When we talked last night, Phoenix told me the brothers who tried to mug him were small fry."

Giles and Artemis left the room along with Henry Case.

"I'm sure you two know what to do, don't you?" asked Athena.

"I'll continue to monitor the news reports," said Alastor, "if a major news story breaks, I'll be in touch."

"The only people we haven't heard from are the Prime Minister and the Home Secretary," said Minos. "I thought someone might have appeared on TV by now. I'll keep watch for that. Tomorrow, while we meet to discuss the aftermath of these attacks, we can expect statements in the House of Commons. That should be a vibrant morning to end the week."

A message alert sounded on Athena's phone.

"I've received word from Hugh Fraser," she said, "he wants to know if he should come back tonight."

"He's taken time off to attend the two funerals, hasn't he?" asked Alastor.

"Yes, he went to Manchester on Tuesday to Monty Jacks' funeral. Finn's funeral is tomorrow in Staffordshire."

"Does Fraser have family in the north?" asked Alastor, "I know he's divorced, but I can't recall them having had children."

"He hasn't been with us at Larcombe for long, but we

always try to accommodate agents when they ask for leave. Hugh has been with Olympus long enough to earn a rest. I can only guess why he stayed up there between the two funerals."

"I sense you have more than a guess, Athena," said Minos, "nothing sinister, I hope?"

"Ambrosia seemed keen to ally with Hugh Fraser straight after his appointment. It was understandable. The Irregulars were her idea. Hugh oversaw developing that project, and I saw no reason to object to her visiting Larcombe to discuss matters with him. It's not usual for a senior Olympian to drop in here unannounced. Erebus told me that Zeus and Hera came here on rare occasions in the Project's early days. Our mentor was against the others visiting. He reckoned it posed an unnecessary security risk."

"We have details of her visits," said Alastor, "nobody crosses that cattle grid at the gate without us recording the fact."

"Keep me informed of her trips south, Alastor," said Athena, "the frequency and length of her stay might highlight their true nature."

"They're both single," said Minos, "so if it's not to discuss Irregular business, it's not irregular."

"Touché," said Athena. "Thank goodness we found a lighter note to end on today. I'll see you both in the morning."

Athena returned to the apartment; it had been an exhausting day. She needed to be with Hope. The giggles and splashes from the bathroom told her Maria Elena was getting her daughter ready for bed. Athena went to the kitchen to see if she could prepare a quick meal. Events in the past ten hours dulled her appetite.

"You're back," said the nanny, carrying a chubby-cheeked infant into the lounge.

"I need a cuddle," said Athena, "today has been dreadful."

Maria Elena handed the warm, fresh-smelling bundle to her mother. Hope wanted a cuddle, too; ten hours was a long time without setting eyes on either Mummy or Daddy.

"I didn't watch much of the news," said Maria Elena, "it wasn't right for Hope to see. Instead, we watched children's TV, played games, and walked around the vegetable patch. There's always plenty to tell her. She takes everything in even if she can't say the words yet."

"Thanks again for filling in at short notice," said Athena, "tomorrow might bring better news. Phoenix will be home, and we should be able to cope after the morning meeting."

Maria Elena said goodbye and left. Giles had rung her to say he had to work underground until midnight. So she had another evening alone to catch up on her favourite box sets.

Phoenix and Rusty got ready to leave the safe house to begin another evening's fun in St. Johns Wood.

The riders they targeted had terrorised the streets around the Abbey Road Studios for weeks. Nearby attractions were a magnet for tourists and gave the gang ample opportunity to snatch mobile phones, cameras, and handbags. Phones and cameras were easily disposed of for cash in the local pubs. However, bags were where they earned the real money. If the tourists carried bundles of money, the credit cards and sometimes passports proved invaluable. They always found a ready market for those.

"Why do tourists flock to these old studios?" asked Phoenix, "that waxworks place is only half a mile away."

Rusty didn't comment. There was no educating him sometimes. Phoenix's phone rang. The same old ringtone. It had to be Giles.

"Giles, what have you got for me?" asked Phoenix.

"The team are on the move. Artemis is tracking them on CCTV. They're riding through Maida Vale."

"We're two hundred yards from the safe house. Where does Artemis reckon these kids are heading, and which road gets us there quickest to intercept?"

"They've turned onto Abercorn Place," said Giles, "their next right will take them on to Abbey Road and lead them towards the studios. Are you on Finchley Road yet?"

"Joining it now," replied Phoenix.

"Turn right onto Grove End Road, and you'll be on Abbey Road in no time. Good hunting."

"Thanks, Giles. Keep a close eye on things. Update me if you see something suspicious."

"Will do, Phoenix." Giles ended the call. He and Artemis resumed their analysis of the Grid attacks. They searched for clues to identify which gang initiated the killings. The killers could have come from any direction. Instead, they surrounded the final pockets of non-Grid enthusiasts and obliterated them.

Rusty drove them along Grove End Road and reached the junction with Abbey Road. Traffic had become lighter now; the rush hour was ending. The pause before the night-time rush was all too brief. London never sleeps, and hundreds of pedestrians cover the pavements.

"We can't use the same ploy as last night," said Phoenix, "it's too busy. But, we can follow them and move in when they're preparing to strike."

"That's risky," said Rusty, "if they spot a tail, they're only two minutes from Edgware Road. If they reach the Westway, they'll disappear in traffic in no time, and we'll have lost them for the night."

"It looks as if we use Plan C then?" said Phoenix.

"I didn't know you had prepared a Plan C."

"We've got the masks; why waste them? We locate the three riders, follow as close as we can without drawing their attention, and before they move in on anyone, we strike."

"What, right in the middle of this crowd of people?" asked Rusty.

"Giles, can you hear?" asked Phoenix.

"I'm right on your shoulder, as instructed," Giles replied.

"There are biker gangs out there who are active on social media, aren't there? Bikers who are mad at these punks are giving bikes a bad reputation—time for a little misinformation. Start spreading the news. A vigilante group is due to take the law into their own hands. The true bikers will if the police don't chase these riders."

"I'll get on it straight away," said Giles.

"Hold fire until I've hit somebody," said Phoenix.

"Your targets are sixty yards to your left, Phoenix," said Giles, "they're cruising, searching for fruit to pick."

"We've got them, Giles, thanks,"

The riders and their pillion passengers paid too much attention to passing foot traffic to notice the van. There were so many targets and so little time. They planned one rapid strike each and then a sprint home through Maida Vale. They might earn enough money for a great weekend if they struck gold.

They donned the pig masks and prepared the stun guns in the van. The first bike accelerated. Their target was ten yards ahead. The rider slewed the motorcycle in front of a stationary pair of Japanese tourists. He was taking a photograph of his wife. She looked over her shoulder to ensure they didn't get in anyone's way.

The two riders behind slowed and spread across the lane to prevent traffic from passing.

Both the rider and his passenger struck. It was no simple snatch and a dash from the kerb at high speed. The two thugs produced steel rods ten inches long. The man and his wife threw up their arms to protect their heads. While the pillion passenger grabbed cameras and phones from the couple, the rider took the handbag from the woman. He even wrenched the rings from her fingers.

Passers-by stopped in horror as the tourists slumped to the ground. Their attackers remounted the bike and made to flee the scene. The outriders prepared to follow but were alerted by the sound of a vehicle closing at speed.

Rusty had put his foot hard on the accelerator. The van hit both bikes with a glancing blow as it powered between them; riders and passengers crashed to the ground. Phoenix watched as members of the public rushed forward to help the stricken tourists. They would need to spend the rest of their visit to the capital in the hospital, but it could have been worse.

There were no helpers for the other members of the gang.

The lead attack bike struggled to pull away.

"When he dropped the scooter, his engine died," shouted Rusty, "We've gained valuable seconds when he had to hot-wire it again."

The traffic lights ahead had turned red. The rider wasn't in the mood to stop, but it wasn't his lucky day. A Harley-Davidson idled on the near side of a London Transport bus at the head of the queue. The hairy biker didn't move for anyone. The railings on the curved bend prevented the scooter from escaping via the pavement. Rusty closed right up on the rear of the bike. They were trapped. If only for the seconds before the lights changed.

Phoenix and Rusty leapt out, and each zapped a target with the stun gun. They thrust the semi-conscious bodies into the van. The lights changed as they returned to their front seats. The bus passengers weren't sure what had happened. Maybe it was for a TV show or a student prank? The biker had turned to look behind. He realised what was happening and gave the agents the thumbs-up as he roared away.

Traffic behind them grew impatient. Horns blared, but Rusty took his time; they were in no rush — time to return to the safe house with their captives.

Someone else could remove the scooter. The lads in the back didn't need it.

"There's no point dissuading these two from nicking the odd iPhone, is there?"

Phoenix shook his head.

"We'll truss them up nice and tight and relieve them of the items they stole. Then we'll bag those, together with the weapons, taking care not to leave any prints. Finally, I'll check where the nearest police station is, and we can dump them on the front steps."

"Aggravated assault is the least the police can charge them with," said Rusty. "I'd hope for a lengthy custodial sentence given the prolific history this gang has gathered."

The changeover at the safe house only took five minutes. Phoenix looked for the closest Metropolitan Police station; it stood on Fortune Green Road, less than two miles away.

Rusty took a leisurely drive up Finchley Road and slowed as he approached the drop-off point.

Phoenix jumped out of the passenger seat and opened the rear doors. He dragged the two thugs across the pavement and onto the flight of steps in front of the building. Rusty had stapled a bag containing the tourists' belongings to the rider. The pillion passenger wore the bag with their steel bars.

Another case was solved unless the Met and the Crown Prosecution Service got something wrong with the paperwork.

Thirty seconds later, the van disappeared into the distance. Rusty headed for the M40. A short trip on the road to nowhere. The M25 gave them access to the M4 without too much of a detour.

"We'll be home in time for a late supper," he said.

"I'm glad this mission's over," said Phoenix. "I didn't enjoy terrorising that twelve-year-old last night."

"I know what you mean," said Rusty. "But this menace needs tackling; otherwise, more lads will see it as a lucrative alternative to earning an honest living. There are hundreds of these scooters and mopeds on the road. We had one following us now. He may have been back there earlier after leaving the police station, but I've lost him now. He was too far behind to miss catching a red light before the roundabout where we joined the M4."

Miguel Fernando still rode on the M25, searching for the dark van with tinted windows in vain. The twenty-five-year-old mechanic had moved to London from Sheffield five years ago. In the evenings, he worked as a courier. His daytime job involved breaking up stolen, used cars for parts. The gang Miguel worked for set up bogus hire companies and loaned prestige cars such as BMWs, Audi, and Range

Rovers. The engine parts got exported in container loads heading for Africa and the Far East.

Miguel called his boss as Phoenix and Rusty made their way back to Bath.

"I've seen a van matching the description you gave us. They were on the M25, but I lost them. When I first spotted them, they had left two bodies at the cop shop in West Hampstead. I took a picture on my phone that I can send you. It won't do you much good, though. They wore pig masks. Will I get that bonus?"

The Olympus agents arrived at Larcombe after ten o'clock. Home safe for now, but was that photo the first crack in the Project's security?

Chapter Four

Friday, 3rd October 2014

Phoenix awoke to the sound of rain lashing against the bedroom window. The sunny and warm spell at the end of September was a distant memory. Autumn heralded its arrival. Athena was asleep beside him. Hope stirred in the nursery, but she seemed content for now.

He got out of bed and stretched. There was something he had thought of last night; what had it been? The van; that had been it. He needed to tell the transport section to dispose of it. In case the tail they picked up last night on the M25 had noted the registration. Rusty hadn't covered it while they motored around North West London.

Athena risked opening one eye.

"What's the time?"

"Seven," Phoenix replied.

"I'd love to stay here," she groaned.

"I'd love to join you, but today won't be any easier than yesterday."

Phoenix left his wife wrestling with her conscience and went for a shower. He studied his face after a shave and wondered where the years had gone. Time was catching up with him. Was forty-six classed as middle-aged these days? Rusty was much the same age. He didn't appear to have aged in the past four years, but neither could he stay in this game forever.

"Are you nearly finished?" asked Athena from the other side of the bathroom door.

"I'm decent if you're coming in," he replied.

"If you're decent, what's the point?" she said as she entered.

"Are you hungry?" asked Phoenix.

"For you, always," she replied.

Along the corridor, they both heard Hope was now wide awake as she yelled for attention.

"I'll cook us a hearty breakfast," said Phoenix, "you carry on, I'll collect Hope, and she can watch me in the kitchen."

"Life's not fair, is it?" said Athena, giving him a pout.

"When I look at you and Hope, life's damned good," said Phoenix as he made for the nursery.

Family time always got squeezed between sleep, meetings, and crises. Phoenix and Athena knew they must make the most of the time the Project left them free to relax. They enjoyed the ninety minutes this lull in proceedings offered. When Maria Elena arrived to start another day, she found the three in the kitchen smiling and happy.

"It's going to be better today, no?" she asked.

"We live in hope," said Phoenix.

The couple left the nanny with their daughter and walked to the meeting room. Everyone was eager to start. Today was Friday. If they got through today without another crisis, at least they might get the weekend to recharge the batteries.

"What's the latest on the Grid's attacks yesterday, Giles?" asked Athena.

"Nothing new overnight, Athena. No further deaths. I imagine the Grid are congratulating themselves."

"What progress on locating the killers?" asked Phoenix.

"Slow but steady," replied Artemis, "we have a list of suspects for each strike. It will be a painstaking task to reduce the numbers until we've formally identified the culprits. We could be ready to act a week from now."

"That fits in with our meeting next Wednesday in London," said Athena, "if we take names to Zeus for him to approve, that's preferable."

"We'll be busy next weekend, Rusty," said Phoenix.

"That's inadvisable," said Athena. "Eight different regions with direct actions needed? You need to work with Rusty on the planning, but we'll delegate responsibility to the most relevant teams to carry out the attacks."

"Can we not do the Bristol job? It's on our doorstep," asked Phoenix.

"You know what you're not supposed to do on your doorstep, Phoenix," said Henry Case. "If you must undertake a mission, it should be in Devon or Wales."

"I'm not ready for my pipe and slippers yet," replied Phoenix. "I vote for Hampshire, where they butchered that family."

"If I decide it's the right move, then that's settled," said Athena, "let's move on."

"Has everyone heard the Home Secretary's statement?" asked Minos.

"Phoenix and Rusty returned too late to catch it," said Artemis, "why don't you read it out to us, Minos?"

"Here goes," said Minos, "but I'm not sure I can match the earnest expression on her face when she delivered it. The full impact of these terrible incidents has yet to be assessed. I know the whole country's thoughts will be with the families of those who died. The emergency services responded in their usual quick and professional manner, for which we are eternally grateful. I was briefed by the police and the security services earlier this evening. The government will continue to receive updates on an ongoing incident. The top priority is the security of our people, and I urge everyone to keep calm. If you have information on who carried out these attacks, please report it to the police. We shall work together to defeat those who threaten the rule of law. The families of the victims of the men killed might raise an eyebrow at the government's concern for their families. The world's a better place without them in it. Even if other killers sent them on their way."

"You could have written that Minos," said Giles, "textbook stuff from Whitehall. Patting ourselves on the back for the excellence of our services, appealing for unity, but never initiating direct actions."

"It would make people sit up if she came on and said help us find these murdering bastards so that we can kill the lot," said Phoenix.

"Her statement won't put the fear of God into the Grid," said Rusty.

"The Grid will keep calm and carry on," said Henry.

"A good result yesterday, well done," said Colleen O'Riordan.

"It achieved what we expected," said Tyrone, "with fewer killings than I thought it might take. I followed up on the message the attacks sent, suggesting that the gangs joined the Grid within twenty-four hours or suffered the consequences. Each of the eight had agreed by midnight. Whoever was next in line to take over knew the score."

"The increased income will be useful to the cause," said Colleen.

"I'm estimating the numbers now. I'll send you a projected balance sheet later."

"Don't bother," said Colleen, "I don't understand it; give me the bottom line. The bigger the number, the better."

"I received good and bad news last night," said Tyrone. "My request for news or photos turned up something on the organisation, cramping our style of late. Reassuring to get a bite within two days. I told you there was something."

"You still believe in this secret organisation?" said Colleen. "Go on then. What did you hear?"

"Two Japanese tourists got mugged near Abbey Road last night by a moped gang. The couple spent the night in the hospital. A dark van injured four of the gang and wrote off their scooters. Two men in pig masks grabbed the guys who did it and took them away."

"So, this van is the only link to this outfit? It could have been an accident. The driver may have been distracted by the muggers."

"A young guy photographed the men, and the van, in West Hampstead. He rang to say they left the muggers on the steps of the police station."

"Are you sure it wasn't the A-team? That was what they did," laughed Colleen.

"Before my time, Mum," said Tyrone. "We can't see their faces because of the masks, but it confirms their existence. We can piece together the clues. The word's out on the streets, every sighting, every memory that photo triggers will get us closer to discovering who they are and where they're based. Have faith, mother. I know they exist. I'll prove it to you in time."

"What was the bad news?" asked Colleen.

"That moped gang was a set-up. Frank Rooney told me he had someone expendable. The gang had made a nuisance of themselves for weeks; that put them on this organisation's radar. So we inserted two new faces. They all look the same when they wear those helmets. The ferocity of the attack worked perfectly. There was no way they would ignore that. The idea was to get these two riders taken to their base. I never anticipated them handing the riders over to the police. It appears these guys have a social conscience. So, it's back to square one on the Trojan Horse scheme. It might need a more scientific approach."

"If they have a conscience, it means they are weak. Much easier for us to deal with the problem. Sometimes you overthink," said Colleen. "Keep it simple, as you did yesterday."

Monday, 6th October 2014

Geoffrey Fox buttered a slice of toast when the phone rang. He stopped and took a sip of his coffee before answering.

"Hello?" he asked.

"Good morning. Am I speaking with Mr Geoffrey Fox?" It was the voice of a young lady.

"It is," he replied, "how may I help you?"

"You honoured us by placing your house in Vincent Gardens, Belgravia, with our agency. I'm calling to inform you we have received an offer. It represents the full asking price of four million, seven hundred and fifty pounds."

"Happy days," said Geoffrey.

"Indeed, Mr Fox. We'll advise your solicitor this morning, and the sales process will proceed in its sweet way. These things have a mind of their own, don't they? We don't anticipate any undue delay; the Qatari buyer is well-known to us. He has bought a whole raft of properties in Central London. Your house is one of his cheapest acquisitions. His security staff will probably occupy it while he stays in London."

"How the other half lives," said Geoffrey, eager to get back to his coffee and toast.

When the call ended, Geoffrey salvaged his breakfast by toasting more bread and boiling the kettle for a fresh cup. Grace would have scolded him for lazing around half the morning. He wanted to run along the corridor to tell his daughter the news, but he knew she would be in meetings.

After he had washed up his breakfast things, Geoffrey dropped in on Maria Elena and his granddaughter.

"What are you two up to?" he asked.

"It's quiet today," said the nanny.

"I've had good news. My house in London has sold. I need to look for a place near the coast. I wonder if my daughter wants to go for a drive later today, to see what's on the market?"

"Easier to Google it," said Maria Elena.

"Ah, well, I'm no expert, my dear," laughed Geoffrey.

While Hope played on the carpet before them, Geoffrey and his new friend searched for Burnham-on-Sea bungalows on her iPhone.

Within thirty minutes, Geoffrey had three properties on his list. Prices ranged between four hundred and six hundred thousand pounds. Now, he needed his daughter or Phoenix to drive him to the coast to take a closer look.

"What time will they return from the meeting?" Geoffrey asked.

"I make us lunch for half-past twelve," said Maria Elena.

"I'll ask her then," he said, "catch you later."

Hope gave her granddad a little wave as he left them to return to his apartment. Perhaps Mummy would take her with them this afternoon. A trip to the seaside was special.

Athena and her senior agents discussed the weekend's events in the meeting room. Giles and Artemis reported zero activity from the Grid.

"They are still involved in their usual villainy, but intergang rivalries have ended," said Giles.

"Before the bodies of their victims," said Rusty, "that's insensitive."

"The government hasn't announced any new initiatives in the past forty-eight hours," said Artemis. "The police are still carrying out fingertip searches at the scene of every murder. Arrests don't look imminent."

"We will have two-thirds of the names confirmed by Tuesday evening, Athena," said Giles.

"You always were several steps ahead of the police, Giles," said Athena.

"Makes you wonder how he got a job here if that's true," said Phoenix.

"I never got caught, so my record was clean Phoenix," said Giles with a smile. In addition, the relatively quiet weekend had allowed him to spend quality time with his fiancée. That always helped put a smile on his face.

"Has anyone spoken with Hugh Fraser since his return?" asked Athena.

"Fraser attended both funerals as planned," said Henry. "I believe Ambrosia accompanied him in Rugeley."

"Zeus or Hera must have sanctioned that," said Phoenix. "Ambrosia has been working hard."

"What's next for our Irregulars?" asked Artemis.

"As we find accommodation, we add more people to those areas that could be terrorist targets," said Henry. "We're building on what we learned from Edinburgh and Birmingham. It will be the New Year before we can get sufficient veterans approved by myself and Hugh stationed across the country. We can then add the Grid to the list of things they're watching. We were quick off the mark at New Street but not fully prepared. Two people died because of that."

"Understood, Henry," said Athena, "the Irregulars are like the retrained agents and the new intakes. It's a slow process, but the more people we have in the field, the better chance of competing against the forces that threaten the nation. Many thanks, everyone. We'll break for today."

The others returned to their posts or planned their afternoons. As Phoenix and Athena walked along the corridor to their apartment, they bumped into her father.

"Daddy, will you have lunch with us today?" asked Athena.

"Maria Elena invited me," Geoffrey replied. "I'm hoping to persuade you to go for a drive this afternoon."

"I hoped to catch up with Hugh Fraser after lunch," said Athena, "but I suppose we could go somewhere once that's over. Where were you thinking?"

"A Qatari billionaire has snapped up the house. Maria Elena and I found three possible bungalows in Burnham-on-Sea on the internet. The sooner you and I look them over, the sooner I'll be out of your hair."

"That was quick," said Phoenix, "don't rush off on our account, Geoffrey. We don't mind having you around the place, and Hope loves the attention."

As they entered the living room, Maria Elena sang in the kitchen. Lunch was on its way. Hope knelt on a chair by the window, and grubby finger marks smeared the glass. She scrambled to the floor, but it was too late. Hope knew she was in trouble.

"Well, young lady," said Phoenix. "Maria Elena will need to take you into the kitchen with her in the future. You're too adventurous to be left alone for a second."

"At ten months, you were a handful, Annabelle," said Geoffrey.

He picked up Hope and carried her through to the kitchen.

"We need to wash our hands before lunch, Maria Elena," he said, sitting Hope on the worktop next to the sink.

Hope gave a big sigh. You know I'm not allowed up here, Grandad, she thought, there might be sharp things. I'm in enough trouble; I'll never get strapped into the car seat this afternoon.

Geoffrey wiped her hands clean and dried them with a cloth.

"There we are. Just the windows to clean now."

Maria Elena had carried the food through to the living room to Phoenix and Athena. She left them to decide what drinks they needed but gave Hope the usual cup of her favourite orange drink.

"Will you need me again today?" she asked.

"No, that's fine," said Phoenix, "we'll look after her until the morning. Then, we'll see you at the usual time."

After the nanny had left, Athena was keen to go through

the details of the house sale and the forthcoming house search.

"We'll all go," said Phoenix, "it will be great to get away for a while. What about Fraser? Did you want to ring him and schedule a time? I want to be there. It might help us understand what's going on with Ambrosia. I hate turning up to Olympus meetings unprepared."

"Good idea, I'll call him now. We should be home by this evening. I'll arrange to meet at seven-thirty."

"There's never a thing on TV at that time, is there?" said Phoenix, "Hope will be asleep from the effects of the travel and the sea air."

Athena went into the kitchen to make the call. She rejoined them two minutes later, nodding to Phoenix that the meeting would go ahead. Geoffrey had fetched a jacket, despite the warm weather.

"You won't need that in the car, Daddy," she said.

"We never got sea breezes in Belgravia, darling," he replied, "I'm getting on in years. I feel the cold more than you youngsters. Rain's forecast, anyway."

Phoenix put a cardigan on his daughter, which made her happy. She felt dressed up, the same as her Grandad. Phoenix drove them to Burnham. Geoffrey sat in the front with him, and Athena sat alongside Hope in the back.

"Before you ask, we don't need any music, Phoenix," said Athena.

He shrugged. His favourite Judas Priest album was still in the last van he'd driven.

"We'll sing a song," said Geoffrey, "does everyone know the words to Wheels on the Bus?"

Phoenix groaned.

Hope had fallen asleep by the time they passed Chew Magna. Peace reigned once more. They soon arrived in the seaside town and hunted for the properties in which Geoffrey was interested. Maria Elena had printed off the details of what lay inside the four walls. Geoffrey was keen to see the location for himself, and how it fitted the tranquil setting he sought.

Phoenix had hardly come to a halt at the first bungalow before Geoffrey said he'd seen enough. It was too near a road, and the view was restricted.

"Typical estate agent," he muttered, "economical with the truth. This description should read, two oak trees obscure forty per cent of the vista.

Phoenix drove them to the next address. Maria Elena provided excellent directions.

"This is better," said Geoffrey, "we might ask to view this one later in the week."

As they approached the final bungalow, Hope cried out. She was excited.

"Do you like this one, Hope?" asked Geoffrey, "yes, it's idyllic. You have good taste, the same as your grandmother. Good, but expensive. This place is the most expensive of the three I chose, at five hundred and ninety-five thousand pounds."

"You can get a few improvements done and still clear four million," said Phoenix as they walked to the gateway. Athena was fetching Hope from the car.

"Money isn't everything, old chap. I'd sooner have Grace here to share this place."

"I know, Geoffrey. What do you reckon then, a shortlist of two?"

"No, Hope's reaction when she saw this place was good enough for me. We'll drive into town, find the estate agents and make an offer. Everything I've seen online of the interior is fine, and the place is in good decorative order. I won't need to do a thing."

"It looks super," said Athena as she joined them.

"This is the one, darling," said her father, "I've decided. Let's get the offer in pronto. I don't want to risk losing it."

An hour later, they were walking along the front at Burnham as the rain clouds gathered. It was a race against time. Could they reach the ice cream kiosk before they got soaked to the skin?

"That was fun," Geoffrey said as they returned to the car. The sky was as dark as night. The rain beat a tattoo on the car roof. Hope still smiled as she polished off the tub of ice cream her mother fed her.

"Typical English weather," said Phoenix, "four seasons in one day."

"Only when you visit the seaside, Phoenix," said Geoffrey.

"Two of you got what you came for," said Athena, "you got your bungalow, and Hope's eaten her ice cream."

"Ninety-nine per cent of which went in her mouth," said Phoenix. "Thanks to you for feeding her with that wooden spoon. Sharron had ice cream everywhere when we went on holiday on the South coast. Over her face, on her dress, and in her hair."

"You've never mentioned that before," said Athena.

"We couldn't afford to go away often," said Phoenix, "my memories are few but precious."

Geoffrey said nothing. There were things in Phoenix's past he wasn't a party to, and this was one. His daughter would tell him who Sharron was in time if it was appropriate.

"Time to head for home?" he asked Phoenix.

"Home for you, for now," replied Phoenix, "we'll move

your furniture from London before you know it. You and Hope have made a good choice. It's a great location."

Hope agreed with her father. The bungalow was perfect. Her grandfather had a panoramic view of the sea from the back of the property. The cliffs made it impossible for anyone to approach from that direction. He'd spot anyone well before they reached the gateway, whether in a car or on foot. Oh, and the ice cream was lush.

Phoenix decided the rainy finish to the afternoon wasn't spoiling his rare trip out. So he took the A38 back to Bath, stopping in Paulton for a great pub meal. It was half past six when they got home. He looked at the faces of his passengers; Athena and Geoffrey were half asleep. Hope's head was on her chest; she was snoring. The sea air and the children's meal had done the trick, as he had predicted.

A rapid crossing of the cattle grid in the gateway made the grown-ups wake with a start.

"Home, sweet home," he said, "we can put Hope to bed in plenty of time to meet Hugh Fraser at half-past seven."

"Many thanks for today, Phoenix," said Geoffrey. "It won't be easy, but I'm starting the next chapter of my life. With you three coming along for the ride, I'll be fine.

"I'm sure you will, Geoffrey," said Phoenix. "We're only an hour away if you need us, and Hope can't resist a trip to the seaside."

After a short dash to the door, they were inside the main building when the rain came on harder. Athena kissed her father as they left him at the entrance to his apartment. Phoenix carried the sleeping Hope to the nursery and prepared her for bed. Athena joined him, and they stood by the cot.

"We made that," said Athena.

A Frequent Peal of Bells

"Did you find it odd she made such a fuss over that bungalow?" asked Phoenix.

"At first, I thought it was an involuntary response, or she'd spotted a cat in the garden,"

Athena replied as they turned to walk through to the lounge.

"And then?" asked Phoenix.

"Of the three we viewed, it offered the best defensive position. Was that pure luck? I have no idea."

"That's my girl," said Phoenix, choosing to believe their daughter was a child prodigy. If he could persuade her to share his taste in music, everything would be perfect.

Athena hoped her father never needed to defend himself against anything.

They arrived at Hugh Fraser's quarters in the stable block at seven-thirty.

"This takes you back, doesn't it?" he said to Athena.

"Should we knock, in case he's entertaining?"

Phoenix knocked on the door.

"Come in," called Hugh. He was alone.

"We both felt it wise to discuss progress to date on the Irregulars and to consider the best spot to deploy them," said Phoenix.

"Ambrosia may have told you there's an Olympus meeting in London on Wednesday," said Athena.

The pause before Hugh Fraser replied was only slight, but both Phoenix and Athena noticed it.

"I've written a report on the first mission for the Irregulars," he said, ignoring the opportunity to reveal his relationship with the senior Olympian. "The losses we suffered were tragic. We must learn from that. I'll give you copies to take back to your senior team. I hope you agree with my recommendations."

"Do you have a number yet for the next batch of suitable recruits?" asked Phoenix.

"Eighteen more are ready to go into the field with immediate effect, Phoenix. If you have a list of preferred sites where you want them allocated, I'll liaise with Alastor and match them to the available accommodation. Is it wise to continue our concentration on railway stations? Or should we extend our network to cover air and seaports?"

"We can clarify that at the meeting," said Athena. "Has Ambrosia talked to Zeus on this matter already? Do you know?"

"I believe Ambrosia has been in touch with both Zeus and Hera," replied Hugh, "but whatever she discussed with them wasn't shared with me."

The verbal game of ping pong continued for what felt like ages to Phoenix. Whatever they threw at Hugh Fraser, he batted back without revealing too much. Could he ask him outright whether he was sleeping with the Olympus goddess? It wasn't anyone's business but their own. Were they plotting to undermine his and Athena's status with the organisation? Now, that was a separate question, one he couldn't ask but one for which he needed the answer.

"I'll give you a suggested distribution for those eighteen in the morning," said Phoenix. "We'll take those copies of your report back with us now, please. We can pass them to the rest of the team at the morning meeting."

As the couple left the stable block, Athena seemed troubled.

"I thought we were doing the right thing appointing Piya as our latest recruit to the top table. Her background was solid, and her fortune is more than welcome to bolster our funds. There were moments after she paid us that first visit, I queried the wisdom of allowing her free access to Larcombe."

"Erebus found Zeus and Hera at the outset. Their money helped form the Project. Perhaps they weren't as disciplined in their selections in those early days. Next, Poseidon and Demeter slipped through the net. Hermes was proposed by those two, and Zeus accepted, not knowing he was Demeter's son. Since Erebus died, you and I have added a further layer of protection. We consider each applicant on their merits. Piya Adani ticked the boxes. As Ambrosia, she promised to add a dimension to the Project it lacked."

"That was something Erebus wished for," said Athena, "he even questioned naming the gods from Greek myth. He thought it elitist, and the upper echelons were too representative of the white establishment."

"Apollo and I have altered that aspect," said Phoenix, "Ambrosia adds her ethnic contribution into the mix. Her upbringing nurtures her ambitious nature. That ambition so far has always been positive. She may wish to make a fast ascent up the Olympus hierarchy, but Zeus and Hera will resist attempts to steer the project differently. They don't want a repeat of those perilous times last year."

In the stable block, Hugh Fraser was talking with Ambrosia.

"Phoenix and Athena have just left. They asked many questions; they suspected something was going on between us. I told them nothing."

"We are free to be with whoever we choose," she replied. "My work behind the scenes with Zeus and his wife is of more concern to them, I imagine. I aim high in everything I do. Too many of the gods around Olympus' top table are lethargic. Their money grants them entry, but they have no fight left in them. If we stand still, we will fall further behind the Grid. The terrorists will also move ahead with new methods of hurting this country. I can't stand by watching that happen. Olympus needs more dynamic leadership. With your help, I aim to reach the summit."

"I'll help in any way I can, Ambrosia," said Hugh.

"You already have, darling," she replied, "those three days last week were heavenly. I can't wait for us to be together again."

"When that will be is entirely in your hands," said Hugh, "I'm on duty here at Larcombe for the foreseeable future."

"Then, with your permission, we must show Zeus and the others we are more than colleagues," she replied.

"Of course," Hugh replied.

"Athena can hardly raise objections to my visiting you whenever I wish if we announce it in front of Zeus."

"What do you mean?" he asked.

"We're going to a wedding party at The Dorchester on Wednesday evening. A party for two of the Olympus gods. I don't need to attend it alone. However, I shall warn Hera I'm bringing a partner. She will keep our secret from Zeus until the evening."

"Send me the details of where you're staying. It will be an honour to escort you," said Hugh. "I'll drive up to London in the late afternoon."

"We'll watch how the gods interact on a social level. It will be easier to spot alliances to be wary of in that environment and differences we can exploit."

"You can be devious at times," said Hugh.

"To get what you want, Hugh, it's imperative. Sweet dreams, darling."

Later that night, Hugh Fraser found sleep elusive. He wondered whether their relationship was genuine or she was using him.

Hugh decided it was too much fun to matter.

Chapter Five

Tuesday, 7th October 2014

"I have returned."

Ahmed Mansouri looked at the simple message a second time. It came through on his phone. He destroyed his collection of burner phones when they fled to the mosque. There was only one person this could be; Bakar al-Hamady had returned to the UK.

His younger colleague Omar Harrack knelt in another room, praying. He must tell him to prepare when he returns. The call could come at any time.

The elderly Syrian stood on the platform at Liverpool Lime Street. Bakar al-Hamady had taken a calculated risk. After he flew to Paris, he travelled to the Netherlands. Friends sheltered him there until he felt safe to return. The authorities had domestic matters occupying them. A small window existed in which he might slip back into the country.

Bakar flew to Belfast and then boarded an overnight

ferry. An eight-hour crossing delivered him to Birkenhead at six-thirty this morning. A replacement passport had been costly in Amsterdam. Whether his arrival had been in Northern Ireland or the mainland, it was genuine enough to gain entry. However, he went unchallenged. There was wisdom in travelling overnight; staff were half asleep. A taxi trip through the tunnel under the Mersey brought him to Lime Street Station. The train he waited for went to Bristol.

He contacted Mansouri and Harrack before he boarded. This service took him to Stafford, where he changed to continue his onward journey to Temple Meads. Bakar al-Hamady wanted to avoid New Street until the right time. When he reached Bristol, he would call Mansouri's number once more. Then, they needed to meet to arrange to purchase more mobile phones. Every communication had to be covert now. Even when the authorities were under pressure, one diligent officer lay in wait to intercept a suspicious message.

The Syrian would reach Bristol at midday. He studied the layout of Temple Meads while in Amsterdam; Bakar knew its history. The famous British engineer Isambard Kingdom Brunel planned a line that connected London to the West Country. Paddington station was one hundred and fifteen miles to the east. Construction of Temple Meads began in 1839 and opened the following year. Much work was to be done to link the line from Bristol to Bath Spa with the line from London to Chippenham.

Bakar al-Hamady wished he could travel back in time to speak with Brunel. They shared a similar vision. Brunel used one tonne of explosives each week to complete his dream. Two and a half years to produce a tunnel of under two miles. It had affectionately been called God's Wonderful Railway.

The Syrian wondered what damage he might do with one tonne of explosives on the Grade I listed flagship of Brunel's GWR in the centre of Bristol.

Inside the mosque in the heart of the Midlands, Mansouri and Harrack gathered together their things. It didn't take long. They destroyed much of their gear in Birmingham when it became too dangerous. The authorities raided houses in the nearby towns where the suicide bombers lived. Everyone was dead. The planned attack on New Street was abandoned. Mansouri lamented the lack of coverage their deaths received.

It was usual for the security services to tell the British public when they foiled a terror attack. They were quick off the mark on those occasions. An apology was far slower coming when a lack of numbers and paper-thin border controls encouraged breached defences.

Mansouri had anticipated the media report of a hunt for the men responsible for the DLR bombing in Canary Wharf. So he and Omar prepared for it and escaped by disguising themselves in female clothing.

Why didn't they follow up on the trail that led from Edinburgh? The death toll was far higher; they should have been on high alert after the first strike. The security services must have identified the potential New Street threat and acted against their colleagues. He wished to hear from al-Hamady again. Why was news of the deaths of the secret service agent suppressed in the media? The body disappeared. Mansouri watched the video posted by Uddin; it wasn't a fake.

The British loved to weep and wail over a few dead bodies. The nation went into several days of mourning while ten thousand children have died in Syria since the civil war began four years ago.

Mansouri wanted to ask al-Hamady to explain. Why order a news blackout? Which arm of the security services carried out the raids on the houses in the Midlands? Something didn't add up. They needed to be cautious when executing their next attack. He planned each one with precision, and those they completed were successful.

Ahmed and Omar had escaped to this mosque with minutes to spare. Birmingham was the key. Canary Wharf and Edinburgh Waverley generated the headlines ISIS craved. The authorities committed as many resources to find the culprits as possible, without result. That was because of al-Hamady's superior planning.

Yet, they did nothing when they uncovered the threat of an attack ten times greater than the last. It made no sense.

His phone rang again. Was it a second message from the Syrian?

"Platform 9 BTM. Come now."

Mansouri heard movement next door; prayers had ended. Omar walked into the room without saying a word. Mansouri showed him the mobile phone screen.

"We need a trip to the shops," said Harrack, "for a new disguise. So I shall travel posing as your wife. We can still be on a train from New Street within the hour. So we will be on the same platform island in Bristol by three o'clock as our friend."

"The wait is over," said Mansouri, collecting his bags, "we can continue with our work."

The two men left the mosque without troubling their hosts; they could return whenever they wished. Their hosts had made that plain. Mansouri marvelled at the speed with which his young companion identified and purchased the dark blue burka in the Grand Central shopping mall. His sisters would have spent a whole morning on such a task.

Harrack followed Mansouri as they entered New Street station. They purchased tickets to Bristol Temple Meads with cash and boarded the train at a quarter past one. It arrived in Bristol on Platform 12 at three o'clock. Not a word passed between them throughout the journey.

When they arrived on the platform in Bristol, Mansouri looked for the Syrian.

"Over there, by the information screen," whispered Harrack. Mansouri led the way. They crossed the island to Platform 9 and joined their colleague.

"Follow me," said al-Hamady, "I'll give you the grand tour. Enjoy the view while you can. It won't stay this way much longer."

The platforms and subway weren't busy on a Tuesday afternoon. But nobody paid much attention to two Muslim men and a woman whose clothing covered every inch of her. Within minutes they reached the entrance to the main building. As they stood with their backs to the gate, al-Hamady listed the points of interest. The ticket office and machines lay ahead. The ubiquitous bookshop stood on the right, next to the entrance to the platforms. Customer Information System screens by the entrance showed arrival and departure information for every platform.

"The signalling to all platforms will accept trains in either direction," he told them in Arabic, "the flexible layout allows trains on any route to use any part of the station."

"Automatic ticket gates control entry to the platforms. Is that correct?" asked Mansouri.

"Yes, those are on Platform 3, over there," replied al-Hamady. "Walk with me. You see the main station restaurant and bar on the left. On the right of the entrance is the subway linking the platforms. Those are reachable either by steps or lift, as we noticed when we crossed from Platform 9."

As the terrorists entered the subway for the second time, they passed the main public toilets. James Protheroe was leaving. James's memory was still sharp despite the hard times he'd experienced since he returned from active duty in Kosovo. Those three had passed him earlier when he was upstairs. They didn't trigger suspicions initially, but he reasoned they didn't move with purpose. It was unusual for people to wander around the concourse unless lost.

James Protheroe followed them as they looked at the ATMs and studied the various catering outlets; this was more than a sightseeing tour. Finally, the older man pointed to the ceiling. They were beneath the passenger information office if his bearings were correct. A few yards further, they were now below the lounge, a lounge filled throughout the day with travellers relaxing before the next stage of their journey.

Up ahead, al-Hamady continued to explain their surroundings to Mansouri and Harrack. Protheroe recognised it as modern standard Arabic but was unable to translate it. The speaker looked around sixty years old, and from his appearance, he was a Sunni Muslim from Syria.

"The third island platform where we met is our first target — platforms 9 to 12 service trains from various sources. Most significant to us are those to and from Paddington and Waterloo. The subway will be next. The emergency services will need to use it to gain access."

"Have we abandoned the suicide bomber approach now?" asked Mansouri.

"We must accept that the New Street scheme is beyond repair," the Syrian replied. "From now on, we revert to a series of bloody big bangs."

Protheroe studied the second man; he might be from several North African countries. He looked much younger, perhaps thirty. The wife was young, too, judging by the way she walked. A loose-limbed and athletic woman with surprisingly large feet. How could anyone tell her appearance with that burka? Hell, she might even be a bloke.

The group turned towards him now. They had seen what they needed to see. Protheroe elected to keep walking past them, his mobile phone in his hand. Nothing unusual about that. He avoided others in the subway doing the same thing. The signal was weak, but he knew he must try to get a photograph.

Protheroe took several snaps as he approached the trio. The two men were deep in conversation. It was impossible to tell whether the burka-clad individual spotted his actions. Nevertheless, Protheroe didn't turn back; he walked to the next lift and made his way upstairs. They weren't visible on the concourse. As he kept watch, he made a call.

"Protheroe here, at Temple Meads. I'm forwarding images of possible terrorist activity. I hope you can use them. Something's happening."

"Thanks, James," said Hugh Fraser. "I'll check them out. Don't approach them. Keep watch and await further instructions."

Outside the station, Barak al-Hamady had hailed a taxi. As he got in, he handed Ahmed Mansouri a piece of paper.

"My lodgings are in Bradley Stoke. I have a cousin living there. She will put me up for three nights. You must visit our friends in Lawrence Hill; they will make you welcome. Take this phone; it will be our sole means of communication. Destroy your phone. You must never use it again."

Mansouri nodded. He took care of that before they left for Grand Central this morning.

"Everything will be ready for Friday afternoon," said al-Hamady, as he closed the taxi door.

Mansouri and Harrack watched the cab disappear into traffic.

"I can't be sure," said Harrack, "but a man in the subway lifted his phone as he passed. He may have been searching for a signal, or he may have photographed us."

"Has he followed us?" asked Mansouri.

"He didn't look back. Instead, he went to the lifts."

"Then, it is likely it was innocent," shrugged Mansouri. "No matter, we won't return until Friday. Our new friends from Lawrence Hill can look for evidence that the security services have been alerted. We will take extra precautions."

"Look," said Harrack, "there's a bus to Lawrence Hill. If we run, we can catch it."

Mansouri shook his head.

"We don't want to draw attention to us running. It's unseemly for a Muslim wife. So we shall walk to where our friends live unless another bus is due."

Mansouri asked for directions from a street cleaner. Twenty minutes later, they stood on the doorstep of the address on the piece of paper.

"There are many Muslims in this part of the city," said Harrack, "no one will find us in Lawrence Hill."

The terrorist trio had gone into hiding once more; the planning stage was complete. Preparations for the bombs to be constructed had begun. One hundred hours remained before the heart of the Victorian station would cease to beat.

Wednesday, 8th October 2014

"What time is Biggles arriving?" asked Athena.

"You've got twenty minutes to get ready, say your goodbyes to Hope, and run back to collect your dancing shoes."

"Biggles can wait," said Athena.

Phoenix could be so flippant; this wasn't the plan. They were to drive to London with Hope and drop her off with her grandparents. Then, she and Phoenix would be free to enjoy the evening wedding party. Sometime tomorrow, depending on how late they arrived in Vincent Gardens, they planned to travel home to Bath.

The DLR bombing changed that. Her mother had died of a heart attack at the scene. Her father stayed with them at Larcombe Manor until he moved into that new home on the coast. Little Hope was to remain with her nanny, Maria Elena. They were to travel to London alone.

Phoenix decided discretion was the better part of valour. He could drive up today in time for the Olympus meeting, but they were too busy to hang around in the capital until the effects of a hangover cleared tomorrow.

"We'll give Les Biggar a call at Filton," he said lunchtime yesterday, after the morning meeting. "He can get us to Fairoaks airfield, and then a driver can take us to Curzon Street at ten tomorrow morning. We'll be collected from Marylebone at nine on Thursday morning and taken to the airfield. Biggles can then drop us off on the lawn. We'll be back in time to hear from Minos about what happened at the meeting. Simple."

"How far have I got to walk in heels from the Dorchester?"

"Two minutes, tops," Phoenix told her, "it's the same

distance from the meeting rooms to the wedding party venue."

"How do you know so much?" she asked.

"Research," he replied.

It came back to her then. Erebus worried about her mental state four years ago when terrorist bombers threatened central London. Soon after he joined Olympus, Phoenix kept watch over her while she visited her parents. Erebus feared the nightmares she suffered following her fiancée's death in 2005 might return to haunt her.

This morning, Phoenix was itching to get out into the garden to watch the helicopter's arrival. Athena was running late. Hope was dressed and already eating her breakfast with Maria Elena and Geoffrey Fox. The start of yet another busy day for the Olympus Project.

As Athena bundled the last few items into an overnight bag, she heard the telltale noise of the helicopter. She ran to the kitchen, kissed her father and daughter, and thanked Maria Elena. Then, Athena dashed into the garden; their transport had landed on the lawn. She prayed she wouldn't slip on the wet grass, shielded her head against the rain and made for the open door. Phoenix sat inside, grinning.

"All this fuss for a forty-five-minute flight," he chuckled.

"You can go off, people," said Athena, trying to rearrange her wet and windswept hair.

Les Biggar landed at Fairoaks, and an Olympus car pulled alongside. It was still raining hard. Before they left the dry interior, their pilot reminded them he expected them for a ten o'clock lift-off in the morning.

"No worries," said Phoenix, "we'll be here."

They arrived at the hotel fifty minutes later. After they checked into their room, they walked to Curzon Street,

Mayfair. The rain had paused. In truth, it hadn't stopped for days.

"Bags of time," said Phoenix as they arrived at the London Executive Offices building. It was now ten to ten.

"I remember the first time we came here," said Athena.

"Hard to forget the atmosphere," said Phoenix, "let's hope those dark days are behind us."

When they arrived at the suite Olympus had reserved, Athena saw that several other senior Olympians had come before them. Zeus was talking with Apollo; Hera sat on the other side of the room with Ambrosia.

"You two look as if you're on the naughty step. Has Zeus ordered you out?"

They turned to see Ludovic Tremayne had arrived.

"Achilles," said Phoenix, "good to see you again. But, no, we were checking who was inside."

"Who aligned with whom, I suspect?" asked Achilles with a smile.

"You know us so well," said Athena, opening the door.

Zeus came towards them at once. Phoenix thought Ambrosia seemed reluctant to let Hera follow her husband.

"We were devastated to learn of your mother's death," said Hera, hugging Athena.

Zeus shook Phoenix by the hand.

"We'll discuss our response to that later, Phoenix," he said.

Sir Malcolm Dunseith and Jean-Paul St Clair breezed through the door when the commiserations and greetings were complete.

Dionysus, the Privy Counsellor, oozed class and entitlement. Phoenix imagined he learned at a preparatory school how to enter a room. No social or business occasion, however important, flustered people like him.

Daedalus, the French industrial designer, was so laid back he was horizontal. It was difficult to imagine them as friends in any other setting, yet neither man betrayed any distaste for the vast gulf between their backgrounds. They must have met outside the building or in the lift, deep in amicable conversation as they joined the small crows surrounding their leader.

"It appears our newlyweds have overslept," said Zeus. Hera now stood by his side.

"They still have a minute, dear," she said.

"We'll get the formalities out of the way while we await their arrival," said Zeus. "Can I ask you to check if you have switched off your mobile phones? This room was swept for any listening devices before we arrived. Security remains paramount, as I'm sure you appreciate."

"Here they are," cried Hera, hurrying to the door. At last, Sir James Grant-Nicholls and his bride, Elizabeth, the Duchess of Lochalsh, had appeared.

"Sorry we're late," said Heracles, "we dropped into tonight's venue on our way here. Elizabeth wanted to check the arrangements were perfect for tonight."

"How was the honeymoon?" asked Hera.

"We had a lovely time on Martinique and cruising in the Caribbean," said Aphrodite.

It helps when your husband owns a yacht half the length of a football pitch, thought Phoenix. Nevertheless, he was keen to get on with the meeting. Zeus must have agreed, as he soon encouraged people to take their seats. Ambrosia sat next to Hera. Phoenix and Athena were in their usual spot at the opposite end of the table to Zeus. But Heracles and Aphrodite sat side by side for the first time.

Phoenix was pleased to see that Daedalus grabbed the chair next to him. The Frenchman was becoming a trusted ally. With Ambrosia cosying up to Zeus and Hera, he and Athena needed every bit of support they could get around this top table.

Zeus updated them on the Project's progress around the globe. Unfortunately, foreign missions were fiendishly challenging to undertake, and often their cost was punitive. So he proposed Olympus scaled back its activities overseas and concentrate on the threats they now faced at home.

"I'm concerned over the latest actions attributed to the Grid," he said, "Athena has briefed me on last week's events. Under Hugo Hanigan's leadership, they sought to eliminate the competition and control every aspect of criminal activity in the UK. His progress may have proved too slow for someone in the organisation. Who knows? We must now accept that the new leadership is far more brutal. That poses a headache for Olympus."

"We can apply pressure on the Grid with our increased number of agents," Athena reminded him. "We have regular programmes at Larcombe to train recruits and retraining agents redeployed from overseas. The Irregulars are being fed into the system as quickly as is practical. We approved eighteen men for action in the field in the past few days. I believe our biggest headache is security."

"Someone followed Rusty and me for a brief period on our last mission," explained Phoenix. "We lost them on a series of roundabouts on the outskirts of London, but the threat is real. With their competition eliminated, the Grid has the facility to have eyes everywhere. One slip and a safe house might be exposed, agents identified, and a concrete link with Larcombe Manor established."

"How do we combat that?" asked Hera.

"How to handle that and increased terrorist activity?"

asked Zeus. "Two successful bombings with a significant loss of life. A third major attack foiled. All within two weeks."

"The next strike is imminent," said Phoenix. "Our Logistics Officer received a call from an Irregular on his second day in the field at Bristol Temple Meads. The images he captured were useless because of a poor underground signal. Our people only determined they showed two men and a woman. The clothing suggested they were Muslims, but Bristol has a diverse ethnic population. They may easily be locals, not terrorists."

"Have we increased our surveillance?" asked Heracles.

"We cannot add further resources for a while," said Athena. "I've confirmed the Irregulars have updated photos of our main suspects from the previous bombings."

"I hope you post more people outside the station rather than on the platform," said Apollo, "because if they've reached that far the attack will be underway. It will be too late."

"Our ice-house team switched their focus from the blurred images in the subway to the CCTV on the bus and taxi ranks outside," said Phoenix. "We flew here before we heard the results of that search. We prefer to trace where the bombs are manufactured and eliminate the threat. If these three were our bombers, they must have gone to safe houses in the city. How long they will remain in hiding is anyone's guess."

"I would be happier if the Irregulars didn't get exposed to the level of risk they faced at New Street," said Hera, "these homeless veterans have suffered enough."

"Every Olympus team has received a set of updated protocols from Hugh Fraser, both for working with and protecting Irregulars," said Phoenix. "I told you last time how valuable an asset he might be."

Ambrosia sat higher and straighter in her chair when her lover got a pat on the back.

Athena thought it amusing.

"Ambrosia has been working closely with our Logistics Officer on the Irregulars project," said Phoenix. "I'm sure the hands-on support of a senior Olympian helps to produce the best results."

Athena watched for a response from the tiny Indian woman at the far end of the table. She hoped Phoenix didn't catch her eyes; he would have turned to stone.

"I think it confirms we made another good choice when we appointed Ambrosia," said Hera, squeezing her companion's hand.

"If I can follow up on that subject," said Zeus. "I've reached a shortlist of three candidates for the vacant twelfth seat around this table."

He passed photographs and histories around the table for the others to study.

"Will you carry out due diligence on these three, Athena? I've checked as much as I can, but I don't possess the skills of Minos and Alastor. If they pass that final hurdle, we will vote on the matter at our next meeting in Birmingham on Wednesday, the seventh of January. I wish to bring the meeting to a close now. Then we can relax and enjoy the refreshments arriving in fifteen minutes. You can assess the three candidates as we wait but remember that they may not survive the final cut."

"Zeus and I agreed we should call an early halt to this meeting," added Hera. "I'm sure you wish to have sufficient time to prepare for tonight's party."

Phoenix and Athena skipped through the backgrounds of the candidates.

"The three candidates look to be billionaires from IT," said Phoenix, "and every one of them is younger than me."

"I can see the logic behind targeting men and women who have made their fortunes from new technology. We question the efficiency of our surveillance equipment at Larcombe when we struggle to locate our enemies. If we added someone from the cutting edge of the computer business, it could only improve our performance, could it not?"

The first candidate was *Byron Paterson*, forty years old. Born in California, he taught himself computer technology in high school. The family was poor. His mother had separated from his father and raised Byron and his two younger sisters alone. He got a job as an engineer with a web services provider. His rise to the top was rapid as one internet giant after another spotted his skills — three of his business-related applications featured in the top twenty favourites for seven consecutive years. His net worth was 7.6 billion dollars.

Raymond Ferreira was just a boy at thirty-two. His Portuguese grandparents emigrated to southern Ireland in the 50s. An only child, he grew up in a village outside Wexford, in the province of Leinster. He taught himself to code from eight to occupy his spare time. It may be reasonable for some, thought Phoenix, as he studied the photograph of the smiling Ferreira; I got a comic to read once a week.

Raymond left Dublin University with a First-Class Degree in Computer Sciences. His first job was with Google. A decade later, the internet giant became a client of his own company. Then, with a net worth of 1.8 billion euros, he sold up in 2013 to lead a humanitarian charity. It focussed on disaster emergencies, and in times of crisis, its role was to provide valuable and swift assistance anywhere in the world.

Athena was keen to read about the lone female candidate. The balance of male to female at the top table needed to alter. If *Lily Chan* proved the right candidate, she must persuade Phoenix to vote with her and the other women to increase her chances of selection. Then, they would need only one more convert.

Lily was now thirty-six, married with two small children. Her husband, Shinji, was an investment banker. The family lived in a townhouse a stone's throw from the River Thames in Fulham, London. Lily had held various IT positions in financial services firms in the city. Her husband spotted the investment potential in developing a mobile payments service. Lily struck gold. The firm they set up together now held a value of thirty billion pounds. Her net worth was around three billion.

"What a terrific asset," Athena whispered to Phoenix.

"A computer geek who's clever with numbers?" asked Phoenix, "my money is on Ferreira. He's made his fortune, and now he's quit the rat race to head up a charity. I'm impressed."

"You aren't keen on the American?" asked Daedalus.

"I can't deny the money he brings isn't welcome," replied Phoenix, "but we need people who wish to help others. Unfortunately, I see no evidence of that in this brief biography."

"He came from a poor background and fought to the top," said Daedalus.

"He's not alone in that," said Apollo, sitting on Daedalus' left, "both Phoenix and I did the same. I, too, prefer the look of Ferreira."

A Frequent Peal of Bells

Athena knew it would be tough to persuade the men to vote for Lily Chan.

Perhaps the final decision depended on what Minos and Alastor found when they dug deeper into their histories.

Chapter Six

Once the refreshments arrived, the Olympians put to one side thought of the upcoming vote in January; it was time to unwind. Naturally, the conversation centred on the newlyweds.

Phoenix and Athena moved to a side table to watch; Daedalus joined them.

"Talk of a wedding and a honeymoon doesn't interest you?" he asked.

"You're right, no," said Phoenix, attempting a Gallic shrug.

Zeus left Heracles and Aphrodite to chat with Hera, Ambrosia, and Dionysus. He took Phoenix by the arm and led him back to the main table. Zeus picked up the three profiles he had distributed. They were merely a cover for what he was to say.

"Athena will have told you I have questions regarding the disappearance of Sir James's first wife?"

"She did," replied Phoenix, "and we have a man

working on it at Larcombe. If there's dirt to find, Orion will find it. He's like a dog with a bone."

"I hate to pressure you, Phoenix, but time is of the essence. Hera and I are fond of Aphrodite. So we should hate something to happen to her."

"Do you believe her life is in danger?" asked Phoenix.

"Until they find a body, and the death confirmed to be natural causes or self-inflicted, then it remains possible that Heracles killed her."

"I'll ensure Orion learns of your concerns, Zeus, and that he gives this investigation the highest priority."

"Thank you, Phoenix," said Zeus, "now, we should rejoin the others."

Over the next fifteen minutes, people took their leave. Everyone at today's meeting received an invitation to attend the wedding party tonight. Nobody had said they were unavailable.

Athena slipped her arm through her husband's and steered him towards the exit.

"We need to get to our hotel room," she said.

"Happy days," said Phoenix.

"Easy, tiger, there's much to discuss before tonight's party."

They reached their hotel room in five minutes. Phoenix sank onto the bed.

"Okay," he said, "let's hear it," he said.

"An easy one to start. What did you and Zeus talk about?" asked Athena.

"Fiona Grant-Nicholls, next?"

"How can I persuade you to vote for Lily Chan at the next meeting?"

"If Minos and Alastor give them a clean bill of health, it will be a toss of a coin between her and Raymond Ferreira.

Apollo reckoned it important the next Olympian should be young and male. Lily Chan is young, married, and with two children. If she wishes to make large donations to our funds, I have no objections; but can she give enough time to the Project?"

Athena had to agree that Phoenix raised a valid point. She was desperate to add another woman to the mix. She resolved to ask Minos to search for ways to improve Lily's chances.

"I'll keep trying to convince you," she told her husband, "I'm not ready to give up yet. The final matter concerns this evening."

"I know," said Phoenix, spreading his arms wide in mock despair, "what am I going to wear?"

Athena had been pacing at the foot of the king-size bed, but she bounded up to join him, straddling his body and pinning his arms.

"Do you take nothing seriously?" she asked, kissing him on his forehead, eyelids, nose, and mouth.

"Whatever you want, it must be important," he said, "but I'm not complaining."

"What time is it?" she asked.

"Half-past one," he replied.

"Good, because we need to practice."

"That sounds interesting."

Athena sighed.

"We need to practice names, you idiot. You can't wander into the Dorchester this evening and call Apollo by his Olympian title. Other guests who are strangers to us will be in attendance. Although three couples sit around the top table, that leaves five people who a wife or partner will accompany."

Phoenix considered that for a minute.

"You're right, as usual; let's make a list. Then I'll show you mine if you'll show me yours."

As he wriggled free from her grasp, Phoenix heard another long sigh.

At a quarter to two, they compared notes.

"Annabelle, darling," said Phoenix, "I reckon we've cracked it."

"Relax," she replied. "I won't tempt fate by using your real name. Daddy accepts the idea that a pair of hippies named you, Phoenix, and your alter ego is dead as far as the world is concerned. So, you must answer to Phoenix if anyone engages you in conversation tonight."

"It's a shame that Piya will be the only one of us without a partner," said Phoenix.

"She said nothing at the meeting," said Athena, "perhaps she was embarrassed. But, of course, it didn't prevent her from cosying up to Hera. It was so obvious."

"Did you want to run through these names once more before tonight? To make sure we've got them fixed in your head?" asked Phoenix.

Athena grabbed his arm and led him towards the bathroom.

"If we shower together, we can be in that bed by two o'clock," she said. "If we're dressed, ready to leave for the party by eight o'clock, we'll be fine."

"Lead on, Annabelle," said Phoenix.

In Lawrence Hill, Mansouri and Harrack were in a modest terraced house. Their hosts were at work. Since arriving yesterday evening, they had spoken to nobody inside the property. Each of the four bedrooms housed several people who kept themselves to themselves. Ahmed

Mansouri and Omar Harrack had slept in the conservatory.

Mansouri called al-Hamady late last night on the burner phone he bought. He confirmed they were welcome. There was no point worrying the Syrian over something he couldn't influence.

"The bombs are almost complete," al-Hamady told him, "there will be three in total. You will not hear from me until one hour before you must leave for the station. Only then will I tell you where to plant the devices."

"Can you tell us how they will disguise the devices?" asked Mansouri.

"Be patient. Trust the bomb maker. He has been doing this in Afghanistan for many years. He still has his fingers, which tells you he is an expert."

This afternoon the rain beat a rhythmic tattoo on the conservatory's glass roof. Mansouri grimaced.

"I hate the waiting," said Harrack as afternoon inched towards the evening.

"Why not visit a mosque?" said Mansouri, "you have four to choose from within walking distance. The Syrian was right. We are among friends here."

Omar Harrack was a more devout Muslim than Mansouri. They shared extreme views, but the younger man had far more religious zeal than his colleague. He left the house to walk to the Albaseera mosque thirty minutes away. Omar wasn't bothered. It was better than staring out of the conservatory at a grey skyline and an overgrown garden. As he walked along Queen Anne Road, he passed many others on the pavement. The roads were always busy in Bristol. Traffic built even more as the rush hour approached.

He arrived at the mosque and found the brothers there

friendly. The prayer hall and ritual washing area were both spotless. After prayers, he learned where to find the best halal food stores. A large shopping complex in nearby Cabot Circus. Omar wasted an hour wandering around the shops before making the return journey.

The house had become busier now. Their hosts had returned from work, and there was more noise as families gathered to prepare food in the large kitchen. The time would pass quicker now, he thought.

Forty-eight hours until the call from al-Hamady.

Since Friday, Tyrone O'Riordan had had the photos of the dark van and two masked men. He had not been idle. His mother still believed he was wasting his time. Tyrone reckoned they were the key to the organisation that had been a thorn in the Grid's side for months. If the gang leaders he talked to were right, they had been active for much longer.

Tyrone wasn't one for legends. But, the rumours painted a picture of criminals who escaped punishment by the authorities only to be killed or to disappear later. His mother called it a coincidence. But Tyrone reckoned it was a campaign.

Someone waged war against crime, and it wasn't the police. The government saw to that with their austerity programmes. The police made things worse by wasting time harassing motorists and pursuing historical crimes of abuse. It only made the Grid's job easier. Tyrone had a fund on hand if he needed to offer bribes to keep the police off his back, but it had never been necessary. They were too incompetent even to discover there was money available.

It had taken Tyrone a while to find the person he

needed. Several gang leaders told him of hackers they used and experts on the dark web that facilitated the importation of firearms and drugs. Keeping a low profile was something at which they excelled. Their whole career depended on never being discovered.

At last, his search had been successful. Simon Gonzalez was twenty-four years old. Gonzalez possessed the computer skills to hack into the White House and the Kremlin to send Christmas cards in July. However, it worried Tyrone that the lad hadn't come up with a better codename than Gonzo.

Tyrone couldn't persuade Gonzo to meet him in person. Instead, the hacker used an intermediary. A motorcycle courier roared past as Tyrone walked to the Glencairn Bank on Monday lunchtime. When Tyrone reached the front door, the courier called out, thrusting a jiffy bag in his hand when he turned around and left as soon as he came.

Inside the jiffy bag, Tyrone found a mobile phone. As he removed the phone, it rang. It was Gonzo. Tyrone looked both ways along Gresham Street but didn't spot anyone who resembled a computer hacker. Not that he knew what one looked like.

The message read, 'Send instructions. The price is ten grand.'

That told Tyrone what he needed. It was no longer relevant what Gonzo looked like. Tyrone realised this kid didn't appreciate the actual value of information on the men in the photograph. Inside his office, he sent the photo and instructions to Gonzalez. If the courier returned in fifteen minutes, the money would be in the jiffy bag. He had stashed the burner phone inside the bank for safekeeping. The instructions were simple.

'1. Name these two men. 2. Where was this van twenty-four hours before and after this photo?'

A Frequent Peal of Bells

The photo carried the date and time stamp that would give this hacker his starting point. Then, if he were as good as his reputation, he would get the answers he craved.

A courier collected the money. No further messages had arrived yet. Tyrone was confident he only had to wait. Either way, Gonzo would only disappoint him once. It could be a better option than the Trojan Horse if he were successful. Gonzalez could be the man on the inside, gathering knowledge for the Grid, and his enemy would be none the wiser.

Phoenix and Athena left the hotel to walk to Park Lane a few minutes after eight o'clock. Phoenix was suited and booted. Not the clothes he enjoyed wearing, but one had to make an effort on occasions such as tonight. Athena looked magnificent. Her long hair fell in dark curls on her bare shoulders, and the maroon-coloured dress fitted where it touched.

Around her neck, she wore the diamond necklace her mother had worn at Larcombe Manor when she and Phoenix married.

The wedding party occupied the breath-taking opulence of Dorchester's magnificent ballroom. The venue that had often been the setting for London's more exceptional social gatherings. The classic Art Deco interior accentuated a room steeped in history. Heracles and Aphrodite had the financial clout to make an impression. They knew how to throw a party.

When Aphrodite had first mentioned this evening, Phoenix imagined it might involve the Olympians plus a few close friends. As they entered the building, it was clear that although the wedding in Scotland had been a quiet affair, tonight would be different. The five hundred guests already here would be pampered in style.

"What a fantastic place," exclaimed Athena.

"Aren't you glad we got out of bed to come here?" asked Phoenix.

Athena ignored him. The smart suit might improve his appearance, but she would never rid him of his upbringing. Not that she ever wished him to change. They were positive proof that opposites attract.

When the elegant door staff vetted their invitation, the couple joined the queue to be greeted by their hosts, James and Elizabeth. Phoenix took the opportunity to take in his surroundings. He wasn't interested in the chandeliers or the fixtures and fittings. No matter how much they must have cost. It was the people he wanted to study.

Could he recognise anyone? Elizabeth was a Duchess with royal connections. James was a captain of industry who graced the business world for decades. The people they knew well enough to earn an invitation would be wealthy and connected.

"I've seen many of these people on TV and in the newspapers," whispered Athena. Phoenix was pleased his wife made productive use of the wait.

"I didn't expect them to invite so many people," said Phoenix, "I don't see our other Olympians yet,"

Two couples stood ahead of them in the queue, so Phoenix abandoned his people-watching. Behind them, the line grew. He might need to increase the number of guests. This ballroom looked capable of holding a thousand. Who had that many friends? Phoenix did a quick count on his fingers. He was satisfied with the ten friends he managed.

"Welcome, Annabelle," said Elizabeth, "it's wonderful to see you. You too, Phoenix."

A Frequent Peal of Bells

"It's been far too long," said Phoenix.

The Duchess gave him a cold hug and tutted when she realised what he meant.

"I've welcomed so many people; I'm losing track. This morning seems weeks ago."

James Grant-Nicholls shook Phoenix by the hand.

"So glad you made it," he said.

"We didn't have far to come," said Phoenix, "any idea where the others are?"

James had moved on to the couple behind them, but Elizabeth overheard.

"We asked that they seat you together in the far corner," she told him.

He and Athena threaded their way through the crowds.

"I can see Duncan and Celia," said Athena.

"What a great spot," said Phoenix, "a quiet corner with a partial view of the dance floor. Do you think we received invites under sufferance?"

"I wouldn't worry, darling," said Athena, "that orchestra won't play any tunes you recognise. Let's say hello to the others."

The most senior Olympian and his wife welcomed them. Then they found seats next to Troy Gardner.

Apollo, the ex-boxer and property tycoon, was with his young, blonde partner, Sophie.

"How do you find rubbing shoulders with the great and the good?" asked Troy.

"Terrific," Phoenix replied, "we're a long way from the action, aren't we?"

"James may have thought we could talk more readily this way?" Troy replied. "You haven't met Sophie before, have you?"

"This is the first social occasion I've attended since I

arrived at Larcombe Manor four years ago. I've met no one's partner apart from Duncan and Celia."

"That's not true," said Troy, "look over there."

He and Athena looked towards where Troy nodded.

Hugh Fraser sat with Piya Adani. Ambrosia had indeed been working closely with their Logistics Officer.

"Very cosy," said Phoenix.

"It explained her reaction when you said she was hands-on with the Irregulars project," whispered Athena.

Piya nodded a brief greeting. Hugh Fraser gave a tentative wave; their affair was now in the open.

The party was soon in full swing. The guests took to the dance floor. Phoenix watched as Ludovic Tremayne, Achilles, shuffled his wife, Rosalind, around the room. He knew Athena would want to dance before the end of the night. He dreaded it.

"I love this song," she said as if on cue.

"Oh look, Jean-Paul and Simone are heading this way," said Phoenix, "I'm sure they'll be glad of the company."

Jean-Paul looked as uncomfortable as Phoenix felt. Simone and Athena chattered away in French. Another skill Phoenix hadn't mastered.

"Do you enjoy parties, Phoenix?" asked Daedalus.

"Hate them,"

"James and Elizabeth look happy, considering," said the Frenchman.

"Have you heard something?" asked Phoenix.

"I lip-read," Jean-Paul explained. "I saw Zeus talk with you this morning. He mentioned his first wife, Fiona?"

"Fiona disappeared without a trace," said Phoenix. "We need to confirm whether she's dead or alive."

"If she's dead, you must determine how she died, I assume?"

"Exactly," said Phoenix.

"Elizabeth is very wealthy," said Jean-Paul, "does Zeus believe she's in danger?"

"If James is desperate for money, I should hope Olympus would have discovered it. They are both very wealthy. They honeymooned on a yacht in the Caribbean for a month. If he wanted Elizabeth dead, he had ample opportunity to shove her overboard."

"Strange times," said Jean-Paul.

Phoenix laughed. "Not half as strange as before you agreed to join Olympus, I can assure you. I prefer to call these times interesting."

"Everyone is here," said Jean-Paul, "and everyone has someone special. I did not realise Ambrosia was bringing a partner."

"We suspected an ulterior motive for her frequent visits to Larcombe Manor," said Phoenix, "I like Hugh Fraser. He's very efficient in his work."

"I'm sure Ambrosia appreciates that," said Jean-Paul with a cheeky grin.

"We are not alone in our discomfort, Daedalus," said Phoenix, catching sight of Dionysus.

Sir Malcolm Dunseith and his wife Louise returned to their table. The retired civil servant was still sober, but his wife, it appeared, was not. She sat with a bump, hiccupped, and looked set to slide under the table. Celia Eliot came to her rescue. Dionysus joined Phoenix and Daedalus.

"Sorry, chaps, the old girl isn't used to it," he said, "two glasses of champagne, and she's anybody's these days."

"Don't apologise, Malcolm," said Phoenix, "they'll be serving the food next. It will soak up the alcohol."

Dionysus wasn't convinced. Athena and Simone had

exhausted their topics of conversation and rejoined the men.

"Dance with me," said Simone. Jean-Paul's eyes pleaded with Phoenix.

"I can't save you, Jean-Paul. We may have to join you," said Phoenix. "It will only be one dance. They'll be feeding us in a minute."

"You won't get away that easily," said Athena as they merged with the other couples on the floor.

She was correct, as usual. After the banquet, they danced several times more. Malcolm and Louise watched the other seven couples from the sidelines. At eleven o'clock, James and Elizabeth made brief speeches thanking everyone for coming.

They were leaving early to fly back home to Scotland. Elizabeth insisted the partygoers stay and enjoy themselves. Phoenix looked around the ballroom; not many guests seemed keen to leave just yet.

"I see Piya and Hugh Fraser have latched on to Zeus and Hera now they've left the dance floor," said Athena.

"I think you'll find they're leaving too," said Phoenix, "Ambrosia looks keen on an early night."

"If we want to be fit for duty at Larcombe in the morning, we should follow suit."

"I'm ready to go if you are," said Phoenix, "but I want to catch Zeus before we leave."

He saw the Olympus leader returning from the toilets and intercepted him before he reached Hera's table.

"Were you aware that Jean-Paul St Clair can read lips?" he asked.

"I wasn't, no," said Zeus.

"He knows about Fiona," said Phoenix.

"Ah, I see. If Jean-Paul keeps it to himself, it shouldn't pose a problem."

"We hadn't expected to see Ambrosia here with one of our agents," said Phoenix.

"Ambrosia asked our permission," said Zeus. "She and my wife have become friends of late. Piya is ambitious and gets results. We have high hopes for her with Olympus."

"Until we meet again in January, then," said Phoenix. Athena was doing the rounds of the tables, saying goodnight to their companions. Simone came over to kiss Phoenix on both cheeks. He didn't complain.

"You and Jean-Paul have become chums, oui?" she asked.

"We have, Simone," said Phoenix.

Athena was back, and the two women embraced. Jean-Paul strolled over to wish Phoenix and Athena goodnight.

Phoenix reflected on what Simone had said as they returned to their hotel.

It was true he and Jean-Paul got on better than he did with any of the other Olympians. He needed to re-calculate. Jean-Paul had helped swell the Phoenix friend count to eleven.

Thursday, 9th October 2014

Athena and Phoenix breakfasted early in their Marylebone hotel. The car arrived at nine to take them to Fairoaks airfield, where Les Biggar was on the tarmac with the engine running.

"Enjoy your night out last night, Phoenix?" he asked.

"An experience," said Phoenix.

"He's not anti-social," said Athena, "he prefers chasing villains."

As they flew west, Phoenix gazed at the M4 motorway beneath them.

"I suppose Fraser's back at Larcombe by now?"

"Ambrosia came south by train, according to Hera," said Athena. "She told me last night when I went to say goodnight to everyone."

"As thick as thieves, those two," said Phoenix.

"Your protégé, Fraser is a dark horse too," said Athena. "I never imagined those two being an item."

"As long as it doesn't affect his work, it won't be an issue," said Phoenix.

Their flight home was soon over, and Biggles set the helicopter on the lawn in front of the manor house. Athena looked at her watch.

"Great, we can drop our bags off at the apartment and then attend the last hour of the meeting."

They arrived as Henry Case completed his report on the progress of the training programmes.

"Longdon and Thomas are right on schedule with their trainees," he said, "while Dexter and Vincent have experienced delays."

"What's the problem?" asked Minos.

"Kelly Dexter has missed the occasional day," said Henry, "she's been ill."

Artemis caught Athena's eye and smiled.

It was common knowledge Kelly and her partner, Hayden Vincent, were keen to start a family. It had been the driving force behind their move to Larcombe Manor. However, Kelly hadn't wanted to bring a child into the world while both agents were active in the field.

"What have we missed?" asked Phoenix.

"You both look as if you had a good time," said Artemis. "It takes longer to recover from a late night the older you get, doesn't it?"

"We have good news for you both," said Giles. "If you're up to it, we'll take you to the ice-house to show you as soon as we're finished."

"I wish to take you through our latest reports, Athena," said Alastor, "now you're back. Phoenix can go straight away. Minos and I can discuss their findings with you."

"What you mean is, I won't read them for ages anyway, so I don't have to stay?" asked Phoenix.

"Alastor's right," said Athena, "let's divide and conquer. The quicker we can catch up on the latest news, the quicker we'll be free for the rest of the day. I'm missing Hope, and my father needs the company."

Phoenix accompanied Giles and Artemis on the walk to the ice-house.

"Have you seen much of Orion since he started work, Artemis?" he asked.

"Only the once, on his first day," said Artemis, "it was awkward, but we both appreciate how different our lives are now. We've moved on. It won't be an issue."

Phoenix found it strange to have this discussion with Artemis. He had grown fond of the young woman. Not only because she was his best friend's partner, but her work in the ice-house had been excellent. The skills she had developed in her police career had proved invaluable. Zara Wheeler had quickly adapted to the different focus of the investigations Olympus tackled.

When the four of them got the chance to relax together, she told Athena seeing criminals pay for their crimes gave her the most satisfaction. Too often in her former life, the system had failed the victims.

"I need to talk to Hayden Vincent later," said Phoenix as they reached the lift doors.

"If you want me to guess, I reckon it's morning sickness," said Artemis.

"Really? That wasn't why I wanted to talk to him, though. One of his first tasks has become a top priority after yesterday's meeting. Orion needs to step up the pace. Life could be in danger."

The lift had reached the first level. Giles, Artemis, and Phoenix crossed the busy floor of the Olympus nerve centre. Around them, the surveillance teams were hard at work, gathering data at an astonishing rate. Analysis of that data might produce a key to unlocking the secrets of the Grid and help bring them to justice.

Yesterday, a chance sighting exposed a potential terror attack.

"On Tuesday afternoon, James Protheroe, an Irregular on his first day at Temple Meads, snapped this photo," said Giles, bringing the image up on a large screen.

"Lousy," said Phoenix, "it could be anyone."

"Until this man was caught strolling in Cabot Circus without a care in the world," said Giles, switching to a clear photo of Omar Harrack.

"Harrack," exclaimed Phoenix, "our man from Canary Wharf and Edinburgh."

"New Street, Birmingham too, no doubt," said Artemis. "Rusty missed them at their hotel by minutes."

"Where did they go next, I wonder," said Phoenix. "Bring that first image up again, Giles. Can you please?"

Realisation dawned as they reviewed the image.

"Harrack is the woman in the burka," said Artemis.

"Protheroe reported the woman had enormous feet," said Giles.

"The other two are Mansouri and al-Hamady. The Syrian is pointing out the pressure points. This image is from the subway under the platforms, am I right?"

"Yes," said Artemis, "a prime location for a bomb."

"We need to find out when and where al-Hamady returned to this country," said Phoenix. "He flew to Paris from John Lennon, didn't he? Can we find the bombers arriving in Bristol on CCTV? Try the railway station first. So, on Tuesday afternoon they're on a sightseeing visit. On Wednesday afternoon Harrack has time to waste. We should have time to prepare. The attack will be in the next forty-eight hours, I reckon. I need Hugh Fraser and Rusty to meet me in the orangery at two o'clock this afternoon."

Phoenix left Giles and Artemis to carry out his orders. Things were getting exciting, and he wanted to get back to Athena.

Chapter Seven

Phoenix found Athena eating lunch with Geoffrey and Hope when he reached their apartment.

"We went ahead without you, darling," she said. "Daddy wants to take a trip to Bath this afternoon."

"Need to buy curtains and a few essentials, Phoenix," said his father-in-law. "Not something I've done for a while."

Athena had been right about Geoffrey needing the company. Without Grace, he found many mundane things he hadn't needed to bother with for decades.

"That's fine," said Phoenix. "I'll get myself something to eat. I'll be in the orangery this afternoon. We have an urgent mission to plan."

After Maria Elena returned to look after Hope, Geoffrey went to his apartment to change; Athena asked Phoenix to explain.

"The bombers are back. They've switched their attention from Birmingham to Bristol. We've been off the pace on the other attacks. This feels different. If we get the preparation right, we can foil this latest attempt and take them out of the game."

"I'll catch up with how you get on this evening," said Athena, "take care."

At two, Phoenix arrived at the orangery. Rusty and Hugh were waiting.

"Artemis tells me you have ruined another weekend," said Rusty.

"Maybe not; we might get the job out of the way tomorrow."

"What do you need from us, Phoenix?" asked Hugh.

"Study these building plans. Identify the most likely targets. How many Irregulars have you got available in Bristol?"

"Three, at present. James Protheroe thought he spotted the three suspects on Tuesday. I want to reward him by bringing him in on this next stage. One man is at the airport, and the other has gone to the Harbourside area."

"Recall them. We need to find where al-Hamady and the bombers are staying. Your people need to be in the centre or thereabouts."

"Do you believe al-Hamady will be at the same address?" asked Rusty.

"They won't make it easy for us," said Hugh. "I'd expect him to be miles away from Mansouri and Harrack. The bomb maker will be in another location altogether."

"The ice-house has begun the search," said Phoenix, "we must do what we can to help. Where's the highest concentration of Muslims close to Cabot's Circus?"

"Lawrence Hill?" suggested Hugh.

"Walking distance from where we caught Harrack on camera," said Phoenix.

"Get Protheroe to Lawrence Hill," said Phoenix. "The

other two Irregulars should be at Temple Meads. Warn Protheroe to be vigilant. The bombers have seen him. We don't want a repeat of New Street."

They spent the rest of the afternoon evaluating options. Hugh listed four possible scenarios for the attack method.

Rusty and Phoenix devised counter-tactics their teams might adopt. As the light faded, Giles called from the icehouse. Phoenix listened to what they found so far.

"OK, so Giles confirms al-Hamady arrived in Liverpool on a ferry from Belfast. He took a train from Lime Street to Bristol. Mansouri and Harrack met him there, but where they came from, we haven't established. Giles found al-Hamady on CCTV outside Temple Meads fifteen minutes after the photo in the subway. He spoke to the two bombers by the taxi rank."

"If Giles sends a photo of al-Hamady," said Hugh, "I'll pass it to my Irregular at the waterfront. He can ask if anyone remembers taking the fare once he's at the station. He can get there in twenty minutes."

"We haven't got information on the bomb maker so far," said Phoenix, "it would simplify matters if we did."

"How will they get the bombs to Mansouri and Harrack?" asked Rusty, "or will they collect them? The sooner we locate those two, the better our chance of foiling this attack."

"The shorter period the devices are in their possession, the better," said Hugh, "Each element of the cell operates as a separate entity. Any overlap is minimal. Therefore the risk of being discovered is slim. I imagine the bomb maker will notify al-Hamady when it's ready. He will call the bombers, and they will deliver their packages to the station. All three events will occur within sixty minutes."

"What chance have we got of intercepting those calls?" asked Phoenix.

"They always use disposable, pre-paid phones these days," said Hugh. "They're nigh on impossible to trace."

"We need more information on al-Hamady and our bomb maker," said Phoenix. "I'll ask Giles to get someone on it. Either we prevent al-Hamady from acting on the call to say the device is ready or eliminate the product and its manufacturer."

"Who will take part in the mission?" asked Hugh.

"Rusty will take you, Protheroe and two of our agents stationed in Filton to handle the bombers. I'll target al-Hamady and the bomb maker. I'll decide who I need with me once I know where I'm going. Two of us will be plenty. We have to limit the risk of being identified throughout this mission."

"I'll write up everything we've covered this afternoon," said Hugh Fraser, "and go over every step we agreed. By the morning, you will have a copy to go through as often as necessary to get every step entrenched in your mind. Proper planning and all that."

"Thanks, Hugh," said Phoenix, "I know you get the detail right with the appropriate colour-coding, but my contribution to this direct action needs flexibility. On those occasions, I wing it."

Hugh looked mortified.

"You're new, Hugh. I fought to get you here for that attention to detail. Keep doing what you're doing. For me, it's not so important to get the bombers. Senior people in the cells will find others willing to take their place within days. I want to reach those closest to the organisation's top, such as al-Hamady. He's the driving force, the planner, and this campaign will be thwarted for months if we remove him. As for the bomb maker, he's responsible for many deaths, but Grace Fox's death makes it personal. I swore I would take my revenge when the opportunity arose. That time is now."

"I understand," said Hugh, "you have my word; I'll never stint on the detail. I'll always leave you and Rusty to decide how you want to play things. You have far more experience in that arena. Doing things by the book is how I've lived my life for so long; improvisation comes hard."

Phoenix decided to have some fun at Hugh's expense.

"I didn't mention we saw Hugh last night, Rusty," said Phoenix. "He attended that posh wedding party at the Dorchester."

"Really? How on earth did you get a ticket for that, Hugh?" asked Rusty.

"As a plus one for a guest," said Hugh, gathering his papers. He was keen to leave the orangery before Rusty could probe any further.

"An honoured guest, no less," said Phoenix, "don't be coy, Hugh. Our Logistics Officer has snared the lovely Ambrosia, Rusty."

"Good for you," said Rusty. "I knew you had got divorced. The dating game is a minefield after that trauma, so they tell me. If you want to get back in the game, I guess picking someone from the top shelf is a great way to do it."

"To be honest, I'm not sure I snared anyone," Hugh said. "I thought Ambrosia was out of my league. She's beautiful, intelligent, and loaded. If her late father owned a brewery, she had the full set. As soon as I met her, I never stood a chance."

"She's ambitious, don't forget that," said Phoenix.

Hugh Fraser nodded.

Exactly, thought Hugh, her ambition may fuel her interest; not any great passion.

"I'm not wet behind the ears, Phoenix," he said, "I'll watch my step. What's the worst that can happen? To be seen in public with her last night did my self-confidence no harm."

Hugh left Rusty and Phoenix to head back to the stable block.

"Do you think he's naïve?" asked Rusty.

"I think Ambrosia's a scheming little minx," said Phoenix, "not in the Demeter class, but dangerous all the same. She uses Hugh and the Irregulars to increase her status within the organisation. Her relationship with Zeus and Hera has progressed further in a few months than Athena, and I have managed in two years."

"She's active in targeting those two things," said Rusty, "and be fair, you wouldn't bother with the latter. I reckon you would be happy to exist without being friendly to anyone outside Larcombe Manor."

Phoenix couldn't argue. When you've been a loner for the first forty years, it's challenging to switch to Mr Gregarious, even over four years. Athena despaired of him sometimes, but she understood what made him tick.

As they left the orangery, Phoenix heard a vehicle. It was Athena and her father. The shopping trip must be at an end.

"I'll see you tomorrow morning, Rusty," he said.

"Athena's waving," said Rusty, "she's got the rear door open. I reckon you're in for a spell of heavy lifting, mate."

Colleen O'Riordan had just returned to her penthouse apartment. The afternoon had flown past; she enjoyed pampering herself. The health spa membership was excessive, but she could afford it now, so why not? Tommy would turn in his grave. He moaned if she spent twenty quid on getting her hair done.

Thoroughly relaxed after the treatments they lavished on her, Colleen felt ready to study the latest reports Tyrone emailed her. He was a good boy. Her son explained everything to his mother in words of one syllable, chiefly where computers were concerned.

Colleen could cope with the day-to-day running of the Kilburn gang she controlled. It wasn't any harder than keeping house for Tommy and the children. They were all big kids. Now and again, someone needed a slap to bring them in line.

As for the Grid, she dared to control that, too, no matter how big it became. It wasn't easy to balance the housekeeping accounts and keep the kids in line with gangs scattered across the UK. That's where Tyrone proved his worth.

He was her iron fist when someone needed a slap. His skills in the financial sector allowed her to check rather than micro-manage the money side of things. Colleen understood words of several syllables. She was far more intelligent than Tyrone imagined. She liked to keep that to herself. Her son wasn't the first O'Riordan to think of her as a helpless female.

Colleen always found it helped her get what she wanted. Strident, stroppy women never received what they thought they deserved. They got what their men thought they deserved for being that way. A lesson she learned very early in her marriage.

She sat in front of her computer and read the note from Tyrone. So, this was a memory stick. The idiot notes Tyrone gave her were perfect. Colleen followed the instructions and found a series of files. She opened 'Bank' and viewed folders containing hundreds of photos, street plans, and diagrams of what looked to be a bank vault. Things had progressed well. Colleen searched for a summary, found it in the last folder she viewed, and printed herself a copy to read in bed. She wondered if she would have sweet dreams of a hundred million pounds tonight.

Colleen grew curious. What was in this other file labelled 'Gonzo'? She opened it. There was far less inside this one. Those dodgy photos Tyrone kept mentioning and glossy pictures from a celebrity magazine. They were taken last night at the Dorchester. That magazine wouldn't be on the racks in the newsagents yet; this must be from a digital issue. Who's this Gonzo? Is he in these photos?

According to the captions, these photos came from a society wedding party — two people with more money than sense getting married in their sixties to avoid loneliness. Colleen didn't need that complication.

The deep massage this afternoon stirred a few emotions she had suppressed for too long, but the eighteen-stone gay masseur didn't put his hands anywhere he shouldn't. More's the pity. Colleen wanted someone young and fit, and their role would *not* be to stop her from getting lonely.

"Very posh," she said, looking at the female guests' dresses and jewellery. Tyrone had enlarged one photo; Colleen clicked on it. The bride and groom were dancing. He was a Sir somebody, and she was a Duchess. Behind them, seated in the corner, sat a group of people. A man was led towards the dance floor by a tall woman in a gorgeous maroon dress. The diamond necklace around her neck had to be worth fifty grand.

Colleen looked again at the man. Good looking and a few years younger than her. He was punching above his weight with the woman he accompanied. He must be rich. Why did Tyrone think this was important enough to send her? She glanced at the photos of the men involved in the moped gang business in West Hampstead.

Tyrone was still trying to find proof of a secret organisation at work in the country. Was he clutching at straws as she kept telling him? It was a leap, but when she compared the man's appearance in the various images, there was something familiar. Inconclusive, but maybe Tyrone had a point. It wouldn't hurt to follow the trail from this wedding party.

The photos were first-class, professional shots. An expert could enhance the images of the other guests near where this couple had sat. As for the hosts, they would plaster their details over the magazine's pages. How did they connect to the couple in question? She could shortcut that process by finding a Dorchester employee who needed to earn quick money. Colleen had to have the guestlist for that party.

The stable block at Larcombe Manor was often a hive of activity. The building contained the living quarters for various agents. Henry Case, Giles Burke, and Hugh Fraser lived next door to one another. At multiple times in the past, they entertained female companions. Sarah Gough, Maria Elena Urbano, and Ambrosia were familiar with the spartan surroundings in which their lovers lived.

Kelly Dexter and Hayden Vincent had moved into enlarged accommodation when they took over the training programme. They were not as comfortable as in their previous home in Shrivenham, but they were together and in far less danger than on active duty. The two agents met in

Helmand province. Times with Olympus were different from those in the military but no less hairy.

"Have you done the test?" asked Hayden.

"Twice," replied Kelly, "both times, it confirmed what we hoped. I'm pregnant."

"We have to tell them," said Hayden.

"Are you pleased?" she asked.

"Over the moon," he replied, "but we still have to tell them. You can continue training full-time when this horrible morning sickness is over, but they need to arrange cover for the training programme during your maternity leave."

"I don't think Athena took much time out," said Kelly. "She got Maria Elena to help her with Hope within a week of the birth. I'll return to my training role as soon as possible, but childcare is a problem."

"That's why we must talk to Phoenix and Athena," said Hayden. "We can't drop our little one off in Bath every day. It's out of the question for us to have a live-in nanny. If we raise the matter straight away, they have six months to consider opening a creche. Maria Elena can tend to our child when we're working. Hope will need less and less attention as time passes."

"It's a bit of a cheek," said Kelly.

"Henry Case is getting married next year, so who knows? Artemis is broody, according to Rusty. The place could fill with kids in two years. It wouldn't be a luxury, more a necessity."

Kelly Dexter decided her partner was right. There was no time like the present. She would make the call and tell Athena their good news. She would do it tomorrow.

Further up the corridor was Orion's office. There was no staff accommodation provided for the ex-policeman. He was a day visitor. His window on the world was small, and looked out on a forest of trees and bushes that delineated the start of the estate's boundary. He was denied the views across the lawns the others enjoyed.

Phoenix needed the freedom to move between the main building and the ice-house. When he visited the stable block, he avoided the hours when Orion was at work. Cosmetic surgeries since 2010 reduced the risk of his identity ever being uncovered, but it was wise not to take chances.

Orion had followed up on the leads he established on the Fiona Grant-Nicholls disappearance this afternoon. The time had flown past; it was five o'clock. That was the witching hour. Hayden Vincent warned him to leave Larcombe by then. He pushed the paperwork to one side and pulled on his jacket — time to head home to Erica and the kids.

As he joined the driveway that led to the main entrance, he spotted a group of people outside the front door. A car had parked with the rear door raised. Annabelle Fox supervised two men carrying bags of shopping. One elderly gentleman, he guessed, would be her father. The other man had his back to him. He looked familiar, but it wasn't the security man who had interrogated him. Nor one of the senior officials he met while on earlier visits.

Former Detective Superintendent Phil Hounsell arrived home on the other side of Bath none the wiser. The name would come to him in time. Every good copper was the same with faces. Once seen, never forgotten, particularly when that face belonged to a criminal.

Friday, 10th October 2014

A Frequent Peal of Bells

It was nine o'clock in the terraced house in Lawrence Hill. Ahmed Mansouri had been awake since dawn. His colleague, Omar Harrack, was nervous. He had visited the bathroom three times already. The rain had continued throughout the night. The birds screeched in protest as the neighbour's cat tormented them.

The wait would soon be over. When the call came, he would carry out the task as planned. Ahmed sat in the conservatory, closed his eyes, and envisaged the station. He retraced every step they took with al-Hamady around Temple Meads to remind himself of the layout. He tried to predict where the Syrian would order them to place the pressure cooker bombs.

Pressure cooker bombs were relatively easy to construct. Except for the explosive charge, most materials required were easy to buy. The weapon would be triggered using a simple electronic device. This bomb maker preferred to use a mobile phone. New Street was supposed to be a series of devices that exploded over several minutes. The suicide bombers were to have detonated their vests on the most crowded section of their platform.

In Bristol, al-Hamady had opted for three massive explosions. The blast's power depended on the pressure cooker's size and the amount and type of explosives used. The containment provided by the pressure cooker meant the energy from the explosion was confined until it exploded. That produced the bloody big bang the Syrian desired and generated lethal shrapnel.

Omar had returned.

"How much longer must we wait?" he asked.

"Why not revisit the mosque, Omar? Go to prayers. We won't hear from Bakar until one hour before we must leave.

I shall come to the mosque to collect you if you have not returned when he rings me."

"I don't wish to travel in the burka this time," said Omar, "if anything goes wrong, I want to run without drawing attention."

"Why should something go wrong?" said Mansouri, "you worry too much. Bakar has planned everything. Nothing went wrong at Canary Wharf or Edinburgh."

"Everything has felt wrong since Birmingham," said Omar.

"New Street was unfortunate," Mansouri agreed, "but the bomb maker didn't make a mistake. We didn't make a mistake. The fault lay with one or all the suicide bombers. They died because of their carelessness."

Omar sat beside Mansouri. His colleague was skilled at putting his mind at ease.

"I'll wait until ten o'clock," he said, "and then I'll attend Friday prayers."

Ahmed gave a massive sigh of relief.

Athena chaired the morning meeting at Larcombe. She was aware Phoenix and Rusty had to leave on a mission at any moment.

"What have you been able to tell them, Giles?" she asked.

"We traced al-Hamady's movements from Birkenhead to Bristol," he replied. "We've discovered the taxi driver who picked him up outside the station. They drove to Bradley Stoke, north of the city. He asked the driver to stop on the corner of one of the sprawling housing estates."

"So, we don't have an address, then?" said Henry Case.

"Not yet," said Giles, "but Artemis is still searching. I told her to stay in the ice-house. She's more valuable there this morning than at this meeting."

Athena nodded.

"What progress on the bombers?" she asked.

"We have boots on the ground in Lawrence Hill. I'm optimistic we will have an answer before the end of the morning."

"Last but not least, the bomb maker," asked Athena.

"Nothing yet, I'm afraid," said Giles.

Omar Harrack left the safety of the terraced house at ten o'clock. He followed the same route to the mosque as on Wednesday. There was a break in the clouds, and a thin sun appeared for the first time in days. Omar felt more comfortable now. His stomach had settled.

The nerves remained, but Ahmed had reassured him. The Syrian's plans had served them well so far. British security forces had never suspected a thing. The fools they entrusted with the other bombs caused the failure at New Street. Today would be the start of the next bombings designed to cripple the rail network.

Omar passed rows of houses and shops lining the street. Here and there were businesses; some commercial, others industrial. He saw signs of people struggling to keep their heads above water everywhere. The buildings were intact, unlike in Aleppo and Homs, but desperation showed on many faces he met. As a devout Muslim, Omar tried to change things for his people. Desperation fuels anarchy, and this country, too, cried out for change.

Friday prayers were a momentous occasion. The mosque was filled with happy worshippers. Omar enjoyed the social nature of the day's session. Men there on Wednesday recognised him. When prayers ended, he wondered whether Ahmed was on his way to collect him.

He looked for him outside the mosque, but he was nowhere in sight.

Omar had company on the return journey up Days Road and Queen Anne Road. He ignored the man on the far pavement when he searched for Ahmed. Dylan Griffiths had a guitar slung on his back. He busked for an hour near Cabot Circus and switched positions before the police moved him.

Dylan was homeless until a few weeks ago. Although he now worked as an Irregular, he continued to perform as a street musician. Dylan wore the same tattered camouflage jacket and faded jeans he always wore. Music lovers dropped coins into his hat when he played — especially those who followed the artist from whom he got his name. Dylan played and sang as well as anyone with a recording contract.

He spotted Omar Harrack outside the mosque. The photo he carried of the terror suspect from Canary Wharf was accurate. Undoubtedly, this was the man Hugh Fraser asked him to find and follow. They headed up to Lawrence Hill. No big surprise; the place had the highest concentration of Muslims in the city. Dylan knew he must follow his man right to the door. That address needed to reach Hugh Fraser.

Omar turned into Hanover Street. Dylan waited on the pavement opposite the turning. When Omar reached a terraced house with a royal blue door, he went indoors. Three minutes later, Dylan crossed the road and walked up the right-hand pavement. He looked at the door and checked the number. Dylan continued walking with purpose as if he knew where he was headed and found his way back to civilisation. He called Hugh Fraser, passed on the address, and forty minutes later, he sang 'Like A Rolling Stone' in Corn Street.

Omar and Ahmed still awaited the call from Bakar al-Hamady inside the house.

At Larcombe Manor, Phoenix and Rusty had received the news they needed. Hugh Fraser joined them at the garage. Rusty sat at the wheel of a dark-coloured van; its signage suggested the trio onboard had installed smart meters.

"Where did you ask our Filton team to meet us?" asked Phoenix.

"They should be at the end of the street before us," said Hugh. "If our suspects are on the move when we arrive, they'll follow them."

"No news is good news," said Rusty as they hit the Keynsham by-pass. "Have you ever known this stretch of road to be quiet?"

"Imagine how manic it must have been before the by-pass," muttered Phoenix, "when Horace Batchelor appeared on Radio Luxembourg every night."

Rusty didn't have a clue what Phoenix was saying. Fraser's Dad mentioned using the popular infradraw method when he tried to win the football pool jackpot. He couldn't tell the young Hugh how it worked. But Hugh never forgot how to spell Keynsham because of the number of times his Dad recited the advert.

That's K-E-Y-N-S-H-A-M, Keynsham, Bristol.

Radio Luxembourg broadcast it several times, every night, for years.

Chapter Eight

"Are those our guys in the car up ahead?" asked Rusty when they reached Lawrence Hill.

"It is," said Hugh, "I told them to stand by while we enter the house. I'll call them if we need help."

"No, get them to join us now," said Phoenix. "This has the hallmarks of a multi-occupancy place—four bedrooms, with half a dozen living in each. Everyone is fighting for the same bathroom. We can't risk several of them having weapons."

Hugh called the Filton crew forward.

Phoenix handed the two men official-looking cards and boxes that purported to contain smart meters.

"Grab a toolbox. Knock on the door and gain entry. Do a quick recce. Say that you're popping outside for the ladders. I want to learn numbers and if we face any real opposition. Also, find out which room our targets occupy."

Phoenix counted off the three answers he needed on his fingers.

"No problem," came the joint reply. One of the men

rang the bell; a middle-aged Muslim woman answered the door. The two men were inside the house in seconds.

"Ready?" asked Phoenix.

"Can't wait," said Hugh, "I've been office-bound too long."

"Here we go," said Rusty as one agent reappeared.

"There must be twenty people living in there," he said. "We've gathered the women and small children in the front room. I told them they wouldn't disturb us then, and we'd be out of there quicker. One of the younger ones spoke a little English. She said their men were at work. There are only two guys at home. They've been living in the conservatory for a couple of days. They don't have contact with anyone else in the house."

"That's Mansouri and Harrack," said Rusty, "they don't suspect a thing?"

"They didn't come out to see what was going on," said the agent, "my mate's upstairs, in case they try to escape over the back fence."

"You keep the women quiet," said Phoenix, getting out of the van. "We'll take care of our targets."

Hugh and Rusty followed Phoenix through the hallway. The agent re-entered the front room. Rusty heard a low murmur of voices, but the women didn't sound frightened. The agent closed the door behind him.

At the far end of the hallway, they found the door to the conservatory locked. Phoenix turned to Rusty and gestured with his foot. One well-placed boot removed the obstruction. Phoenix and Fraser rushed inside, and Rusty stood guard at the door.

Ahmed Mansouri and Omar Harrack had been sitting in the early afternoon sun. The warmth had made them sleepy. When the door burst open, they had to become fully awake before being alive to the intrusion. The two agents had enough time to fire the two shots that thudded into each man.

The silenced weapons caused no reaction in the front room. The sounds of traffic outside in the street were more noticeable. The children continued to play on the floor. The womenfolk talked to one another in their language. One of the Filton agents stood by the door and waited for a knock.

"Clear," called Hugh, knocking on the door. The other agent ran downstairs.

"Is that it?" he said, "did I miss the fun?"

"I'm afraid so," smiled Hugh. "Keep the ladies occupied for a few minutes longer. We must take these two to the van. Can you fetch the rolled-up carpet from the back?"

"Okay, will do," said the agent, "but what do I do with these meters?"

"Tell them they gave you the wrong kind. You'll come back another day."

Hugh returned to the conservatory. Phoenix and Rusty collected everything the two bombers had brought with them; it didn't amount to much. A collection of male and female clothing. One mobile phone. A well-thumbed copy of the Koran. Two wash kits. Two knives. A few sheets of paper with hand-drawn maps of Bristol and detailed layouts of Temple Meads.

"Let's get the bodies out of here," he said. "We can study that in the van. The carpet will be in the hallway by now."

Rusty helped Hugh carry Omar Harrack to the van. The burner phone rang. Phoenix picked it up and read the message,

"Jackpot," he said.

A Frequent Peal of Bells

"Don't worry, we'll manage," said Rusty when they returned.

Phoenix ignored him and held up the phone.

"They missed the call," he said, "we were just in time."

When Mansouri was inside the van with Harrack, Hugh ensured the Filton agents had covered their tracks. The women didn't query the reason for the visit. Instead, they appeared satisfied with the agents' excuse for the wrong piece of equipment. If luck were on their side, their husbands would never learn a thing.

The conservatory was a mess but blended in with the rest of the house and garden. Mansouri and Harrack had arrived without warning. The fact they left the same way was no big deal.

While the Filton crew headed home, Rusty looked at Phoenix.

"Don't keep us in suspense," he said, "what did the message say?"

"Two bombs will be delivered here in forty-five minutes. It tells them where to plant them."

"Who's bringing them?" asked Rusty.

"The bomb maker," replied Phoenix.

"Are you sure?" asked Hugh.

"There's a third bomb; they designed each bomb for carrying inside knapsacks. It made no sense for one of these guys to carry two. So the Syrian visited the bomb maker and took the third bomb. He will place that himself."

"We must get to Temple Meads to stop al-Hamady from delivering that final device," said Hugh.

"How many Irregulars do you have on-site?" asked Phoenix.

"Three," replied Hugh, "one outside, one on the concourse, and Protheroe in the subway."

"There are drawings of the station layout among the things Mansouri had in his bag," said Phoenix. "If they've marked potential sites on either drawing, you can eliminate two from the details in this message."

"That leaves us only one place to protect," said Hugh. He grabbed the sheets of paper. Phoenix handed him the phone to note the locations.

"I'd rather tackle al-Hamady in that house in Bradley Stoke," said Phoenix, "but we've never traced it. If we three join the Irregulars at Temple Meads, there's a risk that al-Hamady will spot one of us. He could detonate his device before we killed him."

"What bombs do you think they're using?" asked Rusty.

"A pressure cooker bomb would be my choice," said Hugh. "The knapsacks are easy to carry, keeping their hands free. They are then dropped off at the optimum place and detonated when they get clear. I suspect they're to explode at different times."

"The same as in Edinburgh, yes, that makes sense," said Phoenix.

"I'll call Protheroe," said Hugh, "I hope the message gets through. These drawings pinpoint the subway as the missing location."

"Rusty, can you tell me how to handle the two bombs coming here?" asked Phoenix.

"I trained you how to do that in 2010 when you first joined Olympus," said Rusty. "Don't tell me you've forgotten?"

"You were always there in case something went wrong."

"I'm here now."

"Not for long. Please go to Temple Meads with Hugh. I trust you to intercept al-Hamady before he gets close to the platforms. Stop him and disable his bomb."

A Frequent Peal of Bells

"This is about Grace, isn't it?" asked Rusty.

"Get going," said Phoenix, "or the delivery boy will be here. He'll look at the smart meter installation van outside and disappear. We don't want to be chasing a car loaded with explosive material driving around the centre of Bristol."

Rusty knew there was no point arguing with his friend; the bomb maker was due in less than half an hour.

They would be at Temple Meads in fifteen minutes. The Irregulars might have missed the crafty beggar; it was time to move.

"Good luck," said Rusty. He and Hugh Fraser left Phoenix in the conservatory.

Phoenix heard the van pull away from the kerb. Noises in the hallway and upstairs told him the women and children had returned to their rooms. Everything had returned to normal. Nothing outside or inside the house should alert the bomb maker now. He could sit and wait for him to arrive.

Forty-five minutes after the text message had pinged on the burner phone, the front doorbell rang. First, Phoenix heard a woman's voice. Then, a deeper male voice grew louder as someone approached the conservatory door. Phoenix moved position in his chair. His gun was free of any obstruction, ready for whatever came next.

The door opened, and a swarthy-looking elderly individual entered. He smiled.

Phoenix thought the language he spoke was Pashto. But, what he asked the woman in the burka facing him, he didn't know.

The Afghani bomb maker placed the two knapsacks on the floor with care. He continued to talk, and Phoenix watched his eyes darting around the room. Hugh and Rusty had done their best to clean up, but some blood spatter remained. It was time to end this pantomime.

Phoenix raised the gun and shot the bomb maker dead. Two bullets to the heart. Even in death, the look on the Afghani's face was one of surprise. Phoenix removed the burka and threw it into the kit bag along with the rest of Harrack's clothes.

They had avenged the deaths of Grace Fox and the others in London and Edinburgh.

Phoenix looked at his watch, and it was two-forty.

Rusty and Hugh would be at Temple Meads. The time al-Hamady told the bomb maker to text Mansouri had to be significant. So did the forty-five minutes before the delivery. He opened the first knapsack with care.

One hurdle cleared. There were no booby traps on the knapsack itself. Phoenix thought back to the lessons he had received from Rusty. A pressure cooker bomb often contained an air-fuelled, highly sensitive peroxide explosive. The container in the knapsack did not carry a strong smell of bleach. That was a plus because if this bomb contained an anti-lift device that triggered secondary circuits, he'd already be dead.

Phoenix considered the options. This device could detonate in various ways, but it wasn't as volatile as it might have been. The pressure cooker would contain shrapnel. That might be odd metal scraps, marbles, nails, and razor blades. The dead man on the floor had handled the knapsacks like heavy carrier bags.

His bombs might make a big bang, but somewhere on the outside, he must have placed a timing device or a phone. Phoenix inched his fingers around the outside of the container. There it was, a mobile phone. The screen showed the trigger set for three-thirty.

A Frequent Peal of Bells

Phoenix checked the second knapsack. He found a phone in the same spot. He soon learned the timer for this one was for three-twenty. Terrific. Time was running short. Rusty had constantly reminded him of the lesson on this make of bomb. It was one thing learning how long before it exploded; it was something else to open and dismantle it.

There was only one thing for it; he must remove it to a place of safety.

Phoenix retrieved the car keys from the bomb maker's clothing, closed the conservatory door, and carried the knapsacks outside. The blame would fall on the missing house guests when they discovered the body.

Phoenix reckoned the men of the house would call the landlord first.

If things progressed without anyone carrying out any checks, so much, the better; many occupants of the property were probably illegal immigrants.

A small white van parked outside responded to the key fob. It was brand new. It appeared there was good money in the demolition business.

Phoenix drove away from Hanover Street. His first call was to the ice-house.

Artemis was on duty.

"Direct me to the nearest spot where I can ditch a van. Somewhere with no houses or people within a mile."

"How long have you got?" she asked.

"Thirty-four minutes," said Phoenix. "I won't need to worry about the second bomb."

"Pray the traffic isn't heavy and take the A369 to Portishead. Make for Beach Road and then take to the grass. Remember to jump before the van goes over the cliff."

"How long will it take to get there?" asked Phoenix, dreading the answer.

"Thirty minutes tops unless you get stuck behind a tractor," said Artemis. "Stay calm. You'll be fine."

"Stay calm, she says," said Phoenix, "how did you guess what I was carrying?"

"I was up close and personal with a car bomb that would have demolished half a street the day I met Rusty," she replied. "Your voice gave you away."

"Have you heard from Rusty?" he asked.

"They haven't intercepted al-Hamady yet; he's not inside Temple Meads. Giles and I know there's a third bomb. It must aim to explode later than those you have with you. It's still cutting things fine if al-Hamady wants to get it to the subway and then make his escape."

"Warn Hugh and Rusty that these containers are too difficult to handle without unacceptable risk. They must move them to as safe a spot as possible."

"I'll ask Giles to pass on the message. He's watching for al-Hamady on CCTV cameras at Temple Meads. When is the second device set to explode?"

"Half-past three."

"The third one is likely to show another ten-minute gap. The terrorists are targeting the emergency services and the public just as they did at Waverley station. If our team grab al-Hamady in the next five minutes, they should have fifty minutes to reach a haven. I'll start the search for the best site."

"Does Athena know what's happening?" asked Phoenix.

"She knows where you were going but won't know about this latest development. Do you want me to call her?"

"I'm not planning on this being my last conversation with you or anyone else. There won't be any need for tearful farewells today. Don't alarm Athena. If traffic's bad, we'll need another option, though."

"I'll stay on the line and assess the local terrain as you get closer to the coast. I think you need the company," said Artemis.

"Thanks. What can we talk about for thirty-one minutes?"

"Do you have time to tell me who you are?" she asked.

"Things aren't that serious," he replied. "Anyway, when you look back over the year we've worked together at Larcombe, does it matter?"

"I guess not. I've had a thought. How do we know that the third bomb is the same make and model?"

"They designed the three bombs for carrying in a knapsack, according to the message sent by the bomb maker. Al-Hamady collected the third bomb. Does it make sense for it to be different?"

"It makes life simpler for Rusty and Fraser if they simply had to disarm it rather than destroy it," said Artemis. "They then have options on how to tackle al-Hamady. He could come here for interrogation. We don't want to kill him in the subway. It would be hard to explain away to the authorities and the media."

"The sooner they spot him and neutralise the threat, the better," said Phoenix, "why is it taking so long?"

"Giles is talking to Hugh Fraser now. Hang on," said Artemis.

"Great, let me know what's happening. By the way, I'll be on the Portbury Hundred soon. Are there any large open spaces there?"

"As a last resort, yes, but you will still have twenty-two minutes to cover a little over eight miles. There's not much to choose between the options you have, Phoenix. Questions will be asked whether you blow up several fields or ditch the van into the Bristol Channel."

"I'll leave that for you and Giles to handle," said Phoenix, "you're the experts in misinformation. Deep in the water is the best bet. If nobody sees me send it over the cliff, you could spread a rumour of a WWII bomb."

"Fake news, do you mean?" said Artemis.

"Ask Giles for an update, please," said Phoenix.

"I'll hand you over to him. Here he is,"

"Phoenix? I understand you have a pressing problem?"

"Don't worry about me, Giles. What's happened at Temple Meads.?"

"There's no sign of Bakar al-Hamady. I feel as if I've searched every camera in the city."

"It makes no sense," said Phoenix, "surely, the third device must be for Bristol?"

"Hang on, Artemis has heard something. Dylan Griffiths, the Irregular who notified us where Harrack was living, has filed a report. A car cruised past him by the taxi rank outside the station two minutes ago. He is positive the driver was al-Hamady. The car left without stopping. He may be running."

"Follow up on that, Giles. Put Artemis back on, please."

"Phoenix, how's traffic?" asked Artemis.

"Not too busy. I've been able to hit forty-five on a few stretches. I'm keeping an eye open for speed cameras."

"You're close to my old HQ there. The Hundred is fifty miles per hour limit, so you're okay until you get to the roundabout. There's always a car stationed on it with a speed gun because the limit drops to thirty. The fines they rack up are legendary."

"I'll watch myself, don't worry,"

"Let's discuss this third bomb again," said Artemis. "If

A Frequent Peal of Bells

al-Hamady has enough time to cut away from Temple Meads, it can't be the same device."

Phoenix smacked his hand on the steering wheel.

"Stupid," he exclaimed, "it *is* still Bristol. He's got enough time to reach Parkway. If he spotted something suspicious at Temple Meads, such as Griffiths, he could divert to Parkway. How far is it?"

"Seven miles," said Artemis, "he will be there by twenty-past three."

"Send Rusty and Hugh after him. We can't let him reach Parkway. Let's hope you're right and that bomb differs from the rest."

"How are you coping?" she asked.

"I'll be fine. I'm trying to understand what the plan was. We assumed the drawings we found at the house represented the final plan. That made us accept that the third bomb was destined for the subway while the two I had on board were for different platforms overhead. There must have been a verbal agreement to change tack — something not to be communicated to Mansouri and Harrack until the last minute. Only al-Hamady and the bomb maker were parties to it beforehand. The bomb maker was to tell them where to place the two bombs when he made the delivery."

"Our original timings might still be correct," said Artemis. "If his device goes off at three-forty, he has ample time to hide it and get away."

"What should we do in this scenario?" asked Phoenix. "We're sure they're delivering a bomb. Hundreds of passengers will be at the station. An anonymous phone call to evacuate the station would save lives. The IRA made those calls now and then. Property damage remained, and the message was received loud and clear, but it saved lives."

"Has Olympus faced this dilemma before?" asked Artemis.

"Not with time running out, no," he muttered, "and it's thirteen minutes until this van goes boom."

"I'll call Athena for a decision on Parkway," said Artemis.

"She will need to get it sanctioned by Zeus. There won't be enough time."

"Giles says Rusty is at roadworks. The car Dylan Griffiths described isn't in front at the traffic lights. They're losing any ground they may have made."

"Rusty has to prevent al-Hamady from delivering that bomb," said Phoenix.

It was frustrating for him not to be at what he considered the sharp end. Whatever was in the knapsacks behind him was an inconvenience. He wanted to take out al-Hamady himself.

"Are you okay?" asked Artemis. "I hate it when you stop talking. You're too near the town now to use any other options. The cliffs are your only hope. You are ahead of the clock, not by much, but you have enough time to ditch the van and get away. I ordered a car to come to collect you when you were joining the Portbury Hundred. He'll be there ten minutes after you say goodbye to the van."

"You're a star, Artemis," Phoenix replied. "All I have to do is look inconspicuous near Beach Road while hell breaks loose."

"There are plenty of fields, hedges and trees in the vicinity. I'm checking the satellite view. The area is quiet. The summer is over, and it's rained throughout the week. I doubt you'll see any more than a man and his dog."

Phoenix checked his watch once more. Artemis was right; he would arrive at sixteen minutes past three.

Thoughts of what Rusty and Hugh Fraser were doing had to be put out of his head so that he could concentrate. He trusted them to make the right decisions.

Phoenix prayed they stopped al-Hamady so that whether they should have phoned a warning never arose.

"I'm on Wyndham Way now," he said, "talk me through these streets,"

"It's right and left at the end of Wyndham Way. Take Nore Road until you reach a right turn up Beach Hill. Then it's left at the top towards the cliffs. A car park for the coastal path is on the left. It's empty today."

"Thanks, I owe you a drink after this," said Phoenix. "If we survive today, the four of us will spend the weekend on 'Elizabeth' at Lymington."

"She's a beautiful yacht," said Artemis. "I saw her while checking on Hermes last year with the harbour master."

"I'm climbing Beach Hill now," he said, "I'll sign off until later."

"Before you go, when you ditch the car, don't head back to town. Carry on walking across the golf course to the Windmill pub. I'll call the driver to meet you in the car park."

"Artemis, after the drive I've had this afternoon, I'll be in the bar having a drink."

Phoenix turned onto Beach Road and then into the small car park.

Artemis had been right; the place looked deserted. Strong winds buffeted the van, and the rain hammered against the windscreen. What mug would be outside on a day such as this? There were four minutes left.

Should he accelerate towards the cliff and jump out at the last second? It was risky. He wasn't getting any younger. Phoenix decided to use the tools he had available. He brought a knapsack from the back of the van, placed it on the accelerator, released the handbrake and slammed the door shut as the van surged forwards.

Phoenix didn't wait to hear the crunch when the van landed. He ran towards the pub in the distance taking advantage of every bit of cover available. He would still get soaked by the time he got there. The ground shook under his feet. The blast that followed was tremendous; he found himself on his hands and knees, and his ears were ringing.

Phoenix struggled to his feet, took shelter under a tree, and looked back.

Giles and Artemis would find it difficult to hide what had happened. A long stretch of the coastal path had disappeared. Thousands of tons of earth and rocks had slipped into the waters beneath. Nobody would ever lose a ball in the rough on the left of that hole again.

Phoenix made it to a cluster of trees and bushes opposite the car park. People had ventured outside and looked across the headland to see what had happened. He heard voices.

"Another cliff fall," said one customer.

"There was a bang, wasn't there?" asked another.

"I thought it sounded like a bomb."

"Around here? Perhaps a WWII mine broke loose from the seabed and crashed onto the rocks."

"Good thinking," muttered Phoenix.

The rain dripped down the back of his neck. A car turned into the road leading to the pub as Phoenix stepped from his hiding place.

The driver flashed his headlights and turned the car around. Phoenix got in. The pub's customers were staring towards the sea. Nobody noticed them leave.

"Are you patched-in with the ice-house?" asked Phoenix.

A Frequent Peal of Bells

"Yes, sir," said the driver.

"Giles? Can you hear me?"

"Got you, Phoenix. I see the satellite view of the damage you caused. It's the least of our worries."

"Did Rusty not catch up with al-Hamady? What happened?"

"It seems al-Hamady suspected Temple Meads was compromised. What alerted him, we don't know. Maybe he expected to see the bomb maker outside the station to confirm the other two were safe inside. Instead, something altered his plans."

"He reached Parkway?"

"He was three minutes ahead of Rusty and Hugh. When they arrived, they found his car abandoned. He had entered the station with a knapsack on his back, walked into the main waiting area and detonated whatever device it contained."

"He realised it was likely he was the only surviving member of the cell, so he committed suicide," said Phoenix.

"I was listening to the news as I got here," said the driver, "shall I turn on the radio again?"

Phoenix nodded; it was his worst nightmare. A phone call could have saved these people. The two men listened to the news as they travelled back to Bath. Every witness interview was a hammer blow to Phoenix.

"I had just reached a ticket window when I saw a flash of yellow light."

"I never heard an explosion, just glass and masonry falling. There was blood everywhere."

"All around us, people were shouting and screaming."

"When I arrived, people came out of the station with blood pouring from their wounds."

"Rescuers are inside now searching for survivors under the rubble."

A news reporter gave a summary at four o'clock.

"Members of the security services joined the police officers at the scene of this terrible incident. A single person carried out this terrorist attack. A Middle-Eastern man in his sixties entered the waiting room, called out in Arabic, and detonated a bomb in a bag on his back. They haven't established a link to earlier attacks in London and Edinburgh. Investigations will continue. The death toll is over forty, with perhaps two hundred injured. The emergency services have been marvellous here this afternoon. Conditions inside the waiting area have been traumatic. The building's structure sustained severe damage, yet paramedics and firefighters have refused to withdraw despite the concerns of their superiors. Their bravery sends a message to ISIS or whoever sanctioned this attack. You will never break the indomitable spirit of the British nation. Every minute I've spent here at Bristol Parkway, I've witnessed that spirit at work. It's humbling."

"Turn it off," said Phoenix. They had reached the gates of the estate.

The driver dropped him at the front door. Phoenix climbed the stairs and walked along the corridor to the apartment. Athena and Hope sat together on a settee. She stood and carried their daughter to meet him.

"You should have told me," she said.

"I didn't want you to worry. I was perfectly safe," Phoenix replied.

"What more could Rusty have done at Parkway?" asked Athena.

"We knew the Syrian was carrying a bomb. We could have sent a warning."

"Artemis called me to the ice-house. I reviewed the timings of every step you and Rusty took during both missions. It was impossible to stop without taking a unilateral decision. Protocol demands I ask permission from Zeus to do something that endangers our security. Any warning risked exposure by admitting we had knowledge that wasn't shared by the authorities."

"She told me there wasn't time," said Phoenix, "but it still hurts so many died."

"Hundreds more would have died if you hadn't killed Mansouri and Harrack."

"Can we at least raise the matter with Zeus in January?" asked Phoenix, "another occasion could arise. We need a set of conditions that allow us to take that unilateral decision. They can question us on our actions at the next meeting."

"I have no clue what his thoughts are on the matter," Athena replied. "It's a tough call to make. We will discover in the next twenty-four hours whether our actions today have gone unnoticed."

Phoenix hugged his wife and daughter. Today had been a trial. What lay ahead for Olympus was uncertain, but he could cope if he had these two in his life.

Chapter Nine

Saturday, 11th October 2014

The media spotlight was firmly on Bristol Parkway in the morning. A further sixteen deaths were confirmed overnight. The number of injured had risen to two hundred and thirty-six. Parkway opened in 1972 and was the first in a new generation of park-and-ride stations. It had become the third busiest station in the West Country after Temple Meads and Bath Spa. After yesterday's terror attack, it would be out of action for weeks.

There were echoes of concerns expressed after Canary Wharf and Edinburgh Waverley. Why didn't the security services prevent the attack? They spent thousands of hours poring over the wreckage on those sites. They took reams of witness statements. Why wasn't security at railway stations across the country increased?

The praise for the emergency services continued to feature in every newspaper and on the rolling twenty-four-hour news channels. However, the questions over the bombing campaign mounted.

At Larcombe Manor, the free weekend many hoped for was curtailed. Phoenix looked forward to a pleasant trip to Lymington to get re-acquainted with their yacht, 'Elizabeth'. After yesterday's fun and games, he hoped Rusty and Artemis could join them.

Everything changed when Athena called an emergency morning meeting.

"Are we at risk, Giles?" she asked. "Was there anything from yesterday's actions that linked to Olympus?"

"Nothing from Parkway, as our people arrived too late to stop al-Hamady. We might have caused more problems for ourselves if we had been in time. The bomb wasn't on a timer like the others; witnesses say he activated the trigger himself."

"Rusty arrived three minutes after al-Hamady," added Artemis, "he would already have been at Parkway. Even if they caught him outside the building, it's hard to see how they could have disabled him without being seen."

"Temple Meads Transport Police didn't have cause for concern," said Phoenix, "the bombs never reached there. Unless they realised the Irregulars, Rusty, and Fraser were working as a team, they would be none the wiser."

"Which leaves Portishead," said Athena, "what's our position there?"

"Two local TV channels have sent reporters and camera crews to the site," said Giles. "Rock falls around the coastline are common. Erosion is a big problem. If a hotel or a holiday chalet falls into the sea, it's headline news for twenty-four hours. Yesterday's fall was different. Eyewitnesses report hearing a massive explosion. They've cordoned off the area around the site. Experts have said there's a significant danger of another fall."

"That's good news, surely?" said Alastor.

"Phoenix chose a good spot to send the van over the top," said Artemis, "the only way to view the damage is by boat. I saw nobody on the headland in that awful weather, but a white van was sighted on Beach Hill two minutes before the explosion. The lifeboat was launched at first light this morning to check for signs of a vehicle."

"I hoped it got buried under the rocks," said Phoenix.

"The explosive power of those two bombs would have destroyed the van," said Henry. "Any lightweight wreckage they found floating on the surface could have come from anywhere. The metal components from the van and the bombs would be on the seabed."

"Spread over a great distance," added Giles. "Our main concern has to be to deflect attention from the explosion. One eyewitness suggested an old mine hit the rocks."

"I heard him say that," said Phoenix. "That's where we can focus our misinformation. How do we get our hands on another mine to cause a big bang, maybe five miles up the coast?"

"eBay," said Minos.

"It's not like you to joke over such serious matters, Minos," said Athena,

"I'm not joking," he replied. "I saw one for sale the other evening."

"We won't pry into what you were looking for, Minos," said Rusty, "but if it's still for sale, I suggest we grab it."

"What other concerns did they raise in the media, Giles?" asked Athena.

"We knew there were at least two men involved at Canary Wharf. We noted the apparent disinterest shown by

A Frequent Peal of Bells

Mansouri and Harrack as they left the area. The surrounding crowds stopped to discuss what had happened. The security services had them both on their radar, but neither man's name was ever associated with that attack in the press. Some commentators have found evidence to suggest the same men were at Edinburgh Waverley. The red-tops concentrate on yesterday's shocking scenes and the bravery of the paramedics. But, at the higher end of the profession, investigative journalists ask why this man acted alone?"

"The authorities have yet to name the suspected bombers of the DLR," said Artemis. "But, Waverley was at least a three-person attack. The female suicide bomber supplemented the bombs laid by Mansouri and Harrack; they identified Amina Badour quickly. The security services should have found a link between Badour and the other two men. Badour entered the UK with Mansouri. The nature of the attack led us to believe they formed part of a cell even if we couldn't put a number on how many it contained."

"With al-Hamady dying alone yesterday," said Athena, "you're saying brighter journalists are wondering why there weren't more bombs and bombers at Parkway?"

"Exactly," said Giles. "Canary Wharf felt the work of a team, so did Waverley. Unless the team lost members in an attack like Badour, there should have been more cell members at Parkway."

"The last thing we need is for the focus to switch to Portishead," said Henry Case, "and one loose end that could trigger that is our Afghani bomb maker. I understand the logic behind leaving the body in the house. The ticking bombs became your priority. Things may snowball if they call the police when they find the body."

"The Afghani came here legally," said Rusty, "he owned a property in Hanham and drove a brand-new van. So there will be a paper trail. An autopsy will show minute traces of the materials he used. They'll soon put two and two together. That will suggest a link between him and al-Hamady. The cousin that al-Hamady stayed with at Bradley Stoke will be traced. Everything points to Bristol as the centre of operations for the Parkway attack. Occupants of the house will remember the house guests. They will get asked about where they went. Did they kill the Afghani and flee? Or did someone remove the three terrorists?"

"Did a muppet leave a body behind?" said Phoenix, realising how grave this mistake may have been.

"The bombs stopped you from thinking straight," said Athena.

"I know this sounds stupid, but I didn't have a piece of carpet big enough in the conservatory to cover him. Rusty and Hugh came prepared. I couldn't risk lugging him over my shoulder in daylight."

"What can we do?" asked Athena.

"As Henry said, we distract attention from Portishead," said Artemis, "and Giles and I will trace every step our teams took yesterday. We can erase footage here and there. It may prevent the authorities from pinpointing specific vehicles and linking them to the house in Hanover Street and Parkway."

"We'll need a huge slice of luck," said Phoenix. "Or breaking news that moves the media circus on to the next major story."

Tyrone O'Riordan didn't have a yacht. He didn't often take weekends off, either. Instead, his mother relaxed in her

A Frequent Peal of Bells

penthouse while he studied the details of the Grid's next big job. The Albanian gang gave him the first draft of their planned bank raid. There seemed to be loads of pages to read. Tyrone had been to a nightclub last night; he couldn't drink any more coffee. He was hyper.

He poured himself a large glass of Bushmills. The hair of the dog, kill or cure, take your pick.

"There might only be three of them, but they've been busy," Tyrone muttered.

The whiskey helped, but he remained on edge.

His mobile rang. It was his mother.

"I've got something you might be interested in," said Colleen.

A young woman said the same thing to Tyrone last night in the nightclub. That was another reason he found it heavy going this morning. The birds were in full voice when he got home.

"Is it important, Mum?" he asked, "I'm waiting for a call."

"I'm sure you can spare a few minutes for your mother," she said, "I've got a guest list."

"Really? From where?"

"The Dorchester, Tyrone. Try to keep up with me. There were photos of a wedding party in the folder you sent me."

"Oh, so you opened a file on your own, then?"

"Thanks to your instructions, sweetheart. I've got them pinned up on the wall behind my computer."

"Who was on the list?" asked Tyrone, taking more notice.

"Lots of fancy titles and people from the business and finance world. The crowd in the corner tucked away from the others. They came from a charity. No names on the guest list, just sixteen spaces allocated to the Olympus Project."

"Have you looked up who they are?" asked Tyrone.

"They're based outside Bath at a place called Larcombe Manor. It's a registered charity that has been operating since 2007. They look after veterans who have PTSD. I looked up the Charity Commission reports on them. They've passed every inspection, and the results they achieve are amazing."

Tyrone slapped the tabletop hard. His thumping head protested, but this was a breakthrough.

"You're a genius," he cried, "a charity, my ass. What a great cover. All the stories mention them being well-drilled and ruthless. Of course, they are. They use former soldiers and marines, one hundred per cent fit, mentally and physically."

"Happy to help, son," said Colleen.

"We know where they're based now. The charity reports will tell us how many men they have on-site. I'll get someone inside their systems in the next week or two, and they can discover what their strength is outside Larcombe Manor."

"Will that be who this Gonzo character is?" asked Colleen.

"He's putting a name to the guy with the great-looking woman in that photo," said Tyrone. "It's him and his mate we need to get rid of first. I should find their van, but I don't have to pay Gonzo for that. I'll tell him where and when to look. It will be on a traffic camera on the M4 heading west on the evening of Thursday, the second of October."

"The Grid will soon remove its only remaining opposition," said Colleen.

"I'm glad you rang, Mum. You've made my day," said Tyrone, "but I must love and leave you. I'm expecting an urgent call any minute."

Tyrone contacted Gonzo via a message board. The dark web hacker had suggested it if Tyrone needed to get in touch with him urgently. The sooner they got the ball rolling, the better.

Tyrone yielded to his legacy of a thumping headache from last night. He had one more glass of Bushmills and took to his bed. The next time Tyrone awoke, it was seven in the evening. He showered, felt refreshed, and was ready to face the rest of the day. When his mobile pinged minutes later, Tyrone drew in a deep breath. Was this the news he had been expecting?

The text message was brief but to the point.

"We're in."

It came from Aleks Bogdani, the thirty-eight-year-old leader of the Albanian gang.

Earlier today, Tyrone had studied the draft plans for the bank robbery. That was for later. Aleks and his team were now inside a safe deposit vault. A room that would soon be relieved of a sum of money to make his mother's eyes water.

Aleks had used a professional make-up artist to disguise their features with latex prosthetics. The three men wore wigs, but Tyrone couldn't tell from the group photo the cheeky beggars sent him on their phones. They looked like a middle-aged Jewish boy band.

Zamir Tanush was a year older than Aleks. The group's baby, Januz Goga, was a mere thirty-five; this robbery was not their first rodeo. Each man was a seasoned criminal before arriving in the UK. They didn't come here to work; they came to get rich.

Aleks Bogdani stole cars and learned to pick locks before his voice broke. When he was twenty, he studied people. He studied the habits and mannerisms of men who worked in banking and precious stones. Six years ago, he sought people with a range of skills he could use. Tanush and Goga were adept with alarms, cracking safes, tunnelling, and following orders. The team was small but efficient. Nowhere was secure when this trio set to work.

The message they sent Tyrone came from Hatton Garden, a street and commercial centre in the Holborn district of Camden. The area was famous around the globe as London's jewellery quarter and the centre of the UK diamond trade.

Today, three hundred businesses trade here in the jewellery industry. Over fifty shops represent the most prominent jewellery retailers — companies like De Beers, the international family of companies that dominate the global diamond trade. De Beers HQ lies behind the main Hatton Garden shopping street. Underneath the whole district lay an extensive underground infrastructure of vaults, tunnels, offices and workshops.

During business hours, which ended at five today, men in broad-brimmed hats hurried along the street with satchels securely attached to their wrists. Armoured cars cruised next to the pavements, and couriers with armed escorts hurried between vehicles and doorways. Clients from every nation populated the streets and shops while they were open.

Aleks appreciated that the gems got locked away in safes and underground vaults at night. The concentration of wealth in that small patch of the capital's real estate was of epic proportions. Nevertheless, he had promised Tyrone

A Frequent Peal of Bells

O'Riordan he would deliver forty million pounds of gems tomorrow.

The Albanian gang leader spent weeks of surveillance in Hatton Garden. His knowledge allowed him to merge seamlessly into the environment. Aleks visited the area at different times, noting anything that helped or hindered the planning he carried out once the business closed for the day.

Staff, clients, and security guards became accustomed to seeing him around the place. In the final week of planning, he was happy he had gained their acceptance as a *mensch*, a person of integrity and honour. It was time to open a safe deposit account in the target bank. As he stood inside the vault, Aleks was confident he possessed the knowledge he needed to carry out his audacious plan. That evening he called Tanush and Goga.

The three men met only twice after that first call. The police had never caught them in their native country, and they didn't intend that to change. The fewer occasions they were spotted together, the better. Too often, criminals became tagged as known associates, and if an eyewitness identified one gang member, the others got arrested. When Bogdani explained the comprehensive disguises, Tanush and Goga relaxed. It would be a piece of cake.

At the first meeting in Goga's flat in Maida Vale, Aleks showed them bank diagrams. They cost him twenty thousand pounds. The ex-employee of the firm that produced them had now retired and played golf every day in the Algarve. Aleks assured his friends he knew the man's address. If something went wrong, he would never see a golf course again.

The men studied the diagrams and commented on the initial draft plans. Aleks bowed to their superior knowledge in the areas of their specialist subjects and made the necessary adjustments. When Aleks and Zamir wished their friend goodnight, the tinkering was complete. They were ready to pull off a daring robbery that would send shockwaves through the city of London.

That night when he got home, Aleks contacted Tyrone O'Riordan. He offered to provide the Grid with a forty million payday. Tyrone was keen to impress his mother. Aleks heard the excitement in the young man's voice.

Tyrone wanted to increase that sum. He asked whether he could see the plans for the jewel robbery. The night they visited Tyrone's penthouse apartment was the final time the three gang members gathered together to run through the plans.

Tyrone proposed a second job, a bank robbery, to break the record for the largest haul ever on British soil. He wanted to demonstrate the Grid's power, to show they could steal what they wanted whenever they wished.

Aleks, Zamir, and Januz came to Britain to make their fortune. As they descended to the ground floor in the lift after meeting Tyrone, Aleks assured his friends the Grid would only see the expected amounts. Whatever they amassed on top would be theirs alone. He had heard Tyrone's threats, but they meant little to an Albanian gangster. Life was a risk. If Tyrone wanted a fight, he would get one, and Aleks was confident they could defeat whatever Tyrone threw at them.

Two days ago, Aleks finished the surveillance and planning on the bank robbery. They waited to be invited to the penthouse once more to answer questions from the young Irishman. In the meantime, they looked forward to a profitable weekend.

At five o'clock on Saturday, the businesses closed for the weekend. There was no trading on a Sunday. Doors were locked, shutters rolled into place, and alarm systems were activated. The gang broke through one of the bank's entrances at six o'clock. Zamir neutralised the alarm system once they got inside the bank.

Then they breached the reinforced cement wall of the room with the safe deposit boxes. As soon as the vault's interior was visible, Zamir sent the text message to Tyrone. It would be a while before they stood inside the vault and began work. Aleks was happy; the hard part was complete.

The boxes stood on the right-hand side of the room, directly opposite the hole. Januz worked steadily, enlarging the gap until they could crawl through it. Above them, London life continued with its usual rattle and hum. If you want quiet, you should go to the countryside. Very few Londoners took any notice of noise, above or below ground. Somebody always worked somewhere; the weekend was often the best time to get repair and maintenance jobs done.

That had been the attraction of this job to Aleks Bogdani. The sheer simplicity. Big-time robberies had gone out of favour in the years since he arrived from Tirana. Burglaries on this enterprise's scale were so rare that the police had reduced the number of officers they allocated to solving them. In the diamond district, security was light years ahead of what you expect for a family home. But when the threat of a break-in diminishes to be almost non-existent, people get lazy.

Aleks knew false alarms were frequent. He witnessed them every day during his surveillance period. Over the years, the threat level diminished, and police officers' ability to respond followed suit. He knew the protocol. When an intruder alarm is activated, local security personnel should make a cursory check. If they believed a break-in had occurred, they phoned the police. If not, they carried on with their regular duties.

The police would have received the interrupted alarm call. The police graded the call and determined whether to respond. If they received a second call from security, they sent in the cavalry. It didn't take a genius to work out that the local security was lax in its cursory checks with the volume of false alarms the system recorded.

As for the police, they needed to consider the background of competing for urgent calls and available resources. Add in the frequency of false activations of the alarms across the diamond quarter, and police attendance became a low priority. That was why the odd squawk from an alarm, or the muffled sound of a drill, didn't generate panic. The world kept spinning on its axis. It was probably nothing.

"You're the largest, Zamir," said Januz, "try crawling through the hole."

It was tight, but the big man made it. The others handed tools through to him, and then Aleks and Januz joined him. They stood and gazed at the ten rows of sixteen boxes that faced them.

"How do we know where to start?" asked Zamir.

"Ignore number 114," said Aleks, "that's mine. I'll open it at the end."

Aleks started in the middle, and his colleagues moved to either end. Then, one by one, boxes were levered open. Their contents emptied onto a side table on the far wall. They stopped when they covered the surface with cash, bags, ring boxes, securities documents, deeds, and letters.

"Now we throw the rubbish into a sack," said Aleks. "Open every velvet bag and box. Fill the plastic containers and stack them in the backpacks. As soon as we clear this table, we open more boxes and fill it again."

The second round of boxes took longer than the first. They grew weary. There seemed to be so many boxes that only contained coins and documents. They couldn't predict which boxes to leave well alone. Zamir asked Aleks whether this would be as lucrative a haul as they hoped.

"We persevere," he said, "the next box you open might be full of diamonds."

As they picked through the items on the tabletop, Januz found a bag containing a fabulous necklace.

"Wow, what might this be worth?" he asked.

"In a Mayfair shop, it retails at five million," said Aleks. "When we take it to a fence, we might get ten per cent of that. If it's that good, somebody will have owned it before. It will be recognised. That thing will be more trouble than it's worth. Throw it in with the rubbish. We need items we can convert to cash without the hassle."

Zamir soon discovered Aleks had been right to persevere. He opened a velvet bag that felt different from the others. He tipped the contents into a plastic container. The bag of uncut diamonds was the boost they needed. Januz grabbed a similarly marked bag and opened it. They had struck the mother lode. Aleks joined in the hunt for more of the same bags. They found seven in total.

"We must keep going," he said, "I know we're tired. These disguises are hot, and the air here isn't great, and I don't think we've got forty million yet."

He checked his watch. It had been ten hours since they entered the street above them. He wanted to be out of this place before noon.

"Come on, Zamir. Don't stand there looking at the

backpacks. We'll count the cash soon. If we reach the limit, we discard it and only collect gold and diamonds."

"Surely, cash is best?" asked Januz.

"You're not thinking, Januz," said Aleks. "We will only be able to carry a maximum of fifty kilos on our backs. The diamonds will be the highest value per kilo we collect. The contents of those seven velvet bags could be worth twenty-five million. We concentrate on finding more of these."

They emptied twenty more boxes and divided their contents between the keep and the discard pile. Nobody found any more uncut diamonds, but there was no shortage of gems and cash.

"Now we count the cash, Zamir," said Aleks, "only fifty English notes and one hundred euros. The five hundred notes are too risky. The police think they're associated with organised crime."

Zamir and Januz looked at Aleks, grinning from ear to ear. They counted the cash as instructed. They had over eight million pounds, plus two million euros, and split the amounts across the three knapsacks.

Aleks lifted one. It was heavier than he had hoped. The other two were lighter, but not by much. Zamir was strong; he could cope with this one.

"There's time to open a further twenty," he said, "pick them at random. We might get lucky; who knows? We don't have time for any more than that, and we'll struggle to carry the stuff out. Ditch the cash; go for gems."

"It would be madness to go to this trouble and then get stopped by the police because we're bent double with the strain of our haul," said Januz.

All three men laughed, despite the tension of the moment.

After a short rest, they opened random boxes. Aleks

opened box 114 and retrieved the cash he had stashed when he opened his account. Januz found gold coins, rings and bracelets. Zamir came across dusty old wills and compromising pictures of a young actress.

"We could blackmail her," he said to Aleks.

"Think again," said Aleks, "the pictures are black and white. She retired years ago and wouldn't pay us a bean. If we published these photos, it would do her a favour. Remind people how attractive she was in the old days. Ditch them. The police can enjoy looking at them when they investigate this theft."

They opened the eighty-fifth box and sorted through the contents. The items were boxed or ditched, while Aleks added more plastic containers to the two lighter bags.

"Zamir, can you manage this one?" he asked.

The big man lifted it from the floor and slung it over his shoulders. He staggered forward two steps and then grinned.

"Only kidding," he said, "I'll be fine."

"Okay," said Aleks, "let's take a few minutes clearing this mess. Wipe every surface. We mostly wore gloves, but we handled bags and necklaces that went into the sacks. We must take them and dispose of them before we leave."

Ten minutes later, they crawled through the tunnel pushing the knapsacks in front. Zamir went back inside the vault and grabbed the rubbish sacks. Then, with the bags on their backs, the three men returned to the door they had entered eighteen hours earlier. It was a quarter to twelve.

Aleks opened the door an inch. He couldn't see anyone. He saw what they needed,

"Waste bins, twenty yards up the lane, Januz," he said, "throw the sacks in there and set everything alight. We're heading in the opposite direction back to the car. Don't run to catch us. We'll wait for you."

Aleks and Zamir left the building and strolled along the lane to the corner. They spotted a few pedestrians and vehicles on the move, but nobody paid attention to two Jewish gentlemen in this part of town. Finally, they reached the car and got inside. Januz appeared at the end of the lane. A police car cruised past and stopped twenty yards further up the road.

"Don't panic," pleaded Zamir as he watched his friend glance over his shoulder at the car. He continued his slow walk. The two officers were out of the car now; one talked on his walkie-talkie. Had he received a message concerning them? Januz slid into the back seat and puffed out his cheeks.

"Let's get out of here," he said.

The police officers reached the entrance to the lane.

"Did anyone see you ditch the sacks?" asked Aleks.

"The place was deserted. The waste bin was smoking well when I left."

Aleks started the car and moved away.

"Somebody reported the smoke. That explains the call. We're still alright. Let's get back to my place and recount the cash."

"Aren't you going to tell the boss we've finished the job?" asked Zamir.

"Are you kidding?" asked Aleks, "that's why I wanted to get away early. I'll call when I have a good idea of what we've got here. He'll get his share. We'll hang on to as much cash as possible without raising his suspicions."

They had executed the plan to perfection. The business owners and the police were unaware of the problem. No one would discover the robbery until Monday morning.

A Frequent Peal of Bells

When staff arrived, they would find the vault compromised. Eighty-five of the one hundred and sixty safe deposit boxes opened. Cash and velvet bags were scattered on the floor.

It suggested to the police that a small team had been at work. Although the gang had time to break into the remaining boxes, they reached the limit of what they could carry. There was nothing but heartache for those who stored documents, deeds, love letters, and risqué photos in the vault. The police had found a burning waste bin at the far end of the lane; its contents were irretrievable.

As for the five million pounds necklace, Januz had rescued that before throwing the sacks into the bin. It was in the inside pocket of his jacket.

Chapter Ten

Monday, 13th October 2014

Tyrone O'Riordan finally heard from Aleks Bogdani at midnight last night. The success of the robbery was great news: one down and one to go. Tyrone couldn't wait to ring his mother with the news. He wasn't sure what time she got up now. She was a lady of leisure. He waited until half-past nine.

"Good morning, Mum," he said, "and how are you this fine morning?"

"Have you seen the news?" she snapped.

"Why, what's the matter?"

"That jewellery robbery you mentioned is all over the news. It's causing a right stink."

"Have they said how much they took?" he asked.

"Too early to tell," said Colleen, "they've got to check which safe deposits got opened and who owned them. Not everyone will be honest about what they stored in the vault. I bet the taxman would be keen to find out."

A Frequent Peal of Bells

"Do they have any idea who was responsible?"

"The police plan to question the bank's employees and security guards. The burglars knew their way around. They aren't sure how many people were involved, but they were professionals with sophisticated equipment. The police believe the robbers had help from someone inside to break into the vault. Two questions for which they want answers. Why the security personnel didn't realise something was happening and was there a brief spell when an alarm sounded?"

"I wish I'd got up earlier to watch it now," laughed Tyrone, "what's happening there now?"

"There are people outside the bank. They're eager to learn which boxes got opened."

"I heard from the leader of the gang late last night. Everything went to plan. They got in and out without being seen. We should hit forty million, no bother. I'm meeting with Aleks at noon. He's made an appointment to deliver the cash. We'll get that paid into the Grid's accounts."

"How much cash was there?" asked Colleen.

"Eight million, four hundred thousand," replied Tyrone.

"Is that it? Where's the rest coming from?"

"Diamonds, uncut and cut. We need to sell those on the quiet. Gold bracelets, rings and chains. They will melt those for scrap value. The sooner the actual ornament disappears, the better. Unless someone is daft enough to try to cheat us, we'll scrape up to forty million. When they finish the bank job, you'll see the hundred million I promised."

"It sounds too easy, Tyrone," said Colleen, "it's only twenty-four hours since the robbery. How can you be sure the police won't find clues? I hope there's no way to link these Albanians to us?"

"Quit worrying," Tyrone replied, "these guys are

experts. Nothing can trace back to me either. I met them here once, and my place is more secure than the Bank of England."

"That's not where they're going to go next, is it?" asked Colleen.

"Don't be daft, mother. You don't need to know where. What's important is the Grid will soon be the most-feared organisation in the country."

"I like the sound of that, Tyrone," said his mother, "I want people frightened of what we can do if they don't fall into line. I spent half my life under your father's thumb. It's my time in the limelight now. More than anything, I need people to show me respect."

Tyrone promised to keep his mother informed on how the disposal of the other items stolen in the raid progressed. He needed to get over to the Glencairn. Today promised to be a lucrative day for the Grid's bank.

In her penthouse apartment, Colleen O'Riordan continued to watch TV. The rolling twenty-four-hour news channels showed wall-to-wall coverage of the jewellery robbery. Commentators interviewed various experts on the effects of the weekend's raid.

"It will impact many people's lives," said one, "some may go out of business."

"The public's view of Hatton Garden security has been damaged, perhaps irretrievably," said another.

As she made herself a fresh pot of coffee, they questioned the Metropolitan Police Commissioner at the scene of the robbery.

"Commissioner, how much have the large cuts to police services in the past four years contributed to this weekend's robbery?"

A Frequent Peal of Bells

"I expect further budget reductions regardless of who wins next year's general election. There's a risk to public safety if we don't take radical action. This robbery is a throwback to the old wild west. I doubt we'll see another. Criminals are moving from the shotgun robberies of the past to more sophisticated offences. Cybercrime is where the police need to catch up today. That makes the notion of jurisdiction less and less meaningful. Electronic fraudsters will replace the robbers of the past. If we continue to pursue cuts, we could see the end of neighbourhood policing vital to preventing crime. We will respond to an emergency but little else."

"Other services had to make cuts. Are you saying the police should be a special case?"

"No, you must remember cuts to other services jeopardise the assets we access. Councils fund CCTV cameras. As they face more cuts, they must decide whether they can afford to keep them."

"Were CCTV cameras on this street switched off to save money? Is that why the police didn't respond to the alarm?"

"Many of the cameras in this quarter are funded by the business community. The alarm or lack of alarm scenario is still under investigation. I couldn't possibly comment at this time."

Colleen switched off her television. She needn't worry. Thirty years ago, Tommy and his father would have feared a knock on the door from the Sweeney. They were bigger rogues than the criminals, but they didn't bother with budgets, inter-service cooperation and media bullshit.

While this lot remained in charge, Tyrone, the Albanians, and every other gang working for the Grid were as safe as houses.

At Larcombe, the morning meeting followed the robbery in Hatton Garden with interest after their mid-morning break for coffee.

When Athena opened the meeting at nine o'clock, the focus had to be on Portishead and Parkway.

"What did you manage to do for us, Giles?" asked Athena.

"I'll start with what we didn't do, if I may," said Giles. "We didn't bid for the WWII mine in the end. Events elsewhere meant the spotlight shifted. They've dismissed the rockfall as just that. There was little activity in the area over the weekend. People stayed away from the cliffs in case there was a further collapse. The whole headland is considered unstable."

"I made an anonymous call to the Immigration people," said Artemis. "The house in Hanover Street was raided yesterday morning. Police removed twelve illegals. They discovered the body of an Afghani man in the conservatory. The police answered a call this morning and identified him as Musa Iqbal, aged sixty. He ran a wholesale delicatessen supplier in Hanham."

"With a sideline in manufacturing IEDs," said Phoenix. "How many more are not on the security services watch lists?"

"Several detainees gave the police descriptions of Mansouri and Harrack," added Giles. "The police are looking for them concerning Iqbal's murder."

"Good luck with that," said Henry Case. "After you brought them here via Parkway, we buried them in the pet cemetery on Saturday morning. A team of trainees dealt with that while I attended our emergency meeting."

"We can leave the police to continue their fruitless

search. Lawrence Hill won't cause us any further headaches. Which leaves us with Parkway," said Athena.

"Two more deaths since we last met," said Artemis, "and doctors fear others in the hospital may not survive. The Prime Minister is due to visit Parkway this afternoon. He's arriving by car."

"Not much choice," said Rusty, "they won't be running a normal service this month."

"The question remains over the number of bombers," said Giles, "it may crop up again. I'll continue monitoring the situation. For now, the Hatton Garden robbery has demoted it in the pecking order."

"Thankful for small mercies," said Phoenix.

"Not so small," said Minos, "they say it could amount to well over fifty million."

"We prayed for a blockbuster to shift the focus away from Olympus," said Athena, "and we got it. I'm not complaining."

"The robbery bears the hallmarks of the Grid," said Phoenix, "I told you they would pull off a super crime of some description. This one qualifies as special."

"We didn't get much rest this weekend because of Parkway," said Athena, "apologies for that. I suggest we take this opportunity for a coffee break."

As the team mingled by the refreshments table, Phoenix joined Rusty and Artemis.

"Unless WWIII breaks out, we're going to Lymington next weekend. I'll ask for volunteers from the marine boys here to crew 'Elizabeth'. We'll sail around the Isle of Wight and back. Please say you'll join us?"

"We'd love to," said Artemis, "will you bring Hope with you?"

"Of course, and Geoffrey would appreciate a change of air, too," said Phoenix

"Pray for fine weather," said Rusty.

"Why? Who's not got their sea legs?" asked Phoenix.

Rusty and Artemis pointed at one another. Phoenix laughed.

"I wanted to say thanks for keeping me sane on Friday afternoon, Artemis. I should have bought you a box of chocolates."

"You can buy chocolates at any time," she replied, "the chance to spend a weekend on a luxury yacht is rare. I might learn something."

"You keep telling me you know everything," said Rusty, "I reckon Phoenix would say you know everything you need to. A subtle difference, but an important one."

"Are you ready to carry on with the agenda?" asked Athena, joining them.

"Saved by the bell," muttered Phoenix.

Minos turned the TV to the news channel and listened to the Police Commissioner's interview.

"Have they found any clues yet?" asked Henry.

"If you listen to this chap, it's hard to know whether the police are even inside the building," said Minos. "He's the same as every politician and senior civil servant there's ever been. They never answer a question."

"This gang were a professional outfit," said Henry Case, "in and out, no clues left behind."

"Let's analyse what we learned from the media reports," said Alastor. "They haven't allowed cameras inside the bank, but there was mention of an inside job. That suggests they saw detailed plans of the exterior and interior of the building, the alarm systems, and the vault itself. That enabled them to find a weakness in the external security of the bank."

"Why not say they found a door that opened without the alarm alerting the bank's security and the police?" said Phoenix.

"Sorry, I was listening to the Commissioner for too long. I caught the bug; they got in with ease. The vault door wasn't an issue. We've heard they tunnelled through the wall to gain access. They knew the floor area they had available. They only needed enough inside to work without getting under each other's feet. I've been in vaults such as that, and four is the absolute maximum. Two or three would be far better."

"That's sensible," said Rusty, "but how much weight are we talking for fifty to sixty million? Could two or three men carry it out? Where did they park the getaway car?"

"Giles, Artemis, you've got clues to follow," said Athena, "start the search for the gang. If we add to the list, we'll send the details to you."

Giles and Artemis returned to the ice-house.

"If this team belongs to the Grid, who are the likely candidates?" asked Athena.

"I think we can confine the search to London," said Minos, "they had access to the informant, didn't have trouble finding a parking space, and knew the district well."

"You've got several candidates," said Alastor, "either British White or Black. The Yardies are a distinct possibility. The Eastern Europeans stick to arms, drugs, and people trafficking. The Bulgarian Mafia turn its hand to anything if it has violence attached. I'm not sure the Chinese, Vietnamese, or Bangladeshi gangs would be keen to get involved in a bank caper."

"So, we could want three black or white men in the area

between five o'clock on Saturday and nine o'clock Monday?" asked Rusty.

"We haven't narrowed the search, have we?" said Henry.

"How long do the police reckon they worked inside the bank?" asked Phoenix.

"Giles and Artemis can tell us when there was activity near the bank on Sunday," said Rusty. "They would have taken time to get in, cut the alarms, and tunnel through the wall. Once inside the vault, they had to get the boxes open. Then they had to transfer what they wanted to keep into bags and scrap the rest. How many boxes did they open?"

"The police haven't mentioned a number yet," said Alastor, "nor did the spokeswoman for the bank."

"Who provided the estimated haul of over fifty million?" asked Phoenix.

"The spokeswoman," said Minos, referring to his earlier notes.

"That's fair enough," said Phoenix, "I reckon that means we're talking close to a hundred boxes."

"With three men working flat out, the earliest anybody would be on the street outside is eleven in the morning," said Rusty. "We need Giles to make eleven o'clock the start point for the search."

"How long for?" asked Henry.

"Until they spot them," said Rusty.

While the morning meeting was in progress, it started a new week for Orion. Life at Larcombe Manor proved to be as enjoyable as he had hoped. The outlook from his office window wasn't as picturesque as the rest of the estate, but he

A Frequent Peal of Bells

got more work done as a result. Hayden Vincent was a good boss. He passed Orion a folder every Monday morning at nine o'clock. On Friday, he expected a similar folder with reports on closed cases and progress reports on those outstanding.

If a resource was required to complete a case, he only had to add a request to an item, and it would arrive at the start of the following week. Between nine o'clock on Monday and five o'clock on Friday, Hayden didn't bother him. Orion wished he had bosses like that during those decades he'd spent in the police force. There were always budget restrictions, new initiatives, and those mind-numbing internal consultations.

Orion tried to remember whether anything produced by those consultations ever amounted to much. A glossy brochure with promises of positive change, and that was that. He assisted in concerted drives to reduce crime, protect the victims, making people feel safe in their homes, to no avail. Nothing changed. Nobody had to account for the failure. How could they? They were tied up in meetings discussing the latest hot topic and wouldn't be available for comment.

That malaise wasn't confined solely to the police. It was present across the board. The authorities showered the public with promises things would be different. Then, by adding more glossy brochures to the growing pile, they hoped they would get blind acceptance; those at the bottom had been a success. Orion smiled at a memory from his days at Portishead.

He had always wanted a French saying on his office wall. *Plus ca change, plus la meme chose.* Things were so much different here at Olympus. For them, change was continuous. Things got done. He delivered positive results every week except with the hunt for what happened to Fiona Grant-Nicholls.

Orion had researched everything on the young Fiona before her marriage to James Grant-Nicholls in 1982. He found little out of the ordinary, considering her background. It was unusual for someone such as him, born to parents who never thought themselves to be other than working-class. It was typical for the only daughter of a well-to-do Cambridgeshire family who lived in the same country house for eight generations.

Fiona had attended a girl's fee-paying preparatory school in Cambridge, aged eight. At thirteen, she moved to a mixed-sex public school in South Norfolk. That introduced her to a world that included boys. Her parents soon discovered the Pony Club was a less attractive leisure pursuit for Fiona than it had been since she was six. Her school reports mentioned her caught smoking, drinking, and engaging in activities unbecoming a young lady. These admonishments never resulted in expulsion for Fiona, but her squeaky-clean image became tarnished.

Fiona scraped the grades necessary to earn a place at university. There was no question of it being Oxford or Cambridge as her parents had hoped. She studied Art history at Essex University. But, perhaps, studied might be stretching a point. The attractions of the social side of university life proved more compelling. The smoking continued, more cannabis than tobacco as the three years progressed. Her drinking increased too, and with her inhibitions impaired by alcohol, her fellow male undergraduates had a field day.

Fiona thought she met James at a party in Chichester in April 1981. He believed mutual friends had introduced them on New Year's Eve 1980 in Trafalgar Square. Whichever it was, the sexual attraction had been immediate. Based on Orion's conversations with her contemporaries, James was inexperienced, and Fiona was legendary.

"She couldn't get enough," one flatmate told him, "anyone, anytime, anywhere."

"James was lovely," said another, "He thought he had died and gone to heaven when someone showed him affection."

"James was thirty years old. He was making great strides in the business world," one of his work colleagues told Orion. "James was one of London's most eligible bachelors. Fiona was twenty-one, wasting her chances of a decent degree and sleeping around. I didn't see the attraction. Between you and me, I'd had her months before they hooked up together. She was too easy to count as being memorable."

Orion struggled to understand why what should have been a brief fling survived until 1982. Let alone that it ended in a marriage that year. The wedding photos showed nothing unusual. The bride was radiant, and the groom smiled in every picture. Both sets of parents looked overjoyed. The bridesmaids gazed longingly at the handsome James or his brother Cameron, the best man. The answers didn't appear to lie there.

What happened between the wedding and September 2013? Had there been thirty-one years of wedded bliss? Orion searched the internet for evidence. He found nothing. James Grant-Nicholls continued to rise the corporate ladder. He became the archetypal captain of industry; he received a knighthood. Every newspaper article and every media appearance featured James. Fiona earned a mention from time to time, but she never appeared in print or in person in her own right. It was as if she had become a non-person.

The research Orion received last year indicated the couple had no children. There were no details, except that Fiona couldn't have them. That was said to weigh on her mind, and she drank to blot out the misery. Everything was anecdotal. There was no medical evidence to confirm why she failed to conceive. There were no convictions for drink-driving. He found no photos in the press of her falling out of a nightclub at four in the morning.

Orion read the report's suggestion that Sir James took out injunctions to keep Fiona's troubles out of the press. The instances of drinking, drug abuse, and affairs with men and women certainly sounded like things celebrities paid to suppress. Unfortunately, there were plenty of examples of that in the recent past. If only he could find corroborating statements out there.

He traced the friends, family, and neighbours of the couple. People from all walks of life in both England and Scotland. Nobody had a bad word to say about Fiona. From 1982 to 2002, nothing supported the theory that the couple drifted apart because of her behaviour. Someone had talked to the writers of this report. Who had that been? Was it Sir James? Did they swallow what he told them without checking the facts? It didn't represent typical Olympus handiwork. This sounded shoddy compared to every other case he'd handled since his arrival.

Orion had checked the couple's financial status. Sir James was more than wealthy; he was filthy rich. He had provided Fiona with a monthly allowance after they separated in 2002. Before that, they had a joint account, but Fiona had no restrictions. She liked to spend money, but there were no apparent signs that her expenditure was out of control. Orion had seen enough examples of people's spending habits with an addiction to drink, drugs, or gambling. He couldn't see it between 1982 and 2002 in the financial history of Fiona Grant-Nicholls.

When he dug deeper into her circumstances after the separation, he saw a different pattern. The monthly allowance didn't always arrive in her account on time, or she only received part payment. That didn't tally with her husband's wealth. The amounts may have been high in Orion's eye, but they were small beer to Sir James.

It had to be deliberate. Sir James made his wife suffer for having walked out on him. That led to her so-called mountain of debt. Then, a year after the separation, she had been charged with driving under the influence. Orion checked the official court report, word for word, rather than the sensational version in the press. He wondered whether a payment to a reporter spiced up things.

There was no disputing the fact Fiona was under the influence. Yet, she carried prescription drugs at the time of her arrest. Orion checked the list of items in her handbag. A competent solicitor would have checked whether the opiate-based drugs aggravated the roadside reading in her possession. Orion didn't know whether she had smoked cannabis that day or snorted cocaine. He knew she had taken tramadol for severe pain for ages.

If only he could find Fiona and talk to her. How long was James abusing you? That would be his first question. Did it start straight after the wedding? Or was it after you found you couldn't give him children? Which bones did he break that still cause you intolerable pain?

On February the twentieth, 2004, Fiona went to Musselburgh. Orion thought about what courage that must have taken, given what he now believed. She faced the lion in his lair. James said Fiona wanted more money, and he had refused. They argued, she left, and the lassie at the off-licence says she sold her a large bottle of vodka. That was the last time anyone saw Fiona alive.

Orion knew the passage of time was against him. Over ten years had elapsed since that sighting in the off-licence. He would struggle to find the female assistant, and good luck trying to get her to recall one distraught middle-aged customer from that far back. He wished he still had Wayne Sangster to use as a sounding board. His partner at Hounsell Security Services didn't always know the answer, but he listened. That was often enough for Orion to come up with the solution himself.

Wayne lived in the flat above the Wishing Well café on Kilburn High Road, Camden. Finally, he had plucked up the courage to contact café owner Bridie Carragher. She took a shine to the big man when they hunted for Carrie Ditchburn. That hunt didn't end well, but the Galway girl wanted to give Wayne more than her famous Guinness cake. It just took longer for them to get together than it should.

Since joining Olympus, the two friends hadn't spoken. Maybe, he could ring Wayne tonight. Give him the gist of the story revealing no names, and see if he has any ideas about where to start. Meanwhile, he must start on the fresh batch of cases Hayden left him.

Chapter Eleven

Wednesday, 15th October 2014

While at home with his wife Erica and children Shaun and Tracey, he was Phil or Daddy. There were days when Phil Hounsell felt like a superhero without the butch costume. As soon as he crossed the cattle grid to enter the Larcombe Manor estate, he became Orion, the hunter. What a change from his career in the police force.

It was eight forty-five. Phil sat in traffic outside Bath on his way to Larcombe for another day working for the Olympus Project. He had finally contacted Wayne Sangster last night. They shared memories of the happy days they worked together with Hounsell Security Services. Wayne brought him up to date with the changes in his working life.

Triple S was alive and well. Sangster Security Services now possessed the logo Wayne had always wanted. The white flying horse Pegasus stood proudly on both sides of the black van he used. Under the Triple S business name, it proclaimed that the firm had offices in Bath and London.

"You're keeping our old office as a base then, Wayne?" Phil had queried.

"Yes, boss," Wayne had replied. He had never got used to the change in their relationship.

"Where have you opened an office in London? That must cost a fortune?"

"No, boss. I'm using upstairs in the Wishing Well café as my address. In Bridie's flat. That's my office when I stay there."

"I'm glad to hear you two have realised you fancy one another, at last. Sitting opposite you with our coffee and a slice of Bridie's luscious cake was embarrassing. She would hover over you like a mother hen. I couldn't decide which of you was drooling the most."

"I had to convince her it wasn't just her cakes I fancied," said Wayne, "that wasn't a hardship. We're compatible."

"Spare me the details, Wayne. I'm pleased. Let's leave it at that. Have you got enough work to keep you busy?"

"Yes, boss, Bridie has introduced me to loads of contacts. Customers in need of security advice for their homes and businesses. Then they ask me to find friends and family with which they've lost contact. I'm currently driving to Bath two days a week to sort out cases I'm still handling in the area. If things in London stay as they are with Bridie and me, I'll close the Bath office next year. What's it like working for those people at Larcombe, anyway?"

"I'm isolated from the other things they do there. Whatever that might be. I report to Hayden, the agent you spoke to from time to time. He keeps me busy. Every resource I need is made available. The mood is always positive. Remember when we were coppers? Two steps forward, three steps back. One hand is tied behind your back when dealing with criminals. Villains were getting off when a case went to court. Our successes in those days were rare. With Olympus, every job produces a good result."

"Life's a bowl of cherries, then?" said Wayne.

"Well, I've got a missing person I can't find. That's one reason I called."

Phil summarised the Fiona Grant-Nicholls story for his ex-colleague without using real names and asked Wayne's advice.

"There are only two reasons you can't find someone, boss. They're dead or don't want anyone to find them."

"I followed every avenue I can think of," said Phil, "and I can't find anyone remotely matching this woman's description. The places Hayden arranged to check on my behalf beggared belief. They must have serious surveillance equipment on the site somewhere. I don't suppose I'll ever access it myself. Oh, that reminds me. Did I mention Zara Wheeler, the Detective Sergeant who worked with me in Durham? Zara moved to Bath and followed me to the HQ at Portishead. She left the force before me, but I never heard where she went. Zara's working at Larcombe Manor."

"I think her name cropped up now and again," said Wayne, "I always wondered if you had a soft spot for her."

Quite the opposite, Phil thought, but he didn't want to share it with Wayne.

"Talking of Zara, when I bumped into her on that first day, I spotted a man carrying bags up the steps into the main building. You know us coppers. We get a photo of a suspect in January, and nine months later, we see a face in Tesco or waiting for a plane at the airport. A bell rings, and you know it's them."

"Who do you reckon he was then, boss? Why would they employ a criminal at Larcombe?"

"It nagged at me on the way home in the car. I couldn't

place him. Chatting with you now, Glastonbury popped into my head. That bloke and his girlfriend, we spotted listening to the Stones."

"I remember, boss," said Wayne, "she turned out to be the CEO of Olympus. So, it's no biggie to find her boyfriend living there, is it?"

"That wasn't who I thought of when I saw him first," said Phil. "If I'd seen his face straight off, I would have recognised him as Annabelle Fox's partner. Seeing him from behind, the way he walked, his posture, I don't know, he reminded me of someone from my past."

"A criminal sent to prison because of your dogged determination, or one that got away?"

"That's it, Wayne," cried Phil, "you've hit the nail on the head. The one that got away was Colin Bailey. That's who this man resembled."

"What happened to him?"

"Bailey died. Or he was missing and presumed dead back in 2010."

"At Pulteney Weir, I remember the incident now. You nearly drowned, and he did. Wasn't Zara Wheeler one of the officers who saved your life?"

"Along with Toby Drysdale, that's right."

"Hang on," said Wayne, "if Zara Wheeler has worked for Olympus for longer than you, surely she's met this bloke? If it were this Bailey fellow, she would have said something to her old colleagues on the force. You never associated him with Bailey when we saw them at Glastonbury, did you?"

"There was something that looked familiar," said Phil, "but when I got closer, their faces were different. Maybe, he has a double. We've all got one if you believe the rubbish in the newspapers."

"Ask Zara Wheeler," said Wayne, "see if she sees the resemblance. Anyway, Bridie says it's late, and she wants to go to bed. So, if you want my final word for tonight on the other matter, it seems you've exhausted the places this missing person might be hiding. That means she's dead. Start the search for a body within a mile of the last place she was seen alive. My money says that's as far as she got."

Ahead of Phil, the Wednesday rush-hour traffic began moving again. He and Zara were unlikely to enjoy a long friendly chat based on their last conversation. Nevertheless, he would ask if the opportunity arose. Phil determined to keep his eyes open for Annabelle Fox's partner to see if there were any telltale signs that everything was not as it seemed.

As he drove over the cattle grid, he morphed into Orion. The search for Fiona's body started in earnest today. He would ask Hayden for a helping hand and permission to travel to Scotland. The last vestiges of his Phil Hounsell persona were leaking away. But he allowed himself a smile as he remembered looking at his watch after he ended the call with Wayne last night. It had been half-past nine. Compatible was one thing; overdoing matters was something else again.

Orion parked his car in his allotted space at nine o'clock. In the main building behind him, Athena asked Giles about the ice-house's progress on finding the jewel robbers.

"We've isolated specific images for you from CCTV in the diamond quarter," said Giles Burke. Artemis projected the array of camera stills onto a screen.

"Groups of two's and three's in the area before Saturday drew a blank," Giles continued. "We found no evidence of concerted surveillance of the bank. It must have been carried out by a gang member acting alone."

"The inside help gave him a head start," said Rusty.

"On Saturday evening, we found three possible candidates. A man and a woman. Two African males, and then this trio of middle-aged Hasidic Jews."

"Men in the street in their hundreds every day of the working week," said Alastor.

"Or, these men are hiding in plain sight," said Phoenix.

"Hold that thought," said Artemis.

"Around noon on Sunday, we captured these images," said Giles, "as you can see, the foot traffic is sparse. This couple walking away from a lane behind the bank interests us."

"Two of the men we spotted on Saturday unless I'm mistaken," said Henry Case.

"Weighed down by backpacks containing the haul, or two-thirds of it," said Giles.

"What was in the corner of that last image?" asked Minos.

"A police patrol car," said Giles, "not responding to an enquiry, merely doing what it was named for, patrolling."

"The gang must have been bricking it when that car arrived," said Rusty.

"What happened to the third man?" asked Henry.

"In this image, the officers are walking back towards the bank," said Artemis. "We discovered a call to the emergency services from a concerned flat owner at the end of the lane. A waste bin was alight. The policemen from the patrol car attended the scene, and the fire brigade arrived in due course, but the bin got destroyed."

"The third man's job was to get rid of the rubbish," said Giles.

"That was an expensive bin," said Phoenix. "It contained any excess cash they physically handled, plus items from the safe-deposit boxes the gang couldn't use."

"Have we got a shot of the third man joining the others?" asked Minos, "do we know what vehicle they drove?

Artemis shook her head.

"The car or van must have been parked in a CCTV blind spot. That was deliberate. We only have a camera on the nearest main road. If we analyse traffic travelling away from the diamond quarter in that five or ten-minute segment after midday, it should contain the vehicle."

"How long were the police at the scene of the fire?" asked Phoenix, "Don't start the analysis until at least five past twelve. The gang would have sat and waited for them to leave. They would want to be sure nobody discovered the robbery until the following morning."

"It sounds like a long job," said Athena, "with so many vehicles. Even if we could see the driver and passenger's faces, there would be plenty to check."

"One more stumbling block nobody has mentioned yet," said Rusty, "our gang wore disguises."

Seven faces turned to view again the image of the three men captured on Saturday evening.

"If that's a mask, it's better than any I've seen outside a film set," said Alastor.

"It wasn't the faces that gave them away," said Rusty, "it was their shoes. When did you last see a middle-aged businessman wearing steel-capped trainers? I've worn a pair of those that the bloke on the right is wearing. With rubble and metal flying around in the vault, they couldn't afford to leave a clue from a bloody toe."

"That makes finding them even harder," said Henry, "if

they removed the wigs and prosthetics in the car, we'd never spot them driving on the main road."

"The easiest way to find them is from the make-up artist who provided the disguises," said Athena. "There can't be more than a handful in London capable of doing such a superb job."

"We'll get back to the ice-house and start the search for the car and the make-up artist," said Giles.

"Alastor, where have the police reached with their questioning of the employees?" asked Phoenix, "are they close to identifying the leak?"

"It's ongoing, the police are saying. The crime scene has been cordoned off and populated with white tents. There are scenes of crime operatives crawling over every inch of ground inside and outside the bank. I saw a dozen policemen in that nearby lane carrying out fingertip searches, but nothing concrete established yet."

Phoenix was impatient. He counted off the list of actions he wanted on his fingers.

"Identify the make-up artist. Find out who paid him. Hunt for the three jokers and retrieve as much of the loot as possible. Dispose of the three robbers."

"OK, Phoenix," said Athena, "We know you're itching to get into action. Patience is a virtue."

"Time is ticking, Athena. The authorities are struggling with this case, and the public is eager for a response. The Grid has one hand on the nation's throat. There's a further blockbuster crime to come; I can feel it. That will be the second hand, and the Grid will have reached the tipping point. The authorities will be held responsible for the Grid holding the nation to ransom. The government could fall if we let things get that far. A vacuum left before any general election is the perfect time for a dictator or an extreme faction to strike."

"That's a tad dramatic, even for you, Phoenix," said Minos, "we're a long way from that."

"When unpalatable decisions are not taken, evil smiles and continues to flourish," said Phoenix, "a great man once said."

"Burke," said Alastor.

He raised a hand before an affronted Phoenix could reply.

"It was Edmund Burke. He said the only thing necessary for evil to triumph is for good men to do nothing."

"I rest my case," said Phoenix, "actions speak louder than words. It's the only language the evil at the head of the Grid understands."

Aleks Bogdani had just completed a deal to sell the gold items and the gems they had stolen. The price he had negotiated had been below his upper estimate, but he was happy the scrap merchant hadn't cheated him. There was something in it for both. The dealer had to make a living, and Aleks wanted to hit a minimum of forty million in any way possible. They already had the bonus of two million euros in cash that hadn't reached the Glencairn.

The diamonds were his trump card. He would travel by train to Paris overnight tonight. The onward journey to Amsterdam took a further three and a half hours. His appointment was at one o'clock in the afternoon.

The success of the robbery depended on this meeting. If the seven velvet bags they had discovered contained diamonds of the highest quality, they would each be millionaires several times over. If they were of poor quality,

Tyrone O'Riordan would look for a new gang to commit the bank robbery.

Aleks knew that meant he, Zamir, and Januz would be surplus to the Grid's requirements. Aleks had heard rumours of Tyrone's prowess with a knife. He prayed the men who had stored those diamonds in the vault had bought them wisely.

Friday, 17th October 2014

The final morning meeting of the week had ended. Phoenix and Athena returned to their apartment. Maria Elena had finished preparing lunch for the family and played on the floor with Hope.

"Hello, Maria Elena," said Athena, "have you seen my father this morning?"

"Mr Fox popped in to see us mid-morning. We had a cup of coffee together, and then he said he was returning to his room. He was expecting a phone call from his solicitors."

"Gosh, that was quick," said Athena, "I hope it's good news. We'll miss him around the place, but I want to see him get settled before Christmas."

"Geoffrey's head is screwed on," said Phoenix, "we're only an hour away if he needs us. You would have been far more worried if he'd stayed in London."

"Hope will miss him," said Maria Elena, "I'll get off now if it's okay?"

"Of course," said Athena, "we're leaving for Lymington tonight. You've got the whole weekend to yourself."

"With Artemis and Rusty travelling with you, Giles is on

duty. So, I'm flying home to my parents. I have something important to discuss with them."

"Wedding plans?" asked Athena, "will this be your first visit since you announced your engagement?"

"Yes, my parents are happy. I'm marrying Giles. When we spoke the other evening, my father hinted that my grandmother was not well. She has been such a big part of my life. I am desperate for her to be there."

"We hope you have a great weekend, and there's more positive news on your grandmother," said Phoenix. "We'll see you on Monday morning."

Maria Elena kissed Hope on her forehead before she left.

"Are you hungry, poppet?" Phoenix asked his daughter.

Hope clapped her hands in glee.

"I had better fetch it from the kitchen," her father said.

As the three tucked into their lunch, Athena and Phoenix discussed what they had learned this morning.

"Giles and Artemis have laboured away with little success finding the vehicle the gang used," said Athena. "Giles can get his team to carry on the search over the weekend, but the make-up artist looks like our best bet. So he must concentrate on that."

"Giles has narrowed it to two people," said Phoenix. "Their financials will be pivotal. He'll make quick progress when he learns which one has received a large boost to their income in the past month. I bet we'll have a name by the time we return home on Sunday night."

"It was interesting to listen to Alastor's insights on the continued reaction to the station bombings and the jewellery robbery in the media," said Athena.

"I can't recall such a sustained level of outrage at the apparent ineptitude of the police," said Phoenix, "and the government haven't helped their cause. The media are putting the squeeze on them, that's for sure. I don't imagine it's what they wanted to face in the run-up to a general election."

"It's usually a time for largesse," said Athena. "Genuine handouts and promises for more once re-elected. The opposition would need to counter that by highlighting everything negative in the country. Neither main party seems to offer a solution to the uncertainty and fear that the Grid and ISIS have caused."

"The sooner Olympus acts, the better," said Phoenix.

"I talked with Zeus last night," cautioned Athena, "he's still wary of attacking the Grid. Organised crime and terrorism are under the media microscope in Britain. All eyes are on how the authorities react to their goading. If we carry out unilateral strikes, the public might welcome them, but Olympus runs a terrible risk of exposure."

"The authorities would take the credit to pacify the media, and once the circus has left town, they would turn their attention to finding us," said Phoenix,

"That's what Zeus said," said Athena.

"I can't wait to get away this weekend," said Phoenix, "it will give us a chance to relax. Next week, we can start again. Giles may bring us a ray of hope."

"We can only pray, and now, I want to see Daddy," said Athena, collecting their lunch things together and taking them through to the kitchen. When she returned, Phoenix was carrying Hope on his shoulders.

"Come on," he said, "let's visit Geoffrey."

When her father answered the door, a beaming smile greeted them.

"Good news, darling," he said, "the purchase has gone through. I can move in on Monday the twenty-fourth of next month. I should be in my little Burnham bungalow for Christmas."

"Terrific," said Athena, "we hope you'll still come here for Christmas dinner. Hope would love to see you on Christmas morning."

"I'll accept that invitation if you agree to come over on Boxing Day," said Geoffrey.

"No problem, Geoffrey," said Phoenix, "now, will you be ready to set off for Lymington by five o'clock tonight?"

"I've packed my bag already, Phoenix," Geoffrey replied, "I'm looking forward to the experience."

"Erebus and Elizabeth are always with us in spirit when we go aboard his yacht," said Phoenix. "The old man's presence often helps me solve problems when we visit her at the mooring."

"I can't envisage too many problems with the charity business, Phoenix," said Geoffrey, with a twinkle in his eye.

"You would be surprised," said Athena, "we'll give you a knock when we're on our way to the car."

With that, they left Geoffrey alone and returned to the apartment. It was time to pack those bags and find the toys Hope had to take with them wherever they went.

Tyrone O'Riordan had invited his mother, Colleen, to tea. She accepted at once. Her son either wanted something or had a present for her. He was so like his late father. A man appeared on her shoulder as she walked to the lift to his penthouse apartment.

"You must be Mrs O'Riordan," he said, "I'm here to see Tyrone. I'll ride with you if that's okay?"

Colleen was nervous, but she knew the cameras in the

foyer would alert Tyrone to the intrusion. She stood her ground.

"That accent's not from around here," she said, moving her position so the man now faced the camera over the lift door.

"Tirana," said Aleks Bogdani, "Tyrone's expecting me."

The lift door opened. A green light on the display panel told Colleen her boy was happy to receive this Albanian visitor. The lift ascended silently. Colleen studied the younger man in the mirrored wall. He was perhaps twenty years younger than her and not bad-looking. The white t-shirt and black slacks covered a toned body. He saw her looking at his biceps.

"You like, Mrs O'Riordan?" asked Aleks.

"Now and then," Colleen replied. She had recovered her composure.

Before the conversation could go any further, the lift heralded its arrival at the penthouse with a loud ping.

"Come on in, you two," said Tyrone, "you gave my mother a fright, Aleks,"

"That was not my intention," he said.

"You had a successful trip to Amsterdam, I hear?"

Aleks gave Tyrone receipts for the sales of the gold and gems from a London dealer. He also produced a receipt for the diamonds from the Amsterdam firm.

"Four and a half for the gold and gems," said Tyrone, "and twenty-nine and a half for the diamonds. Wow, that makes forty-two and a half million overall. I told you we would make a killing, mother."

"Is that all?" asked Colleen.

"What? That's not enough for you?" asked Tyrone.

"How do we know this Aleks hasn't cheated us?"

A Frequent Peal of Bells

"I know the penalty for that, Mrs O'Riordan," said Aleks.

"I love your plans for the bank job, Aleks," said Tyrone, "when will you be ready to go ahead?"

"We should let the heat cool down," said Aleks, "the police have made no headway on the jewellery robbery, but there's no rush."

"No rush?" exclaimed Colleen, "we'll decide whether there's a rush or not. Not you; you're just the hired help. We want this country on its knees, begging for someone to save it from the big, bad criminals. Tough shit, there is no one. They'll do as we wish. The authorities are like a punch-drunk boxer on the canvas for an eight count. I want the bank job done before they have time for their heads to clear. A further sixty million pounds will be the knockout blow. Is that understood?"

"Yes, Mrs O'Riordan," said Aleks.

"I thought you two were getting on so well in the lift," said Tyrone, trying to ease the tension.

Aleks saw that the table was laid for an English afternoon tea. He needed a stiff drink. It was time to leave.

"I need to arrange the next stage of the job," he said, edging towards the lift, "it was good to meet you, Mrs O'Riordan."

"Thanks, Aleks," said Tyrone, following him across the room, "don't take offence. My mother can be a firebrand at times. She wants everything, and she wants it now. You've delivered more than you promised. The Grid has no complaints. Let me know when you're ready to discuss the final plans."

As they stood by the door together, Tyrone whispered: -

"I'll make sure she's not here when you come up for that meeting, don't worry."

Aleks travelled back to the ground floor. He was happier being alone on this trip. Aleks breathed a huge sigh of relief. Neither Tyrone nor his mother was aware of the six and a half million pounds he had made on the diamonds he had kept back for him and the others. When they added in euros, he hadn't paid into the Glencairn Bank; they had relieved the Hatton Garden company of fifty-two million.

If the bank job only nudged the sixty million he forecasted, it was a retirement fund to savour. Phase one was complete. They were still unscathed. They could enjoy the rest of their lives in luxury with one last assignment.

What could go wrong?

Chapter Twelve

At five o'clock, Artemis and Rusty came downstairs. In the hallway, they met Phoenix.

"Ready to go?" he asked, "the others have piled into the car. I think there will be enough room for me. The car I booked for you two is outside with the keys in the ignition."

"Did you get enough volunteers for a crew?" asked Artemis.

"Henry didn't even need to twist anyone's arm," said Phoenix, "everyone loves a weekend away."

The people carrier with the crew had already left. Their orders were to get the yacht ready to tackle the Solent in the morning. Phoenix, Athena, and their entourage would arrive in Lymington at seven. She booked tables at a bar and bistro at the marina for an evening meal. It had great sea views and was as pleasant a place as any to spend a Friday evening.

Hope stayed awake later than usual. She was sensible, like her grandfather, and had a snooze on the drive from Bath. Everyone was ready for bed when they climbed aboard 'Elizabeth' at ten o'clock. The crew had worked their magic. The yacht was spotless, and as he settled for the night, Phoenix reckoned Erebus would have approved.

Saturday, 18th October 2014

They awoke to a breezy day with the threat of scattered showers. Phoenix and Athena had no trouble getting Hope to eat her breakfast. Friends and family surrounded her.

Their daughter was in her element; others seemed less keen on eating so early.

"Don't tell me you're no sailor, Geoffrey," said Phoenix. "I heard rumours you lived on luxury yachts every day when you and Grace mixed with the rich and famous in Monaco."

"I think you'll find the rich and famous mixed with us, Phoenix," he said, "no, I'll wait until later. The sea air makes me hungry. Brunch will suit me better."

"Sounds good," said Rusty, "after that meal last night, I couldn't eat again before eleven."

"What's the plan for today?" asked Artemis.

"We'll take the journey in bite-size pieces," said Phoenix, "I discussed it with Adam, our senior steward. He's the man with experience in these waters. If we raced out from Lymington to circumnavigate the island and get home again, we could do it within twelve hours with ease. We'll cross to Cowes and then travel through the Hurst Castle narrows where the tide races and see the multi-coloured sand cliffs of Alum Bay."

"If Captain Birdseye has finished, we should let Adam

get us underway," said Athena. "He's better equipped to tell you where we're heading and point out the sights."

The elegant 'Elizabeth' soon eased her way into the Solent. Adam and his crew made the trip as comfortable as possible for their passengers. The morning slipped past, and brunch was upon them before they knew it. Rusty and Artemis tucked in along with the others. They would soon be in Cowes, and two hours ashore visiting the shops and an old pub would set them up for the next leg of the journey.

In mid-afternoon, they set off again. The yacht passed by the famous Needles Lighthouse where strong cross tides and underwater obstacles proved dangerous to the unwary sailor. However, they easily negotiated Goose Rock and sailed south to St Catherine's Point.

"We'll stop at Sandown for a meal on the way back," Adam told them as they gathered around to watch him handling the beautiful craft. "as soon as we round this point, we're in the Channel proper. You get bigger waves and a steady breeze on the island's south side. Finding the least tide against you and the most wind can be a challenge."

Phoenix, Athena, and Hope loved the experience. Athena noticed her father had quieter moments when she imagined he thought of Grace. But he kept Hope amused and chatted with the crew, so she didn't think she needed to worry too much.

Phoenix watched as Rusty and Artemis sat close together, none the worse for the sea trip. It seemed they had their sea legs after all, but the opportunity to be alone with their thoughts didn't come around that often at Larcombe. They were like ships, he thought, but somehow today, the rest of that saying sounded daft.

The evening meal in Sandown was excellent, and the atmosphere was pleasant. The crew ate aboard 'Elizabeth', but Adam came ashore to remind Phoenix they needed to be on the move so as not to miss the tide. As Cowes disappeared behind them to the southwest and they cruised onward to their haven at Lymington, there were several weary travellers.

Sleep was not long coming for everyone. Tomorrow was another day.

Sunday, 19th October 2014

There were no sea journeys today, just a long lie-in and a late breakfast. There was plenty to see in and around Lymington. Geoffrey remembered a village pub he and Grace had visited twenty years ago. Somehow, it had survived the cull of inns and public houses since the turn of the century and was not only open; but thriving. The old-world charm of the wooden beams hung with horse brasses was a delightful background to the excellent menu.

The party of six climbed aboard 'Elizabeth' to spend the late afternoon and early evening relaxing in the main cabin. Hope played with her toys. Geoffrey chatted with his daughter about the few changes he planned to the layout of his bungalow. Phoenix sat and did what he always did. Phoenix thought about the next mission. Where had Rusty got to, he wondered? He and Artemis had disappeared thirty minutes ago without a word. Everyone below seemed occupied, so he went up on deck.

Rusty had dropped something. Why else would he be on one knee?

As he turned to go below, Athena joined him.

"Daddy's looking after Hope. What's so interesting up here?"

"I went looking for Rusty. I had hoped to get five minutes of his time."

Artemis and Rusty came towards them. Artemis looked flushed; Athena thought she had wiped a tear from her eye.

"What a lovely evening," said Athena. It wasn't, particularly, the clouds were building, and the breeze blew another shower in from the west.

"There is something about this yacht," said Artemis, "I felt it as soon as we came on board."

"It's Erebus," said Athena, "his love for his beloved Elizabeth is everywhere. It can be intoxicating."

Rusty shuffled from foot to foot.

"What's up?" asked Phoenix, "was it those scallops?"

"Nothing like that," said Rusty, "as Artemis says, it's this yacht. Spending a weekend with you and your family made us realise we're missing out on so much. This trip has been the first time since Artemis joined Olympus that we've shared special moments. I suggested we get married. Artemis suggested I ask her properly, so I did. She said yes."

Athena squealed with delight and hugged her friend. Rusty shook Phoenix by the hand.

"I'm so pleased for you both," said Athena, "we knew it would happen one day. We're happy this weekend helped you find the right time.

"Remind me to get that little church spruced up," said Phoenix, "it's going to get more use in the next year than for a century."

"We don't want to wait until next year," said Artemis, "we've been living together long enough. The sooner we can arrange a wedding, the better."

"Let me add, there's no indecent rush," said Rusty. "Artemis has to arrange to get her parents here from Durham. They're not as mobile these days. As for me, you know my family situation. Apart from the crowd at Larcombe Manor, there won't be any others I need to invite."

"The important people will be there," said Artemis. "Inviting any police colleagues I once had is out of the question."

"Especially Orion and his family," muttered Phoenix.

"Did you meet Erica, his wife?" asked Artemis, whose hearing was razor-sharp.

"I couldn't comment," replied Phoenix.

Phoenix wasn't keen on Athena, learning he had once bathed the wounds of a semi-naked Erica in a house not far from Larcombe. It was in a former life. In the past was where it belonged.

"I think we should celebrate with a drink," said Phoenix.

"Not so fast," said Athena, "you and Rusty have to drive back tonight. I propose we pack up now and get on the road. Adam and the crew have done a great job; they can stay and have a few beers tonight. I'll clear things with their superiors in the morning. Tell Adam they needn't report back until lunchtime."

"Should we ring ahead and ask for the champagne to be put on ice?" asked Phoenix.

"What a great idea, mate," said Rusty, "just this once, you know me, I'd be happy with a can of lager."

Simon Gonzalez travelled to Bath by train from London Waterloo. He arrived in the Roman city at three o'clock in the afternoon, when Phoenix, Athena and the others chose their desserts in the New Forest.

The sights of the city didn't interest Gonzo. Instead, his presence had a more sinister motive. Tyrone O'Riordan wanted to know everything that happened at Larcombe Manor. Once Colleen connected the characters at a posh wedding party and the charitable organisation, he contacted him. Last Sunday morning, he was asked to track a dark van back to its base.

Gonzo wanted to tell Tyrone he was looking for a needle in a haystack. If these men drove a distinctive vehicle, it could have saved him hours of work. So on Friday, he isolated the only dark van to reach the relevant part of Bath on the night in question. He learned one fascinating statistic as he ploughed through hour after hour of CCTV film from the M4. Forty per cent of the four million vans on UK roads were black or blue.

Gonzo wasn't used to so much fresh air. His life was centred on a screen a few feet in front of him in a darkened room. He had found the van and established the link between the citizens' arrest of the moped gang and the Bath charity. That was usually enough for most people who employed him. Tyrone was different. He wanted Gonzo to name the two men in the photograph. Find out the number of employees at the Manor. How many patients did they treat if that's what they did? How much activity was visible from the air?

Tyrone didn't take no for an answer. Gonzo wanted to keep breathing, so he took the train for the first time since he left school. The pedestrianised streets near the centre of Bath thronged with people. Half walked somewhere at speed, while the other half idled or stopped without reason. For someone unused to being outside, it was a nightmare.

Gonzo checked the directions to Larcombe Manor on his phone. A physical street map wasn't something he'd ever buy. However, Simon saw plenty in the hands of foreigners surrounding him. Unfortunately, they were most likely to stop dead in the middle of the street.

The Georgian estate was too far out for Simon Gonzalez to walk. He checked for a bus service that would get him close. There was nothing. The bus offered anonymity. He wanted to avoid a taxi, whatever happened. Taxi drivers had a habit of remembering lone strangers heading for rare destinations. Larcombe Manor wasn't on every tourist's radar, nor would locals be encouraged to wander into its grounds.

Salvation lay just around the corner. Well, it was a Sunday. Nextbike had made it to Bath. He would cycle to the city outskirts and take as many photos of the buildings as possible. Then he planned to use the drone in his backpack to overfly the whole estate.

By half-past four, Gonzo had turned into the minor road that led to the Manor. His map showed the winding lane ending at a farm that must have been part of a large sprawling country estate in the past. Halfway along the road, he found the gateway to Larcombe Manor. Gonzo stopped his bike by the stone pillars. There were no high walls or secure gates, only a cattle grid a few metres beyond the gate before you entered a curved driveway to the Georgian house.

He noted the charity's registered number under the Olympus Project sign on the left-hand pillar. Visitors were discouraged. The cordoned-off areas by the gates on either side reinforced the Private signs on both pillars. Using their keys, gas, electric, and water companies accessed meters on the left. Waste bins were sited securely on the right. Gonzo

A Frequent Peal of Bells

imagined that the milkman, postman, and paperboy were redundant. Someone from the charity collected what had to cross this cattle grid.

There were outbuildings visible from the lane. A church spire was almost hidden from view as the ground fell into a valley. What lay in the distance remained a mystery for now. The map showed an estate bounded by a series of wooded areas, which meant this was the only vehicular access. Men on foot could enter from the sides or the rear, but their approach would be detected well before they got near the main building.

It was time to deploy the drone. Gonzo had it aloft within minutes and sent it in a large loop around the estate's perimeter. He studied the ground below on his laptop, searching for men and machines, more outbuildings, and signs of activity that would interest Tyrone.

The lawns and the wooded areas looked deserted. As Gonzo tightened the circle the drone was flying, he saw a walled vegetable garden with several men at work. That made sense if these men were recovering from PTSD. Gardening was supposed to be good therapy. Maybe, Tyrone had gotten it wrong.

A converted stable block next appeared under the drone's camera. Next, an odd-shaped mound came into view, which the hacker couldn't identify. Beyond that stood a row of terraced cottages. Finally, the drone flew over the woods, and suddenly the little church appeared. Gonzo soon had a great view of the rear of the central Georgian building. It was certainly impressive.

He decided on one more spin around the grounds to look at that shape on the rear left-hand side. What could it be?

There was a bang, and his screen went blank. The

drone wasn't responding to his controls. Gonzo realised it had crashed to earth. Had someone shot it from the sky? They disappeared if he had doubts about whether Tyrone was right to suspect this place.

It was time to get the bicycle to the nearest dropping-off point. As Gonzo cycled along the lane as fast as his legs would carry him, he glanced back over his shoulder. He saw a small, white van on the driveway heading for the stone pillars. He kept going. At the end of the lane, he turned left and rode deeper into the countryside. He gambled his pursuers would follow him towards the city. When he reached the top of a slight incline, he looked down at a steep hill. The long, winding road ahead brought him close to the next village.

When he reached the bottom, he threw the bicycle over a stone wall into a field and walked the rest of the way. Despite the risk, he then phoned for a taxi to pick him up outside the only pub and take him to Bath Spa station. So he had plenty to show Tyrone O'Riordan on his laptop when he returned to London. Who said it was the streets of the capital that were dangerous? It was bandit country out here.

Monday, 20th October 2014

Tyrone had received a brief message from Simon Gonzalez late last night. The computer hacker wanted to meet. As he made his way to the Glencairn at lunchtime, Tyrone sensed someone shadowing him. He didn't turn around. Instead, he waited until he climbed the steps to the large glass doors of the bank. The man behind him was in his early twenties.

The ubiquitous hoodie, jeans and baseball cap signified he wasn't a client. He didn't look much of a threat, either.

Tyrone told Gonzo to follow him to his office. Once inside, Gonzo confirmed he had established the link between the Olympus Project and the moped gang attack. He also showed Tyrone the drone film he had captured. When it suddenly stopped, Tyrone looked at him.

"What happened? Is that it?" he asked.

"That's when someone shot down the drone," said Gonzo. "I got out as soon as I spotted the van heading up the drive. If I hadn't, we wouldn't be having this conversation."

"They're as secretive as we suspected," said Tyrone, "what more have they got to hide, I wonder?"

"I can hack into their systems to get personal files, so you can identify the men you're after," offered Gonzo. "Those men at work in the garden *could* have PTSD. Maybe they have a few on-site as part of their cover."

"It was quiet yesterday afternoon. I expected to see more people."

"I didn't anticipate losing the drone," said Gonzo, "but we could try again at night? Then, using a thermal imaging camera, we can gauge how many live and work on the estate. Also, it will give us something to compare to the charity's published personnel numbers."

"Good idea," said Tyrone, "but if they have security systems that can spot and neutralise a drone, surely they'll realise someone has hacked into their systems?"

Simon Gonzalez reacted as if Tyrone had slapped him.

"I can hack into the Department of Defense in Virginia, stay inside for three hours, and then leave by the back door I created without them being any the wiser. Do you think this system will be anything but a walkover?"

"You could have a great future with the Grid, Simon," said Tyrone, "cybercrime will be the biggest earner for organised crime in the future. Why rob a property for a few hundred pounds worth of stuff you need to fence when you can scam them out of thousands via their phone or computer?"

"I'll start on the administration systems for the personnel files," said Gonzo, "and then I'll see what other systems they operate. I noticed there were no high walls or electrified fences guarding the perimeter. To an untrained eye, it looks normal. But I suspect they have high-tech security equipment in one of those buildings."

"I can't wait to learn what you find there, Gonzo. Well done. Keep it up but watch your back."

"Henry," said Athena, "what happened yesterday?"

"I visited Sarah Gough," replied the security officer, "we've had the news we were waiting for that Sarah's new parish has been agreed. She can transfer from Surrey in a month. St Mary's has been without a vicar for a period, and her group of parishes can cover her departure until they find a permanent replacement."

"St Marys? That's north of Bath, isn't it?" asked Minos.

Henry nodded.

"I didn't return to Larcombe until this morning," he continued. "I read the report from the team on duty yesterday just before I came to the meeting. It appears someone flew a drone over the estate yesterday afternoon. Kelly Dexter and Hayden Vincent were alerted when it crossed by the stable block."

"Why did they decide to shoot at it?" asked Athena.

Henry cleared his throat.

"I believe Kelly to be out of sorts at present. I would have said hormonal, but that might be unwise."

"She's pregnant and plagued by morning sickness," said Artemis, "I would have been mad if a kid buzzed my apartment on a Sunday afternoon."

"Are we sure it was a kid?" asked Rusty.

"Kelly blasted it out of the sky as it hovered over the ice-house," said Henry. "There wasn't enough left to learn the purpose of the flight or who controlled it. So the security team patrolled the perimeter, and a van went to intercept an intruder, but they found no one."

"Increase the patrols and review our security protocols, Henry," said Athena, "this may have been a one-off, but we mustn't underestimate the Grid."

"Understood, Athena," said Henry.

"Before we move on, Henry, will this earlier move influence your wedding plans?"

Henry cleared his throat again.

"Sarah is phoning you tonight. Athena," he said, "I believe the twenty-second of November is her preferred date. She starts at St Mary's on the first of December."

"Sarah wants to avoid her congregation finding out she's living in sin at Larcombe by becoming Mrs Case before she starts work," said Phoenix, "is that what you mean?"

"Straight to the point, as usual, Phoenix," said Henry.

"I see no problem, Henry," said Athena. "When we chat this evening, I'll get the number of the friend who will perform the ceremony. Then, I can arrange for the banns to be read here in the church."

Athena moved on to Giles Burke. He looked tired. The poor soul had been working double shifts in the ice-house this weekend. Artemis was in Hampshire, and Maria Elena had returned to Estepona to visit her family.

"How did your weekend go?" she asked.

"I gave up the hunt for the car, I'm afraid. I wasted at least six hours on Saturday trawling through camera footage. If the car with the three robbers was on that main road, they must have removed their disguises before leaving the scene. I concentrated on make-up artists instead. Their work volume is intermittent. They both had short periods of high activity with money transferred into their bank accounts, followed by weeks when they seemed to do next to nothing. Julian Kneiss, a forty-six-year-old, native New Yorker, moved to London in 2001. His last celebrity assignment was for a music video featuring one of the top girl groups in 2013. Then, last month, with no fanfare on his social media advertising which firm he worked for, JK, as he is known, had a sudden twenty-five thousand pounds credited to his account."

"Nothing out of the ordinary on the other candidate?" asked Athena.

"No," said Giles, "she has been flying to and from the continent working with catwalk models in Paris and Milan. As a result, her income has been more regular. When I dug into her background, the occasions when she appeared to be out of work coincided with spells in rehab."

"Time for a talk with JK," said Phoenix, "who do we have that can collect him?"

"I'll send a team," said Athena, "Henry, you can expect a guest tomorrow."

Henry nodded.

"This morning, we have learned that Henry and Sarah will marry in November," said Athena, "over the weekend, there was another pleasant surprise. I'm sure you will want to congratulate Rusty and Artemis on their engagement."

Minos, Alastor, and Henry accepted the news was pleasant, but it didn't come as a surprise.

"I think we've hoped you would make an honest man of him before much longer, Artemis," said Alastor.

"Is this likely to be a long engagement, Rusty?" asked Minos.

"Certainly not," said Artemis, "when Henry started to share his and Sarah's news, I feared the worst. I talked with my parents last night, and we're hoping to get them to Larcombe for the twenty-ninth of November."

"Is Sarah available to do the honours?" asked Rusty, "or are you whisking her away on honeymoon, Henry?"

"We'll be moving her stuff into our new apartment here during the week following the wedding. The honeymoon has been postponed until next Spring, when we originally planned to marry."

"Giles, you're quiet," said Phoenix.

"I'm pleased for the four of you," he said, "but something disrupted our wedding plans."

"What happened?" asked Athena.

"Maria Elena flew home to see her family, as you know. Unfortunately, her grandmother's condition was worse than her father told her on the phone. She is unlikely to make it to Christmas. Her family wish her to return to Spain. Maria Elena is desperate for her grandmother to see her get married."

"How sad," said Artemis, "does this mean you will leave soon?"

"They have procedures to go through in Spain much as we do here in the UK," said Giles, "the earliest practical date will be the fifteenth of next month."

"I don't believe this," said Phoenix, "it reminds me of

London buses. Nothing for ages, and then three arrive at once."

"It will be difficult for any of you to attend," said Giles.

"I shall fly out to join you," said Henry, "we agreed to be one another's best man. I'm not backing out."

"We'll return by the following Saturday for your wedding," said Giles. His concerns eased by the minute.

"We should like to celebrate your wedding with you in some way," said Athena, "have you considered a blessing here at Larcombe? I'm sure Sarah would love to be involved."

"Planning is supposed to be my strong point," said Phoenix, "and my social calendar is suddenly more crowded than ever. Why don't we have a blessing for Giles and Maria Elena in the morning and Artemis and Rusty's wedding in the afternoon of the twenty-ninth?"

"It fits into the calendar," said Minos. "Is there anyone we've forgotten?"

"I think we've exhausted our supply of eligible couples," said Athena. "Several of us have personal matters to arrange on top of our Olympus duties. I suggest we close this meeting today."

Athena grabbed Phoenix by the arm as they made their way along the corridor to their apartment.

"Isn't it wonderful the others are getting settled at last? Despite the number of ceremonies, that means we'll have in our little church?"

"Terrific," said Phoenix, "my worry is the drone on Sunday and what that means for the future. If the Grid plans to attack Larcombe, several of us may not survive next year. Is that the real reason for this rush to the altar?"

A sad couple arrived at the door to their apartment. When Phoenix and Athena entered, Geoffrey sat with Hope

A Frequent Peal of Bells

and Maria Elena. The nanny looked up to see if she could learn something from their faces. She misinterpreted their mood.

"You are unhappy that Giles and I must go to Spain soon," she said.

"That's not true," said Athena, hugging the young girl, "we wish you all the best. We were sorry to hear your grandmother is so ill. Henry will be Giles's best man as arranged. He will be free to fly out to Estepona for your wedding weekend. Giles will tell you about other celebrations when you return as Senora Burke. I won't spoil the surprise. Run along now and see your fiancée. We'll look after Hope this afternoon. You have much to do, I know."

Maria Elena left the family on their own. Athena told her father about the new arrangement.

Hope watched and listened.

Everyone had gone mad around here. Love was in the air.

Chapter Thirteen

Orion had travelled north to Musselburgh on an overnight train from Temple Meads to Edinburgh Haymarket. The twelve-hour journey involved only one change. It necessitated a detour from Waverley due to ongoing reconstruction work following the devastating bomb attack in September.

Orion explained to Hayden what his mission entailed on Friday morning. He asked for assistance from Olympus operatives in the area. Hayden took him along the corridor and introduced him to Hugh Fraser. Hugh was a Logistics Officer, a role that would never be clear to Orion, but it helped to have someone different to engage in conversation.

Hayden told him that Hugh had worked out of Edinburgh before transferring to Larcombe. His old team would be at his disposal while in Scotland. Whatever he needed was available. Orion thought Hugh seemed one of those super-efficient military types with a permanent can-do mentality. A typical Olympus agent from head to foot.

Orion was met at the station by Dougal McLeish, the

new Edinburgh team leader. Dougal asked how Hugh was faring in his new role.

Orion shrugged, "I'm the mushroom guy, Dougal. They keep me in the dark."

Dougal had smiled at that and took Orion to meet the other three team members. Dougal drove the dark blue van to Whitecraig, a few miles from Musselburgh. As they stopped by an estate agent's board by a gateway, Dougal said: -

"James Grant-Nicholls owns this sprawling forty-acre country estate. The main house is late-Victorian, a seven-bedroomed affair extended to provide a large conservatory and an indoor swimming pool. He put it up for sale when he married last month. It's on the market for two million. The locals believe someone is interested in buying the place to develop it as an equestrian centre. We've got plenty of ground to search, Orion."

"We have to start somewhere, Dougal. Fiona disappeared a decade ago. I reckon her body has been on this estate since then. We aren't looking for recent signs someone dug a shallow grave. It's almost lunchtime. Let's find a pub, get a meal inside us, and come up with ideas on where he buried her."

The reaction inside the van told Orion he had found common ground. The world looked brighter when they returned to start the search. The five men split up, and three agents checked patches of land hidden from the nearby roads and tracks. Orion and Dougal avoided areas visible from the house. Nobody believed Sir James vindictive enough to want to look out on his wife's grave every morning.

There was no disputing the couple argued. All four agents agreed with Orion that James had lost his temper, hit out once too often, and Fiona had died. It may have been deliberate, more likely accidental. He wanted to hide the body and stick to his guns when people asked what had happened to her. To this day, James says Fiona never returned to the house after she left the off-licence.

It was dusk before Orion heard a shout from an agent in the distance.

"There's something here,"

Orion and Dougal joined the others under an oak tree by a dry-stone wall. A hollow spot looked out of place compared to the surrounding grassland.

"What do you think?" asked Dougal.

"We dig but take it steady," said Orion.

In less than ten minutes, they uncovered small bones near the surface.

"Fingers of a hand?" asked Dougal. "Scrape away the earth above that. Let's find the rest of the arm."

Orion called a halt when an arm, ribcage and hip bone became visible.

"Time to notify the police," he said, "have either of you got a dog?"

"Take your pick," said Dougal, as a show of hands revealed three dog owners.

"Tell them your dog was off the leash enjoying a run and must have scratched away at the earth. You called out, but by the time you found him, he'd unearthed the bones. You couldn't stop yourself and carried on until you were certain it was a skeleton."

"No problem," said the agent with the most curious dog.

"That's it for us then, Orion?" asked Dougal.

"The police will take it from here," said Orion, "they'll have heard of Fiona's disappearance. It won't take them long to identify these remains. That will implicate Sir James, and his new wife will avoid the prospect of being physically abused."

The men returned to the van and set off back to Edinburgh

"Short but sweet," said Orion, "I thought I might be up here a while. If you drop me back at Haymarket, I'll catch the late train home to Bath."

"I wish our missions were always this easy," said Dougal.

"I'd ask you to elaborate," said Orion, "but you Olympus people are tight-lipped."

They spent the rest of the journey in silence. At Haymarket, Orion shook hands with the four men, and with a brief nod, they returned to the van and left.

Monday, 27th to Friday, 31st October 2014

Orion arrived at Larcombe to start a new week. Hayden Vincent had been pleased with his Scottish mission. When he handed him the file of new cases on Friday afternoon, he told Orion an arrest was imminent.

While he and Erica watched the news on Sunday evening, they saw a handcuffed Sir James Grant-Nicholls, captain of industry, hustled into the back of a police car under a blanket. The arrest was said to be regarding the disappearance of his wife, Fiona and the discovery of a body near the house they shared.

Athena opened the morning meeting in the main house with an update on the news.

"I called Aphrodite last evening," she told the others, "she was devastated. I explained the domestic abuse Fiona suffered throughout their marriage. In time, she will realise she may have had a lucky escape. For now, she's heartbroken."

"To think I had Heracles pegged as one of the good guys," said Phoenix. "He fooled me."

"I called Zeus this morning," said Athena, "we are to meet again in early January. I told him we needed to select two new names to bring our complement up to twelve, not one as we thought. He suggested one male, one female."

"Two women would balance the Gods at six apiece, I take it?" asked Rusty.

"There were three candidates listed at the last meeting, two men and one woman," said Athena, "we haven't vetted them yet. We may need more candidates by January."

"We must choose the best two candidates from the three proposed," said Phoenix, "that's the only choice."

"If we can return to our agenda," said Athena, "what have you learned, Henry?"

"Julian Kneiss, known as JK, the make-up artist, was picked up in London on Friday. He was blindfolded and brought to the ice-house. I questioned him for two hours on Saturday afternoon. I have the names of the three men for whom he prepared the prosthetics and wigs. They are Albanians from Tirana and have been living in the UK for several years. Rusty and Phoenix worked on an action plan in the orangery yesterday morning."

"Did we release Kneiss?" asked Minos.

"Of course," said Henry, "we're not barbarians. We returned him to Pimlico late last night."

"What do we plan to do with these jewel thieves?" asked Alastor.

"We have to find them first," said Rusty. "We only know

A Frequent Peal of Bells

their names and criminal records in their own country. We're still searching."

"I've always maintained the Grid has an agenda," said Phoenix. "One that includes a super crime to make the jewel robbery look tiny. These men are in hiding and will only surface when they are due to strike. Next weekend is crucial. Friday night is Halloween. If they favour disguises, then they will be hard to spot. Giles is helping us in the search in the meantime. We can only wait and hope."

"Giles, what else have you been monitoring?" asked Athena.

"Another drone passed over the estate last night around midnight. We did not attempt to disable it. It was clear from its path they targeted the ice-house. The drone was more sophisticated than the one used the previous Sunday. This one carried thermal imaging cameras."

"The Grid may have been able to determine the numbers of people in the stable block, but they ignored the other outbuildings and the main house," said Artemis. "That's significant."

"Exactly," said Henry, "the ice-house has a protective shield which masks our underground activities. The shield hampers any attempt to gauge our numbers there."

"Good," said Athena.

"Or worse," said Phoenix, "they may think our defences weak, and they can attack us at will."

In London, Simon Gonzalez was at work on the dark web. Last night's foray with the drone revealed nothing. Whatever that odd mound was, it held no secrets, and the Olympus defence systems didn't appear to be as vigilant in hours of darkness.

His first task after he met with Tyrone had been to use the charity registration number he gathered. Next, he hacked into the Charity Commission's files to extract everything they held on the Olympus Project. He took seconds to locate the Olympus website.

The Project set it up in 2007. Erebus hadn't been keen, but Athena and Alastor convinced him a modest site added credibility to the claim they were a charitable organisation. The paperwork Gonzo retrieved from the Commissioners supported that view. Tyrone believed there was much more information hidden from public view.

Hacking into the administration area at Larcombe proved simple as predicted. Gonzo was soon studying a management structure. There were eight managers. The titles of the positions they held were vague.

Three of these eight were Trustees whose names appeared on the website and every Charity Commission report.

Annabelle Grace Fox-Bailey (Chief Executive Officer);
Sir Julian Langford (Executive Director);
Michael James Purvis (Chief Financial Officer).

None of the other managers appeared in any document Gonzo found. There was no record of their pay, yet their charity accounts received a clean audit report every year. As for the others who lived there, he found records for hundreds of men and women who had passed through Larcombe.

Every piece of paper supported the public view that the charity was a terrific asset to service personnel returning from war zones with PTSD.

Athena, Minos, or Alastor could have saved Gonzo a headache. Everything tallied with how the world perceived Olympus. The actual accounts lay in the ice-house, deep in the security systems that Giles and Artemis operated. Erebus wouldn't have had it any other way.

Gonzo scratched his head. There was nothing for it. He couldn't go back to Tyrone and say he'd failed. He must dig deeper. Was there another system somewhere at Larcombe? Could that be what the odd-shaped mound was hiding? It was time to launch an all-out cyber-attack.

Wednesday, 29th October 2014

Security had always been the watchword for Erebus. The man who envisaged the Olympus Project understood the need for its presence to be felt rather than seen.

When Simon Gonzalez accessed the data files in the administration area of the main building, Giles was alerted in the ice-house. He understood the limited value of such data, so he remained patient. Giles sat and watched. He could learn a lot from how the hacker operated. It would identify his methods and enable him to establish a signature.

This knowledge would then add to the Olympus security shield. If Gonzo tried to attack the main computers, he opened himself up to a reciprocal attack. Giles and Artemis could discover where the attack emanated without Gonzo realising he had played with fire.

Patience is a virtue. The attack came at eleven o'clock at night.

Giles had finished his shift and was asleep next to Maria Elena in the stable block when the call came. He rushed back underground.

The system was holding firm. Like a game of chess, as the hacker made a move, the system countered it. The step was far from being defensive. Giles knew minute by minute that the hacker was getting identified. Giles would have seen an identikit picture of his opponent form on the screen in front of him if the identity had been in the form of an image. At three-fifteen, the game ended. The attack had failed, and on the printer next to him, Giles watched as it revealed the source of the attack.

"Got you," he said. It was time to get another Olympus agent out of bed. Why should he have all the fun?

Rusty Scott joined Giles in the ice-house.

"This is who has been causing us the problems on behalf of the Grid," said Giles.

He handed Rusty a name and address.

"Simon Gonzalez, twenty-four years old, former Google employee. I'm off to Lewisham in the morning to collect a computer nerd."

"As soon as, Rusty," said Giles, "take him straight to Henry on Level 3. We need to learn everything we can from Gonzalez. He must know things about the Grid and perhaps that next big robbery."

Thursday, 30th October 2014

Bridie Carragher started another day doing what she did best. The Wishing Well café on Kilburn High Road was a magnet for customers who couldn't give a toss about their waistline. People who enjoyed generous portions, whether from her all-day breakfasts, snacks, or legendary cakes.

Regular clients visited the café at different times during the day to sample all three, washed down with good-sized mugs of tea or coffee. The place was always busy, and the gossip mill made an excellent trade.

This morning, Wayne Sangster took his usual chair to help him watch his partner at work and keep his ears open for a hint of business. The lone Triple S investigator was ready to help if required. There had been a lot of gossip on the jewellery robbery five miles up the road three weeks ago.

They never arrested anybody for that. Nobody was even in the frame. Around here, it wasn't uncommon to hear of things that had fallen off the back of a lorry turning up for sale. Bridie warned Wayne that it was cigarettes, dodgy designer watches, and perfume. She didn't hold with anyone dealing drugs in her café, so they gave it a wide berth.

Wayne caught a snatch of a conversation behind him as he scanned the newspaper and took a sip of his steaming-hot coffee. A foreign accent, Eastern European. He glanced at the mirror on the end wall. A pair of men sat at a window table. One was wiping up the last scraps of his runny egg yolk with a piece of toast. The guy opposite him only drank tea. A newspaper lay folded on the table between them.

The tea drinker lifted the paper to reveal what was underneath. The man opposite him choked. Wayne was too far away to tell what he had seen, but it hadn't been a cartoon or a Page Three model. He was itching to find out. The conversation had ended; the tea drinker was unsuccessful. His potential buyer wasn't interested. Whatever it was, it must have been too costly for his pocket.

Wayne's ex-copper's nose twitched. He smelled money. Could this have something to do with that robbery? Did that guy try to off-load a pricey bit of bling once stored away in someone's safe deposit box in Hatton Garden?

He left his coffee on the counter, and as the door closed on the seller, he said goodbye to Bridie and followed him.

Januz Goga wondered where to try next. This necklace burnt a hole in his coat pocket. Aleks said it was worth five million in a posh Mayfair boutique; a fence would take it for a pittance. Januz had wanted the piece for himself. Ndrita had been his girlfriend for six weeks before the robbery. Januz hoped the necklace convinced her to move in with him. Ndrita took one look at it. She knew he had stolen it and threw it back in his face. He heard language from her he never expected. They had broken up that night.

Now, Januz would take ten thousand for it. To get rid of it before Aleks discovered he had brought an identifiable item from the bank against his wishes.

Wayne followed unnoticed at first. Januz was careless, his mind distracted by the necklace and the loss of his girlfriend. Januz stopped at a crossroads. Which way should he turn? Who could he ask for help? Aleks and Zamir had taught him what to do to stay safe. His instincts took over. As he moved further up the High Road, Januz realised he had a tail. The man looked like a cop. The big guy sat at the counter in the café.

He phoned Zamir.

"Are you busy? Can you pick me up? I'll be in the Wishing Well. Do you know it?"

Zamir agreed to collect him in fifteen minutes. Januz turned and headed back the way he had come. Wayne stood fifty yards away on the opposite side of the road. He made a phone call, too, in case the guy thought he was following him. He rang his old boss.

"I may have a lead on that jewellery robbery, boss," he said.

A Frequent Peal of Bells

"Are you serious, Wayne? Shouldn't you be telling the police?" said Orion,

"I thought the people you're working for might be interested," said Wayne. "The police up here aren't making any headway."

"Wayne, call it in, mate," said Orion, "Stick to missing persons and security advice. That could be dangerous."

"Fair enough, boss. I'll give you a ring next week, maybe." Wayne ended the call as the tea drinker passed by on the other side.

Januz reached the café and went inside. Bridie came over to take his order.

"Are you ready to eat now? I saw you in here earlier."

Januz shook his head.

"Tea, please," he said.

They both looked up as the doorbell rang; Wayne was back. The two men stared at one another; Bridie hugged her partner and kissed him on the cheek.

"You can't keep away from me, can you?" she said, "pop upstairs to your office. I'll bring you a meal once I've sorted this gentleman out."

Wayne went upstairs to the flat. If that was one of the robbers, he knew about him and Bridie. It could mean trouble.

Downstairs, Bridie took the mug of tea to Januz.

"That man has an office upstairs?" he asked.

"Triple S, he runs a security firm," said Bridie, "it's not a proper office. We live together."

Bridie then returned to her cooking. Zamir entered the café and nodded to Januz, who got up and left at once.

"Why did you need me to get you?" asked Zamir.

"I was followed from that café by a fat guy who runs a

security firm upstairs. He may have seen me trying to sell a piece of jewellery."

"You fool," said Zamir, "don't tell me you carried a piece out despite what Aleks warned."

"It was for Ndrita, but she chucked me," said Januz.

"Throw it in a skip, in the river. Please get rid of it today. Aleks has heard the next job must be tomorrow night."

"What do we do with the guy who saw me?" asked Januz.

"We sort it ourselves. Aleks can never find out, do you understand?"

Januz nodded.

Henry Case was entertaining Simon Gonzalez on Level 3 of the ice-house. Rusty had collected him from Lewisham and returned to Larcombe by late morning. Henry spent the afternoon talking with the computer hacker.

To Simon, it was a friendly conversation. He was asked about his motives for trying to hack into the charity's systems. Why was he interested in the rehabilitation of the nation's veterans? Didn't people like him play war games or use their skills for financial gain?

Simon found it easy to talk to the man. That was odd because he had never been a friendly individual. He protested being dragged from his bed by a red-headed giant and bundled into a van with his hands tied. This man waved a dismissive hand and told him not to worry. Then they shared a pot of coffee. He even offered him biscuits.

Henry was a patient interrogator; this Gonzalez character would tell him everything before tonight. The drugged coffee was working its magic.

Friday, 31st October 2014

The media's attention focussed on Westminster. Public outcry over the railway station bombings was not abating. People saw terrorists everywhere, and the Muslim population suffered as a result. It was irrational. A tiny minority was responsible for the attacks, but that did not dissuade the mobs in the streets.

The government might have managed that situation if it was the only problem. The in-fighting between organised crime gangs and the slaughtering of over twenty people left many fearing for their safety. There seemed to be little progress in combating organised crime.

Then there was the jewel robbery. Only a week ago, in one of the biggest hauls recorded in the UK, a gang had stolen between forty and fifty million pounds worth of cash and gems. The police had spent hundreds of hours hunting for clues but getting nowhere.

The government was under pressure. In the media, the opposition parties received as much criticism as those in power. The public had lost confidence in the authorities' ability to keep law and order.

At Larcombe, Athena opened the morning meeting.

"Events in the capital could turn nasty," said Minos. "Whether or not the Home Secretary survives this is debatable."

"You reap what you sow," said Rusty, "we've taken too many steps backwards with this soft approach to policing. This was inevitable."

"We will keep a close eye on how it develops," said Athena, "but we must carry on with Olympus matters now. What have you to tell us, Henry?"

"Our guest provided us with the information we required," said Henry, "he carried out duties for Tyrone O'Riordan as we suspected. Gonzalez handled the drones and the cyber attack. He traced the van that returned from London after the moped gang incident. The most worrying aspect of his work related to magazine photos from the Dorchester event the Olympians attended. Tyrone O'Riordan knows you represented the Olympus Project that evening and now knows Larcombe Manor is the cover for more than a charitable organisation."

"Where is Gonzalez now?" asked Athena.

"En route to the pet cemetery," said Henry, "we couldn't allow him to return to his employer."

"Understood, Henry," said Athena.

Giles and Artemis updated the agents on the ongoing hunt for the jewellery gang. Alastor and Minos told Athena they would have complete background checks on Byron Paterson, Raymond Ferreira, and Lily Chan by mid-November.

In the stable block, Orion watched the clock tick around to noon. It was time for lunch. He wondered what delights Erica had given him today. As he tucked into his tuna salad sandwiches, his mobile phone rang; it was Erica. Incoming calls were frowned upon by Hayden Vincent. It must be urgent.

"What's the matter, love," he asked, "are the kids all right?"

"I'm watching the lunchtime news, Phil," she said. "There was a fire last night in London. A café on Kilburn High Road was fire-bombed. Wasn't that where your friend Wayne lived?"

A Frequent Peal of Bells

Orion ended the call and went into the corridor; Hugh Fraser was in his quarters. He knocked.

"What can I do for you, Orion?" asked Hugh.

"Can you switch the TV on, please, Hugh? My wife thinks a friend of mine may be hurt."

"No problem," said Hugh, and soon they were watching the report together.

"This was the Wishing Well," said the reporter. "the scene of a tragic fire that ravaged the café and adjoining units. Fire appliances arrived at two this morning to find the café ablaze and tried to gain entry. However, the heat of the flames drove them back. When they reached the flat, they found the body of a female, believed to be the proprietor, Bridie Carragher, and that of an unidentified male. Neighbours say Bridie was popular and friendly, without an enemy in the world. She was in a relationship and happier than she had ever been."

"Oh, no, Wayne," said Orion, "I warned you not to get involved."

"The man was your friend?" asked Hugh.

Orion explained how they met at Glastonbury and then worked together before he came to Larcombe.

"Wayne called me yesterday lunchtime," said Orion. "He spotted something fishy and thought it was related to the jewel robbery. He asked if Olympus was interested. I told him to be wary."

"Did he tell you what made him suspicious?" asked Hugh.

"Nothing," said Orion, "I want to help, but he told me nothing."

"I'll pass it on," said Hugh, "there may be clues we can follow with the right surveillance."

"Thanks, Hugh," said Orion. "Wayne was a good friend, and Bridie was his soul mate."

Aleks Bogdani had left to call Tyrone O'Riordan. He wanted to know when the first stage of the robbery began. The Halloween disguises they would use tonight had been shop-bought. JK was out of the country, destination unknown. Zamir and Januz waited in the van while Aleks rang the boss.

"Did you do as I said, Januz?" asked Zamir.

"Yes, I threw the necklace into the Thames from Chiswick Bridge," he replied.

"Pray it never surfaces again," said Zamir.

Aleks returned to the van; they drove to Maida Vale. Stan Kenworth owned the house they were visiting. Stan was at work tonight, but his wife and daughter were home.

"Trick or treat?" asked Aleks as the daughter answered the door. She was fourteen.

"Don't care," she replied, closing the door.

Aleks, Zamir, and Januz barged inside the house. Zamir clamped a big hand over the daughter's mouth as she tried to scream. Stan's wife was watching TV in the lounge with a glass of wine in her hand. Aleks and Januz had grabbed her and made her secure before she could get out of the chair.

With the security officer's family in the back of the van, Aleks drove to the compound where Kenworth worked.

"You each have the photo," said Aleks, "when you see him doing his rounds, shout."

Five minutes later, Zamir spotted him. He was strolling from gate to gate, checking the locks were secure.

Aleks drove the van towards the fence at speed. Kenworth stopped and shone his torch on the van. Aleks turned at the last second, and Januz threw open the side door.

Stan Kenworth saw his wife and daughter in the doorway, bound and gagged. A man held a gun to his daughter's head.

"Do as we say, and they live," said Aleks.

"Don't hurt them," said Kenworth, opening the nearest gate. Januz jumped from the van and zip-tied Kenworth's hands.

Aleks used the security officer's keys to gain admittance to the next compound.

"What's the sequence on the security cameras?" asked Aleks.

He knew the security officer set the timings. Once they had the sequence, they could watch and work out how to avoid being caught on camera by the guards inside the vault.

At first, Kenworth was unwilling to cooperate, but Aleks pointed to the van. Zamir struck the wife across the face with the back of his hand. He learned the sequence straight away.

With help from Zamir, Kenworth told Aleks that the vault was open on Friday nights due to the vast sums of money destined for thousands of ATMs in the capital.

"How many guards are inside the vault?" asked Aleks, "and if you lie, your daughter dies."

"Four," Kenworth had told him.

Zamir took Stan Kenworth to the van and locked him inside with his wife and daughter. He rejoined Aleks and Januz. The keys gave them access to an office building. Kenworth's three security guards stopped for thirty-minute breaks at one, one-thirty, and two o'clock. As each man came to the office block for the only coffee machine on-site,

Zamir overpowered them. They could move on to the second stage now.

Aleks lowered the bag slung over his shoulder onto the ground. He opened it to reveal a Skorpion machine pistol, two handguns, smoke canisters and stun grenades.

"No mercy," he said, "orders from the boss."

The three men reached the vault doors undetected and scattered the grenades inside. Each man entered the vault with their gun raised. The guards quickly reacted but got hit by sustained bursts from Aleks's Skorpion. Zamir and Januz finished off anyone still breathing after the initial assault.

Aleks backed the van into the vault. They dumped the Kenworths on the floor next to the dead guards. The three men loaded cash boxes into the van for the next ninety minutes. After that, there was nothing left to steal. Aleks was ready to go.

"What do we do with these three?" asked Zamir.

"I can help you get away if you let us live," begged Kenworth.

"What do you know that's so valuable?" asked Aleks.

"I can tell you where they keep the security camera recordings in the office building. You may have missed a sequence. Take tonight's with you, and you'll be home and dry."

"Take them to the office building, put them with the others. Fetch the right recordings, and we can leave."

Five minutes later, the van left the compound. Four men died, but the two hostages and the four security guards escaped with their lives.

As the van pulled into a lock-up garage in Walthamstow, Aleks sent a text message to Tyrone.

'Message delivered. All good.'

Epilogue

News of the robbery broke at six o'clock on Saturday morning with the shift changeover at the compound. The streets soon filled with police officers and reporters. The news was a further nail in the coffin for the authorities. No matter how much money they stole. Four men died.

When the first TV broadcasts beamed into homes around the UK, the ambulances had parked in the external compound. The crime scene investigators had much to do before they could leave. One vehicle had arrived for each body. The scale of the enterprise was apparent to the waiting media.

Reporters covered the basic details given by the first police officers on the scene. Six people had been discovered alive in a separate building when extra ambulances arrived under blue lights. The public joined the first responders on the streets around the compound. The crowds surged forward when the security guards and the Kenworth family came out on stretchers.

"How much more do we have to take?" one man yelled at a camera.

"Where's the Mayor of London and the Home Secretary? Enough is enough," shouted another.

"The situation here is volatile," said the besieged reporter. "People are angry. These crimes continue to happen, and yet there are no arrests. Representatives from the company operating this site have arrived in the past five minutes. They drove into the compound under police escort. We hope to learn later this morning how much was taken. But, for now, it's back to the studio."

Athena and Phoenix were asleep when the first reports aired. As they began what they hoped to be a quiet family Saturday morning, events in London caught their attention.

"Here we go again," said Phoenix, "here's the big crime I forecast."

"What is this company responsible for?" asked Athena, "how much could they have stolen?"

"They're the major firm topping up cash in ATMs across London and the Home Counties. When the public learns that, there will be mass panic. Every machine will be empty by lunchtime, and those at work or who had a lie-in will be out of luck. I dread to think how much they hold in one of those places. Do they empty them every Friday and replenish stocks before the next delivery? I'm not sure. The sum could be huge if this vault has been swept clean."

As the days of the month flicked over on the calendar, one by one, the full scale of the robbery and its impact on the country was clarified. At Larcombe Manor, they monitored events and considered possible retaliation, and the scheduled celebrations went ahead as planned.

In the week beginning the third of November, the

A Frequent Peal of Bells

amount stolen in the robbery was confirmed at a record sixty-five million pounds. Stan Kenworth told the police he had feared for the lives of his wife and daughter. That was why he not only opened the gate to let the gang inside the compound but also told them how to avoid leaving behind any incriminating filmed evidence.

The three men wore masks throughout the kidnapping and the robbery. None of the six survivors could identify their attackers due to their Halloween masks. Each witness said the men spoke with an Eastern European accent but could not tell which country they may have come from.

The cash stolen had been in standard denomination notes of twenty, ten, and five pounds. It was untraceable. Experts estimated the gang's van was carrying boxes weighing over two tonnes. CCTV film from streets surrounding the compound was studied, and the van was traced to the outskirts of Walthamstow.

They never found the van, but a lock-up garage burnt down late on Saturday afternoon. Again, kids were blamed for another incidence of anti-social behaviour. The police now believed the gang had used that garage.

Pressure on the authorities increased day by day.

At the Glencairn Bank, Tyrone O'Riordan had transactions to handle throughout the first fortnight in November. Once he received the message from Aleks Bogdani, he sent teams to Walthamstow. The boxes were collected and distributed to Grid leaders across the southeast. Cash deposits were banked in Gresham Street from Monday the third onwards. The operation was slick. It raised no suspicions.

Aleks Bogdani kept nothing back on this occasion. He

and his accomplices had gained enough from the jewellery raid to return to Tirana as millionaires. Tyrone spirited them out of the country on his private jet on Wednesday, the fifth.

Aleks thought it was poetic that the boss had chosen Bonfire Night. Parliament had been the target of Guy Fawkes. History was repeating itself as those in power stood on the precipice. His colleagues Zamir Tanush and Januz Goga were relieved at not having to worry about the police investigation into the fatal fire at the Wishing Well café.

On the eighth, Maria Elena Urbano and her fiancée Giles Burke flew to Malaga. An hour later, they arrived in Estepona. Henry Case and Giles's family flew out on Friday in time for the wedding on the fifteenth.

Maria Elena's grandmother was well enough for the church ceremony but too tired to stay long at the lavish reception. As the bells pealed at Our Lady of the Remedies, the happy couple already thought of their return flight to Bristol. Giles was to return the favour and be best man at Henry's wedding in less than a week.

In several cities across the UK, demonstrations took place where tens of thousands assembled to protest the apparent collapse of law and order. Colleen O'Riordan decided a tiny push was required to fuel the fire. She sent Grid members on looting sprees in shopping centres from Glasgow to Portsmouth.

On Monday, the seventeenth, Minos and Alastor delivered their report on the three candidates for the Olympus top table. Each one received a clean bill of health. It was in the

A Frequent Peal of Bells

lap of the Gods to decide which two they wished to select in January.

Phoenix and Rusty urged Athena to sanction direct actions against the Grid. However, she continued to be cautious. Athena wanted to wait until she believed Olympus could attack with impunity. The hacker had revealed Tyrone O'Riordan's interest in the organisation. However, the Grid's resources were massive. She had to be sure Olympus didn't face exposure to another threat.

Henry Case and Sarah Gough were married in Larcombe Manor's St Michael's church on Saturday the twenty-second. Giles Burke was best man. Athena and Hope were maid of honour and flower girl, respectively. Phoenix sat in the congregation with most of the estate's staff.

The bell ringers from Sarah's new parish set the tone for the coming days as the six bells rang out at an estate wedding for the first time in decades. The rest of the weekend passed in celebration of the happy event.

Geoffrey Fox moved into his Burnham bungalow on Monday, the twenty-fourth. The first thing he saw on TV when he sat in his lounge for the first time was a news flash.

"Following recent unrest in the country and the failure of the government to produce any meaningful response, a group of MPs have tabled a motion of no-confidence. It has cross-party support and reads that this House has no confidence in Her Majesty's Government. The vote will take place next Monday, the first of December. It will be the first such vote in thirty-five years."

Geoffrey switched channels. He wanted entertainment;

he'd spent enough of the past weeks being miserable. It was as if everyone in the country held their breath. Both sides of the House of Commons rallied their supporters. Different factions within the main parties were hard at work. New faces were emerging to sound a note of caution or herald the opportunity for radical change. The result was on a knife edge.

The Grid's leaders looked on and smiled. Was this the time to strike?

The final Saturday of November was a busy one. Across the country, demonstrations occurred again, and there were riots in Leeds and Liverpool. Politicians pleaded for calm and reason, to no avail.

At Larcombe, Giles Burke and his new wife attended St Michael's for their marriage to be blessed. The Reverend Sarah Case officiated. Then, a gathering of the great and the good at Larcombe left the tiny church as the bells pealed in the bell tower overhead.

Later that day, Rusty Scott and the former Zara Wheeler were married. Her elderly parents were ecstatic to see their little girl look so radiant. The 'Mouse' had gone; the 'Hunter' Artemis they saw standing next to her husband was a tower of strength.

As the happy couple stood on the church porch for photographs, the bells pealed for the third time in eight days. Miguel Fernando, the young motorcycle rider who photographed Phoenix and Rusty last month, was in the lane outside the Manor's walls. Tyrone had rewarded him for his initiative. Miguel was unaware of the fate that befell Simon Gonzalez, but Tyrone was keen to maintain surveillance on the Olympus Project.

Miguel waited until darkness fell before he moved from his hiding place. The people on the estate would be inside the main building soon, and the wedding party could begin.

He sent Tyrone a simple text.

"No activity here; only a frequent peal of bells."

Next in The Phoenix series

vinci-books.com/larcombe-manor

Loyalties tested, alliances strained. Will Olympus conquer the Grid's insatiable ambitions?

As Olympus battles the ruthless Grid, buried truths threaten to surface, drawing the authorities' scrutiny. With danger closing in, agents must navigate treacherous waters to protect their secrets before The Phoenix Series reaches its explosive finale.

Turn the page for a free preview…

Larcombe Manor: Chapter One

Monday, 5th January 2015

It was the best of times; it was the worst of times.

Phoenix drove through the entrance to the place he had called home since the first of July four and a half years ago. Stone pillars loomed out of the mist like dark sentinels in a Hammer horror film. The magnificent grounds of Larcombe Manor stretched before him as he rattled across the cattle grid. Damp clouds hugging the ground masked the familiar, welcoming sight of the old buildings and lights of home.

His wife Athena and their daughter Hope would be fast asleep. Friends and colleagues who lived on-site were sleeping or hard at work in the underground facilities of the ice-house. Operations undertaken by the Olympus Project are carried out twenty-four hours a day, seven days a week throughout the year. It was ever thus. Organised crime and terrorism never took a break. So, those who opposed them must remain vigilant.

A Frequent Peal of Bells

Phoenix was returning from yet another mission against the Grid. A fact-finding mission on this occasion. One which he carried out alone. Security for Olympus agents had been an issue recently, and Phoenix was mindful of the need for extreme caution.

The car's headlights fought a losing battle with a dense patch of mist. He slowed to a crawl. He negotiated this sweeping driveway so often that he couldn't believe he struggled to find his way home. Maybe nature was telling him troubled times lay ahead.

Phoenix shook his head. There was nothing new there. He couldn't recall an occasion in the past four and a half years without troubling times. Olympus could only hope they took two steps forward and one step back more often than the reverse. A tumultuous year just ended. What more evidence did they need than to consider how the final six weeks alone turned out?

Phoenix attended three Larcombe ceremonies in the last two weeks of November. First, Henry Case and Sarah married. So too, did his best friend, Rusty Scott and Artemis. Next, Sarah Case blessed Giles Burke and Maria Elena's wedding after their official ceremony in Spain.

The old Georgian manor house filled with couples; Erebus would have loved that. At present, he and Athena were the only ones with a child. Could it be that they needed to convert one of the many rooms into a creche? If so, it promised to keep Maria Elena busy.

Elsewhere, on the first day of December, attention focussed on Westminster. A handful of MPs missed the vote on the motion of no confidence tabled ten days earlier. This vote followed two audacious robberies that shocked the British public. They were the work of the Grid, a network of organised crime gangs that held a stranglehold on every facet of the nation's illegal activities.

Police appeared helpless to prevent these robberies, nor did they make progress in finding those responsible. Terror attacks across the country added to the unease felt by the public; who ran this country? Who could guarantee the public's protection? What had happened to the rule of law? The nation looked to Westminster for answers.

Both sides worked hard to secure success in the days before the vote. Both expected their efforts to allow them to claim victory. Instead, polls suggested a slight edge in favour of the Government suffering a damaging defeat.

Public clamour for action against organised crime and the threat of terror attacks was undiminished. Riots and looting became less prevalent, but chatter on social media remained as caustic as ever. Commentators in the media set the scene for the millions waiting for the result on TV and radio. Wise heads counselled that however the vote went, t was likely to be just the start of the drama, not the end.

When they counted and recounted the votes late into the evening, the Government survived the no-confidence motion by a mere four votes. But, for now, the Tory whips had reined in enough of their rebels to survive.

On the second of December, the Government discussed its response to the severe criticism of its handling of the crisis. A series of riots broke out in Leeds, Liverpool, and Manchester. The Grid orchestrated these to encourage a response in other towns and cities. There was minor damage, and casualties were few.

What caused this failure to ignite a nationwide fire of rebellion was unclear. Perhaps, it was apathy, or it may have been an acceptance that the margin of victory had been so narrow the Government had survived by a whisker.

Pundits predicted a General Election in the spring. Nothing controversial was put before Parliament when things got this bad for the ruling party. They only hoped to limp along until their advisors assessed they at least stood half a chance of winning at the polls.

In Scotland, Sir James Grant-Nicholls languished in HMP Shotts alongside five hundred other criminals. They rebuilt the maximum-security facility in 2012. After his arrest, they detained Sir James there while tests continued on the remains uncovered on his estate.

As Orion predicted, he had helped find Sir James's missing wife, Fiona. The tests also confirmed Sir James had murdered his wife. The happy occasion of the October wedding of Sir James to Elizabeth, the Duchess of Lochalsh, was a distant memory. A joyful event enjoyed by the Olympus hierarchy, which now had dealt a severe blow to the organisation.

The man Phoenix knew as Heracles got remanded in custody due to the serious nature of the case. There was no question of bail. Heracles would appear in court to face the Sheriff and a jury before the end of February. Olympus had to accept the financial benefactor they welcomed among their number from the outset was not the man they thought.

Sir James's new wife, Aphrodite, had started divorce proceedings. She was distraught, but her upper-class background provided her with resilience to such setbacks. She would regroup and recover. Elizabeth's close family gathered to shield her from the gutter press, foraging for a sensational story. Her wider Olympus family made her aware she was welcome to return to the fold whenever possible. Phoenix didn't expect to see her on Wednesday at the next meeting, but he knew it wouldn't be long before she resurfaced.

In the first weeks of December, the hustle and bustle of furniture arriving in various apartments meant the main corridors were never quiet for long. Athena and Phoenix were unaffected, but Geoffrey's move allowed them to concentrate on domestic matters. While Maria Elena Burke decorated her new home, Hope spent more time with her parents. The nanny took over when Giles Burke worked in the ice-house on a day shift. Athena and Phoenix made good use of their free time. Since Geoffrey moved from London to stay with them, their time alone suffered.

Geoffrey's absence eased matters somewhat in other areas too. They were free to discuss Olympus' business. Athena's father had a knack for appearing just as they talked of a proposed mission or debriefed a completed one.

A week before Christmas, they had returned from the bedroom for a late breakfast.

"If we can grab Henry later," said Athena, "we can get him to overhaul our security again. Instigate more frequent patrols of the estate perimeters. Beef up our cybersecurity and allow us to intercept overflying drones before they cross our boundaries."

"Good idea," Phoenix agreed.

A sharp crack interrupted Phoenix's reminiscences as he manoeuvred the car past the walled entrance to the transport section. The mist had continued to confuse him, and the nearside wing mirror paid the penalty.

"Damn," said Phoenix, "oh well, there's a first time for everything."

He left a note of apology for the transport crew chief under the windscreen wiper and returned to the main house. He felt tired, cold and damp, and his bed awaited him; thoughts of the past weeks needed to stop.

Athena stirred when he slipped into bed, but she didn't

A Frequent Peal of Bells

wake. Phoenix heard Hope snuffling in the nursery. Before he fell asleep, Phoenix wondered how old Sharron was before she could respond to being asked to blow her nose.

It was so long ago now he had forgotten. He had lost count of the number of times he and Karen wiped her nose with a tissue. He remembered using a wet flannel to remove dried snot smeared across Sharon's chubby cheeks, her eyes and even in her hair.

When Phoenix awoke, it was after eight. The silence told him both Athena and Hope were no longer in bed. He knew he should get up, but memories that seemed so important last night soon crowded into his head, clamouring for attention.

Everyone had gathered together at Larcombe on the Tuesday before Christmas for a party. The general mood typified many companies and organisations across the country when the holiday season approached.

Festivities had begun at six in the evening. A large bonfire burned on the edge of the lawn. Guests watched from the dining room as it turned from a smoking pile into a flourishing warmth-giving spectacle. After eating, they walked outside onto the patio and then took the steps onto the main lawn.

"The manor house is so beautiful, isn't it, darling?" said Athena.

Phoenix carried Hope on his shoulders. He turned to look at the building. The lighting installed by Erebus a decade ago cast a delicate blue light over the stonework from the ground floor to the rooftops. The more discreet lighting further up the gardens were there for security reasons. But it offered the guests a vast expanse of lawns, trees and bushes to admire.

"It's magical," he replied.

There was a loud bang. Hope, who faced the house too, screamed and cried.

"It's okay, poppet," said Athena, "it's only the fireworks."

The stewards had organised a brief display. Hope, now back on terra firma, hid behind her father's legs and peeked at the array of bright colours in the night sky. Someone should have warned me, she thought.

Sarah Case had found little spare time since the wedding. When she and Henry weren't furnishing their apartment, she carried out duties in her new parish on the other side of Bath. Sarah discovered a church choir with a good number of young choristers.

A final skyrocket that produced a thousand glittering crystals and a loud thunderclap signalled the end of the firework display. Hope was more prepared this time, and as the echo faded, the boys and girls launched into Christmas carols in the dining room.

The guests made their way back from the garden. The bonfire still burned well, but the chill of a December night took its toll. There were smiling faces of people happy to be in the warm. When the carols ended, and Sarah had said a prayer, it was time to enjoy the rest of the evening. Mulled wine for the grown-ups, hot mince-pies, and squash for the young choristers.

Phoenix stood by the patio doors and took in the view.

"It doesn't get much better than this," he said aloud, "I wouldn't want to be anywhere else right now."

"I know what you mean," said Rusty, who had spotted Phoenix and wandered over to join him. "When we're together, having fun, it's easy to forget forces are at work who wish to tear all this from us."

A Frequent Peal of Bells

"While we have breath…" said Phoenix as he saw Artemis heading their way.

"The fireworks are over, boys," she laughed, grabbing her husband's arm and dragging him towards the centre of the room. Rusty groaned as he realised Sarah was arranging party games until the parents arrived to collect the boys and girls of the choir.

Phoenix looked at the dying embers of the bonfire.

"If only," he thought.

"Time to say goodnight to a tired tot," said Athena. Hope was half asleep on her mother's shoulder, sucking a thumb.

"We should have invited Geoffrey over tonight," said Phoenix, "he would have enjoyed this."

"He's wrapped up warm indoors for the night," said Athena, "I called earlier to remind him we're collecting him tomorrow. I can't believe it's Christmas Eve."

They tucked Hope into bed, stood, and watched from the nursery door as she settled.

"Forget Christmas Eve coming around so soon," whispered Phoenix, "New Year's Eve will be on us before we know it. A first birthday. Yet another celebration."

Athena kissed him on the cheek.

"Come on," she said, "let's get back to our guests. The youngsters from Sarah's parish will leave in a few minutes, and we can relax in front of that big fireplace."

"Exactly," said Phoenix. "Give it an hour, and we'll take turns to stifle a big yawn until they take the hint."

"What did you have in mind?" asked Athena.

"An early night," replied Phoenix.

Now, as he lay in bed, he smiled at the memory.

The transport section sent a car to collect Geoffrey Fox from his seaside bungalow in Burnham on Christmas Eve.

The family then had a pleasant time over the Christmas holidays. Geoffrey enjoyed watching Hope tear open presents, some were her own and others their parents, but it kept her amused. He smiled a lot too.

It was the first Christmas without his beloved Grace, and Athena knew it was essential to keep him occupied and let him know how much he was loved. She knew the memories would return, but the less time her father had to think, the better. That night, she shed a tear as she recalled the happy Christmases they shared in London. Phoenix had gathered her in his arms. They needed no words.

Hope didn't give her grandfather much peace when they returned to Burnham on Boxing Day. She wanted to walk around the bungalow and gardens to ensure he was safe and sound. The family walked to the beach in the afternoon and let the fresh air buffet them from one end of the promenade to the other. It blew the cobwebs away from Christmas Day and sharpened the appetite for a meal out in town. In the early evening, they visited a restaurant that Geoffrey discovered on his occasional forays into Burnham.

When they said their goodbyes at the bungalow, Athena drove back to Larcombe because Phoenix had joined his father-in-law in a large brandy.

"Only because it's Christmas, Phoenix," Geoffrey said. "It's rare I touch the stuff these days."

The wink he gave Phoenix when Athena wasn't watching said everything.

As they drew up by the main building at ten o'clock, they bumped into Henry and Sarah Case. While the two female university friends chatted over church services, soft furnishings and the weather, Phoenix took Henry to one side.

A Frequent Peal of Bells

"Have you revisited the security protocols yet, Henry?" he asked.

"Already done, Phoenix," replied Henry. "We had a wake-up call with these drones and that Gonzalez fellow. We reassessed every aspect of how we keep Larcombe safe. Giles and his crew are introducing technical innovations from tonight that will give us an early warning of any imminent incursions. The foot patrols will increase throughout the day and night."

"That's terrific, Henry. I can sleep easy tonight."

"More to the point, Phoenix, Athena can stop fretting."

Phoenix had smiled at that comment. Sarah and Athena's conversation ended.

"Everything OK?" asked Athena.

"Time will tell," said Henry.

Phoenix rolled over in bed and stared at the alarm clock. How did it get to be ten o'clock already? His reverie needed to stop. He got up, showered and made ready to face the day.

As he reached the door to the lounge, he heard Hope's laughter.

"That's what I like to hear," he said as he entered. He was surprised to see Giles Burke making his daughter giggle. Maria Elena was in the kitchen. Athena was absent.

"Hello, Giles," he said, "I didn't expect to see you. Hope seems to enjoy your company, though?"

Maria Elena came through from the kitchen with a drink for Hope.

"Giles can pull funny faces," she said, raising her eyebrows, "at least they're funny for a young child."

"Have you seen Athena?" asked Phoenix.

"You're not in her good books, Phoenix," said Giles, "she meant us to have a morning meeting. Athena told us you got back late. She still expected you to be ready for nine o'clock, given events overnight."

"Ah, the broken wing mirror. I hit the wall in the fog last night. I took one of the best cars on my recce trip yesterday. We've had far too many reported sightings of dark blue or black vans with two agents on board. I reckoned we should vary our transport more."

Giles gave Phoenix a quizzical look.

"No, nothing like that. Nobody knows about the wing mirror except the guys in the garage."

"What was it then?" asked Phoenix.

"The increased foot patrols proved successful. Henry has a guest in an interrogation room in the ice-house. They found evidence of his various hiding places from previous nights. Until last night he had always moved position when they tried to surprise him. His final spot was in the bell tower of the estate church. As the patrol passed, an owl darted away from the tower ledge. The lads must have spooked it. Our unwelcome visitor got a bigger shock as it must have flown past his face, and he couldn't stifle a string of swear words. The two agents lay in wait until he returned to ground level just before dawn and brought him in without a fuss."

"I'd better get over there to see what Henry has learned."

"Up to you, Phoenix, but Athena is watching proceedings from behind the one-way mirror."

"Imagining me trussed up in the chair," said Phoenix, "ah well, I've got to face the music sometime."

As he turned to leave the room, he had a thought: -

"Is Artemis working in the ice-house? As you're here with Maria Elena?"

"No, she was with me when we pitched up to the

A Frequent Peal of Bells

meeting room. She and Rusty disappeared after Athena cancelled the meeting."

"I won't disturb them then," smiled Phoenix. "It will only upset me more if I interrupt them having fun. It might be the spare room for me tonight. I don't need more grief."

Hope giggled as he left the room.

No, thought Phoenix, it had to be Giles and another funny face. No way could she be finding my discomfort a laughing matter at her age.

Phoenix began the long walk along the corridors, down the elegant staircase to the ground floor and then outside to battle his way against the freshening winds. No chance of a repeat of a foggy night tonight.

He reminisced about the days following Boxing Day. Across the country, few families ever complained when Christmas Day fell on a Thursday. It meant a free weekend tacked onto the seasonal celebrations. The gap to New Year that followed was so brief that many had kept holiday entitlements in reserve to avoid returning to work until today.

Phoenix made his way along the path past the orangery and headed towards the stable block. He recalled reading reports from Minos and Alastor on events around the country. The only people working hard were the emergency services and the criminal fraternity.

When New Year's Eve arrived, there was the usual anticipation of a fresh start. As if the time between eleven fifty-nine and midnight was more significant on the year's final day than any other. Phoenix had suffered over forty-five disappointments in his lifetime. Nevertheless, it was just another day until last year when Athena went into labour earlier than predicted.

Phoenix had heard Hope's first cry when the crowds in London counted from ten towards midnight. He first set eyes on Athena with their daughter in her arms as the chimes of Big Ben boomed out across the Thames and the firework display began.

Hope was unaware of last Wednesday night's importance. As soon as she was born, Athena told him she wanted to celebrate the birth of their daughter at the same time. First thing Wednesday morning was wrong, as was first thing New Year's Day. Phoenix had been so keen to sleep after a week of night feeds that he agreed without protest.

So, Maria Elena and Athena contrived to tinker with Hope's routine to have her bright-eyed and bushy-tailed in her party dress at eleven-thirty at night. First, hope attacked the wrapping paper on her presents with gusto. Next, she devoured her jelly and ice cream. Maria Elena carried the birthday cake and one candle from the kitchen and set it on the table in front of the birthday girl.

Rusty, Artemis, Henry, Sarah and Giles had joined the proud parents to celebrate a birthday and another fresh start. Geoffrey Fox elected not to come. He was suffering from a heavy cold, which he blamed on the Boxing Day walk along the promenade. Hope stopped looking at her presents when she heard her mother sing.

Everyone joined in with her singing, 'Happy Birthday', and Maria Elena lit the candle. When they stopped, Hope clapped and then she paused. All eyes turned towards her, wondering what she would do next.

Her nose twitched, and a tremendous sneeze extinguished the burning candle.

"I think someone has caught Grandad's cold, don't you?" said Athena, as everyone collapsed in fits of laughter.

While Maria Elena cut the cake, Phoenix wiped Hope's nose and dabbed at her party dress. Athena switched on the television, and the scenes from the Thames embankment and Trafalgar Square echoed the events of twelve months earlier. As Hope dug into her slice of cake, the others raised a glass to 2015.

The following four days had seen little activity in the UK, but at Larcombe Manor, there had been sleepless nights for Phoenix and Athena. Hope's cold saw to that. She was on the mend now, thank goodness, Phoenix thought, as he reached the entrance to the ice-house.

He descended to Level Three. Henry Case was in Interrogation Room Two; Phoenix entered the observation room next door. Athena sat in a chair alone, her hands steepled under her chin as she rested on the window ledge. Their prisoner looked mid-twenties, possibly from a Mediterranean or South American origin.

"You got up at last, then?" Athena asked.

"It was a tiring journey after a long day," Phoenix replied, taking a seat beside her, "who have we got here and what has he told Henry so far?"

"This is Miguel Fernando, twenty-five, currently living in London. He moved south from Sheffield."

"Have we learned anything important?"

Athena sat back in her chair.

"Henry has just started, Phoenix, don't be so impatient. After our security patrol discovered him, they brought him below and left him in darkness for two hours. Henry treated him to occasional periods of your favourite music at excruciatingly high volume for an hour. Now, he's peeling back each layer of the onion. They need me in the administration offices. If you wish to stay here to watch, you can. I'll see you at lunchtime."

With that, Athena stood and headed for the door.

"I'm sorry," said Phoenix.

"I know you are," said Athena. But, she stepped away

from the door and kissed her husband's forehead, "these first few days of 2015 have left us on edge. Something momentous is looming on the horizon, and I don't know whether Olympus can counter it."

"We must take each day as it comes, Athena. Our cause is. Our intentions are pure. We must respond to whatever the Grid throws at us in equal measure for as long as we can. If the terror threat grows, then that too will need us to oppose it with as much vigour as we can muster."

The door closed behind his wife, and Henry Case continued to interrogate Miguel Fernando in the next room.

Phoenix wondered whether this young man was to be another resident in the pet cemetery.

Larcombe Manor: Chapter Two

Tuesday, 6th January 2015

After the false start yesterday, things got back to normal for the Larcombe Manor senior staff today. Athena chaired the morning meeting, and everyone arrived by nine o'clock. The main items on the agenda were Miguel Fernando, the Olympus meeting in Birmingham tomorrow and Phoenix's report on his fact-finding mission.

"Can you bring us up to speed on your progress with our guest, Henry?" asked Athena.

"Fernando wasn't the hardest nut I've had to crack," replied Henry. "Giles found his juvenile records in South Yorkshire easily, a frequent truant from the various schools he attended before they excluded him. He often appeared in court on burglary charges when he wasn't in class. When he left home and moved to London, they held a street party."

"A typical teenager, based on the latest news reports," said Alastor with a wry grin.

"Fernando found employment soon enough," Henry

continued, "he preferred two wheels to four to get around the city. He worked for Domino's pizzas, did courier work and flirted with the first moped gangs. Before long, he reverted to type. He's been helping dismantle stolen, used cars for parts. The gang Miguel works for creates bogus hire companies and then loans prestige cars. The parts are exported in container loads heading for Africa and the Far East. I convinced him he should tell me about this organisation. Perhaps we could visit them?"

"Give me everything you have, Henry," said Rusty, "I'll put together a proposal for direct action."

"This is minor stuff, Henry," said Phoenix, "okay, this gang has to belong to the Grid. There have been no independent operators since their last cull, but why did Fernando carry out surveillance on Olympus? Surely, they didn't plan to steal our vehicles?"

"That's unlikely," said Henry, "but this young man has had his eyes on you for a while."

Phoenix sat up, straighter in his chair, at that piece of information.

"He photographed you in October when you were in St John's Wood. You were outside the police station. You dropped off the rider and pillion passenger of the gang that attacked those Japanese tourists."

"I get it now," said Rusty. "Tyrone O'Riordan put the word out, looking to identify the people disrupting Grid affairs across the country."

"That's it," Henry continued. "There was a reward for information offered by the Grid's leaders that spread like wildfire around the boroughs. Young Fernando moonlighted with a spot of courier work that evening. He spotted you on the M25, tailed you to the station on his moped, and then lost track of you. He got his reward, but Tyrone O'Riordan wanted much more than the photographs once he had his hooks in him. Fernando came here to replace Simon Gonzalez. He's been snapping away, taking shots of people and vehicle movements since the middle of November."

"We should be thankful his time with us coincided with so many non-Olympus related matters," said Minos. "Apart from weddings and the holiday season, there won't have been anything critical to our operations."

"If you discount the contribution those photos make in establishing our strength in personnel and transportation, then I would agree," said Athena. "Any scrap of knowledge that falls into the hands of our enemies is one scrap too much."

"Fair comment," said Minos.

"How often did Fernando report back to O'Riordan," asked Phoenix.

"Every twenty-four hours," said Henry.

"So, Tyrone will know the surveillance was compromised," said Rusty.

"I bought us time," said Henry, "O'Riordan doesn't sit by the phone waiting for Fernando to call. Instead, he picks up his messages at the Glencairn Bank at lunchtime when he arrives for work on a weekday. At weekends he has been known to answer, but he's often not in his penthouse apartment. He enjoys the social whirl of the nightclubs and casinos."

"Did Fernando agree to send a message to his boss?" asked Athena.

"After a little persuasion," said Henry. "I required him to say, 'It's quiet here', and he managed it perfectly. Losing a little finger has little or no effect on the vocal chords."

"Well, it has been quiet here, as Minos suggested," said Artemis.

"I thought it an appropriate comment, given the circumstance," said Henry.

Phoenix looked up from the tabletop where he had been gazing. He now knew the answer to his question from yesterday. Miguel Fernando lay in the pet cemetery. Hidden deep in the woods at the bottom of the gardens, it was a quiet spot.

"I take it we can move on, Henry?" asked Athena.

"We shall have no further problem from Fernando," said Henry, "as for the Grid, who knows what their response will be? The extra security patrols and technical initiatives will stay in place until they reduce the threat level."

"Or it's eliminated," said Rusty.

"Minos will be in the chair tomorrow morning," said Athena. "Phoenix and I are attending the Olympus meeting in Birmingham."

"A different venue?" asked Alastor.

"Zeus wished to reduce the distances Gods travel," said Athena. "He selected a suitable place near the heart of the country."

"Zeus had no idea Heracles and Aphrodite might be absent for different reasons," said Phoenix.

The room fell silent for a moment. There would be no forgiveness for Heracles and his betrayal. Aphrodite, though, was a firm favourite. She may have been a member of the aristocracy, but she was a warm-hearted, generous person, both of her time and her enormous wealth.

"Do you have the agenda for tomorrow?" asked Henry Case.

"We make the final decision on appointing two new members," said Athena. "I shall tell Zeus that we eliminated two spies working on behalf of the Grid. Other items to be addressed concern the Irregulars. How many can we get into the field? Where should they target?"

"Which brings us to my contribution for today," said Phoenix, shaking himself awake.

Rusty allowed himself a grin. He hadn't seen much of his best friend over the holiday season, but he knew Phoenix hated sitting and waiting. He was a man of action. Meetings were a chore to be endured, not enjoyed.

"On Sunday afternoon, I drove to Northamptonshire," said Phoenix, "on a fact-finding mission."

"Was this trip driven by any perceived threat from the Grid to target Olympus?" asked Alastor.

"No," said Athena, "we stuck a pin in a map covered with a sheet of greaseproof paper. If we asked a member of the public whether they believed crime levels were rising or falling in their locality, many would say it was rising. As for the national picture, they would say it's definitely on the increase."

"My first contact was with a shop owner on a retail park outside Northampton," said Phoenix. "He had been in business in the town for twenty years. In the past three months, a woman was held at gunpoint in a jewellery shop in the town centre. A female drug addict threatened to throw acid at a young assistant if he didn't hand over cash. He knew of numerous cases of anti-social behaviour on the estate where he lived."

"Anecdotal evidence flies in the face of the official statistics," said Athena. "According to the Office of National Statistics, crime has been steadily declining for two decades."

"It was a pure chance the pin found this rural county," Phoenix continued. "The county's official drop of one-fifth is the sharpest fall across the country. So we thought it worthwhile to see if we could understand why the perception and the statistics differed so much."

"This is something Alastor and I have analysed," said Minos. "In part, it's related to how crimes feature in the media. After the recession hit hard, there were cuts in public spending, unemployment rose, and incomes squeezed. The natural response might have been for crime figures to rise, but they didn't. The number of recorded offences fell."

"In rural counties such as Northamptonshire, criminals target the border areas because they assume they will not have as much police presence as large towns and cities," said Giles Burke. "In the ice-house, police teams in the affected counties have access to automatic number plate recognition. The ANPR cameras allow them to spot known criminals as they drive into their patch. These roaming organised crime gangs have thrived in recent years."

"Northampton, Kettering, and Wellingborough have issues with gangs," said Phoenix, "it didn't take long to spot them. The expensive cars and the bling mark them. Locals didn't want to describe the make-up of the gangs in any specifics. Still, it's easy to hear whispers of sexual exploitation, drug dealers setting up in the homes of vulnerable people, guns and ammunition, machetes and swords. Extreme violence is only one street from anywhere you wish to visit."

"Did your fact-finding trip encourage you to mount a direct action against any outfit in particular?" asked Henry Case.

"The intimidation suffered by students at the university spiked my interest," replied Phoenix. "Gang members dealing drugs have ramped up their efforts to target the twelve thousand students on the two campus sites. I suggest we get Hugh Fraser to identify Irregulars capable of mingling with the students and highlighting these vermin. Then, Rusty and I can lead a team to remove the problem."

"Isn't there a danger the Grid will merely replace these drug dealers with people from nearby counties," asked Alastor, "if these roaming gangs are everywhere?"

"Doing nothing is not an option," said Athena. "We must keep delivering a blow to the Grid's operations wherever and whenever we can. We know it's likely to force them to make reciprocal strikes against Olympus, but we've increased our security levels, and every agent knows it's vital to be on the alert."

"I won't hold my breath," said Minos, "but we hope for a sea-change in the government's strategy on crime. If the police and the judiciary swung into action to take our place, they could decimate the number of criminals on our streets. But, at present, that help is light-years away."

"Certainly, it won't happen in our lifetime," said Rusty. "I look forward to visiting Northampton and its environs, Phoenix. Is there a priority attached to this proposed mission as yet?"

Phoenix shook his head.

"We may sort out Miguel Fernando's car gang first. Athena and I will let Zeus and the others attribute priority tomorrow."

"Thanks to Minos and Alastor's background checks, we have the information to figure out which two people to recommend to Zeus and the others tomorrow," said Athena. "Byron Paterson, the forty-year-old Californian, has the skills and the financial clout to help Olympus, and there were no red flags to discount him. However, he's not enough of a people person to match the new dynamic in the Olympus hierarchy. Raymond Ferreira, the thirty-two-year-old Irishman, passed every check, and his charity work with disaster emergency makes him stand out."

"He offers far less in financial terms than Patterson," said Artemis.

"True," said Athena, "but we believe his empathy will resonate with more of the other senior Olympians. Patterson's abrasive American approach might have been too strident."

"Another Donald Trump, you mean?" said Rusty.

"At least Trump's never shown much inclination to go into politics," laughed Minos.

Athena wanted to keep things moving.

"Lily Chan, our lone female candidate, is a thirty-six-year-old married mother of two. Everything checked out in her past, and we desperately need another female at the top table. Two great assets will become our new Olympians, *Chronos* and *Hebe*. Is there anything anyone has to contribute this morning?"

"We noted two statements from government sources recently," said Minos. "It's clear the panic in the ranks after the no-confidence motion inspired them. One spokesperson wanted the public to know tackling terrorism was a national priority. That provoked an announcement that extra resources would be in place following the Charlie Hebdo attack in Paris. Another leaked document reported that they thwarted three terror plots in the recent past."

"More, if you include those that Olympus had a hand in," said Rusty.

"You're on good form today," said Phoenix, "married life suits you."

"It suits us both," said Artemis.

"Especially when you get unexpected free time?" asked Phoenix, raising an eyebrow.

A Frequent Peal of Bells

Artemis blushed, and Rusty smiled.

"Touché," he added.

Athena concluded the meeting, and she and Phoenix returned to their apartment. Maria Elena sat, cuddling Hope. Their daughter's cold had run its course, but she played on her recent illness. After several days where her parents had cared for her more often than their usual work schedule allowed, Hope had realised things were back to normal today.

"Oh, dear, are we having a relapse?" asked Athena.

"I think not," said Maria Elena, "her temperature is back to normal, and her appetite is fine. It's just that she missed you."

"We were only away for three hours?" scoffed Phoenix. Maria Elena stood and handed him her charge. Phoenix gathered his daughter in his arms; Hope clung to him like a limpet.

"You remind me of an advert I used to see on TV," he told Hope as he stared at her cheeky face. "When you grow up, you're going to be a proper little madam."

Hope didn't know what he meant, but having her father's arms around her felt good. But something told her everything would not stay the same here much longer.

"I wish we could stay here with you all day," Phoenix told her, "we have to get lunch and get work done this afternoon."

"She won't want to hear we're driving up to Birmingham in the morning either," sighed Athena.

"Sorry, Maria Elena," said Phoenix, "that will mean another early start for you. I hoped Les Biggar might ferry us to and from this Olympus meeting. He's otherwise engaged."

"I don't mind," said Maria Elena, "Giles is on a late

shift today. He'll return to our apartment at six, so the bed will remain warm."

"Early mornings in the first week of January can be hard for everyone," laughed Athena. "It was no bed of roses last year when we had sleepless nights with this tiny tot."

Athena ruffled the hair on her daughter's head. Hope had stopped clinging now and half-turned, so she could watch and listen as her nanny talked with her mother.

"She doesn't miss much, does she?" said Phoenix, "every conversation we have, she takes in every word. I reckon she understands a damn sight more than we give her credit for, despite her only a year old."

"I'll get that lunch started," said Maria Elena.

Phoenix handed Hope to her mother.

"Fair's fair," he said, "give your mother a big hug for a while. Then we'll think of something we can do together on Thursday or Friday. Perhaps, a drive into Bath to visit the shops? There are bound to be sales campaigns to tempt us to buy clothes or toys we don't need. What do you say?"

If it keeps you both out of danger, it works for me, thought Hope, as she laid her head on her mother's shoulder.

Grab your copy...
vinci-books.com/larcombe-manor

About the Author

Ted Tayler is the international best-selling indie author of the Freeman Files and Phoenix series. Ted lives in the English West country, where his stories are based. He was born in 1945 and has been married to Lynne since 1971. They have three children and four grandchildren.

His thought-provoking mysteries appeal to readers of Sally Rigby, Joy Ellis, Pauline Rowson, and Faith Martin. His action-packed thrillers are a must for fans of Mark Dawson and J C Ryan.

Gus Freeman's cold case investigations are carried out with reasoned deduction rather than bursts of frantic action. In each of the 24 books, unsolved murders are accompanied by romance, humour, and country life. The core message in the 12 Phoenix novels is that criminals should pay for their crimes. Unfortunately, the current system fails to deliver the correct punishment, so Phoenix helps redress the balance.

Acknowledgments

The love and support of my family; without them, this would have been impossible.

www.ingramcontent.com/pod-product-compliance
Ingram Content Group UK Ltd.
Pitfield, Milton Keynes, MK11 3LW, UK
UKHW040119190326
469155UK00004B/1243